See Right Through Me

L. T. Smith

Acknowledgements

Without Astrid Ohletz's love and dedication to the publishing profession, I doubt this book would have ever hit the shelves. Astrid—You are a wonderful publisher, a fantastic listener, a perfect guide, a stickler for paragraphs and dialogue tags (I bow to you), and a genuine, kind-hearted woman. I feel so lucky that you decided to give me and my writing a voice and hope I live up to your expectations.

Also, I would like to thank the woman behind the scenes (you've heard the saying "behind every powerful woman… etc.")—Daniela. Thank you for being such a support—and thank you for letting my furry lads sniff and lick you half to death without complaint. They miss your tickles.

Amanda Chron. Thank you. Thank you. Did I say thank you? You have designed a wonderful cover for See Right Through Me, and if anybody asks, yes, that is me on the front cover beneath the x-ray. You are a superstar, and I know you will knock everyone dead with your designs. The future's bright…the future's Amanda Chron. And yes—I stole part of that from the Orange ad, but mine's more truthful.

Judy Underwood. You are brilliant. Thank you so much for working on my story and making her something I am proud to put my name to. You make me appear to be a better writer than I actually am.

Next, I would like to thank you, the reader. Without your support and positive comments over the years, I would have given up writing a long, long time ago. You have given me the courage to continue swearing and filling pages with my rambling. Without you, what is the point to writing? No pressure there, then. Insert a big smiley face here.

Finally. I hope you like this story. I do. But then again, I am definitely biased.

L.T. Smith

Dedication

To my mum. Although every day you forget a little more, I will keep your memories alive within me. I promise.

Thanks to the NHS. You are all fantastic. Ignore the press.

Chapter 1

TUESDAY. FIVE-FORTY PM. SITTING IN a room with sniffers and moaners and not feeling too bloody happy to be amongst the germ ridden, I can tell you. But it couldn't be avoided; there was no other way. If there were, I would have done it. Believe me.

Radiology. That's where I was, cramped in the smallest waiting room I think has ever been built, unless mice actually have waiting rooms; then there would be competition. Ward G. I think the G stood for Git, because that's what I was feeling like at that moment. People of all different shapes, sizes, and *smells* surrounded me, and all I wanted to do was up sticks and flee. I was okay when I first came in—well, apart from not being able to move my arm to scratch my head and lacking the strength to move my chair away from the letch who was leaning over me, pretending to read my newspaper. Riiiiight. Grabbing an eyeful of what was down my bra, more like. I had serious doubts whether he actually had anything wrong with him in the first place. A huge part of me honestly believed he was there just to leer at the women who came out half naked from the dressing room.

And that was the reason why I wasn't too chuffed now. Not because of him, because of the changing rooms. Why on earth some dickhead architect would think that putting a dressing room inside the tiniest bloody waiting room in existence (okay, mice, you're not included) was a good idea beats me. I wouldn't have been surprised if there had been a shoehorn behind a pane of glass with a sign above it that read "In case of emergency, break glass. Ease person carefully from cubicle. Deposit at reception." Every one of us sardines was privy to the moans and groans of the poor bastard behind the plastic curtain. Then, to add insult to injury, literally, the patient would have to saunter past all of us "cripples" to go to X-ray, with his or her backside hanging out of the hospital gown for all the world to see. Not a pretty picture and one I didn't want to experience. Ever.

"Mrs Sheila Simpson."

Not me, thank fuck.

A middle-aged woman struggled to her feet, her face the colour of clay, and was directed to the dressing room by the nurse. I could hear her emphasizing that all she needed X-rayed was her shin, but the nurse insisted she strip from the waist down, slip on the gown, and then come along to the room at the end of the corridor.

Bollocks. I had to have my shoulder and neck looked at. That meant I was definitely on the verge of a beetroot makeover.

Eventually Mrs Simpson garnered enough courage to enter the cubicle, and the waiting room fell silent again. Grunts and huffing sounds were audible as the poor woman struggled to disrobe. It was at that moment—you know, that time of absolute silence that if someone would have dropped a pin at the far end of the hospital, it would have seemed deafening—that Mrs Simpson farted. All heads spun around to stare at the place the noise had originated and, if I'm not mistaken, I'm sure I saw the curtains flap.

Everything went quiet. Impossibly even more quiet than pre-fart. It still amazes me that no one laughed, but I think the adage "There but for the grace of God go I" was paramount. A muffled "Excuse me" surfaced through the crack. I think I should rephrase that. Okay. A tiny voice whimpered, "Excuse me" through the spot between the curtains where there was a gap.

Letchy bloke couldn't resist and answered, "Better out than in, luv." I bet that made her feel like a princess, and as I turned to him to deliver a look of disgust, he grinned at me and nodded his head. "I wouldn't like to be the one that goes in after her."

Twat. Didn't he understand that getting your kit off and walking past morons like him was bad enough without the added sound effects? Honestly, I *was* going to put him in his place, but just as I opened my mouth, the curtain was drawn back tentatively and a very red face appeared. I could tell he was going to say something else, so I did the only thing I could think of—I stretched. You heard me right. Stretched. And even though the pain in my shoulder stung like a bitch, it saved the day. All his focus was on my breasts, and this gave Mrs Simpson the opportunity to slip away and down the corridor, clutching her clothes in her arms.

That was another thing. Once the poor saps had struggled out of their clothes and scurried off down the passage, they weren't seen again. Was there a huge hole down the corridor, one big enough to swallow you whole and save the NHS money on X-rays? Did they flog your clothes after, and that's why they wanted you to get undressed? Crap. I was formulating my own conspiracy theory, and I didn't like what my brain was trying to conjure. As if it wasn't bad enough that I had to be there in the first place.

Are you wondering that yourself, why I was there? Or don't you give a shit? I bet you wanted to read this story on the off chance that it included rudey scenes or the declaration of true love, didn't you? Well, give me a minute. I am just about to tell you about the events that changed my perception of love...and maybe a little bit more than that. So hang on a tad longer and let me get this out.

Chapter 2

Three Weeks Earlier

T IME DOES SHIFT IN FUNNY ways, especially when you have the power to flit from one scene to another, maybe even shift from one place—or planet. But if you are expecting sci-fi, I'm sorry, although the events later on in my tale I would classify as out of this world. And not just because I had taken too much medication, either.

Okay. Three weeks earlier. What did I do? Did I hurt my shoulder and neck by performing some heroic deed? Land badly when I jumped in front of a moving car to stop a small child from being mowed down? Lift a heavy object off a trapped woman? Or man? Child? Dog? Stop a fight? Step into the shoes of an airline pilot and land a plane full of terrified passengers? I wish I could say "yes" to any of the above, but it has to be a "no", I'm afraid.

Here goes. Just remember one thing before you take the piss—it hurt, okay? They always say hard work can't kill you, and part of me still believes that to this day, but it *can* hurt like buggery, though, as I found out. Now you are thinking I have a strenuous job. Well, I do, but most people wouldn't think so. I teach. Teenagers, to be exact. And no—I wasn't in the midst of a catfight or stopping an intruder from entering the school. In fact, I wasn't even at work at the time. I was at home. Home. The place where most accidents happen. But it was work related, so the waffling I have done does actually key in somewhere along the line.

We had just gotten back from the Christmas vacation, two weeks of doing nothing—no planning, no marking, nothing. And if you teach or know a teacher, then you also know being idle over a holiday is not the wisest of plans. Mainly this is because when you get back, you have to run around like a dipshit—chasing your tail in the process—trying to get things in order to get you through the half term. Usually, this is accompanied by the "For fuck's sake. Why didn't I do a little bit when I had the chance?" The same thing, over and over again. Some day I would learn, and it's a pity I didn't remind myself on the last day of term, as it would have saved the ultimate embarrassment of sitting in a hospital waiting room with a bloke who would make the original Peeping Tom look like an innocent bystander.

I had been working on some resources, trying, if you will, to make the following week a little easier, when it happened. Sitting in the same position for hours on end whilst staring at a computer screen is not my idea of fun at the best of times, but at least I had the opportunity to catch up with some overdue emails (although we usually call that procrastinating). Eventually I'd had enough, saved the work I had done to a memory stick, and clicked to log off.

Then it happened. The "incident" took place. I thought I was being eco-friendly, saving energy and all that, but look where it landed me. All I did was lean over and click the button on the front of my computer. Click from Vista, and then click from somewhere in the Region of Agony. Or should I say "lock" instead of "click"? Because that's what happened. A pain and noise shot through my neck and shoulder, followed closely by a cry from me, and it wasn't along the lines of "Ouch! That stings." It was loud enough to set off the dogs in the vicinity, and all I could do was bounce around with my arm extended and my head canted to one side. I looked as if I was either Morris Dancing or semi-interested in the Nazi party. Do Morris Dancers shout "Fuck!" whilst clanging their bells together?

Two days later I was at the doctor's and being examined by a bloke who didn't suit pink and gave the impression that he read horoscopes on the side.

"I think you may have trapped a nerve."

Well done. Here's your medical certificate. Now, what do the stars say?

"It would be for the best if I recommended you for an X-ray, and then we can go from there."

Where? Uranus? I know I sound like a bitch, but I was in pain, and all he could do was state the obvious. He could have told I had something wrong just by the way I had buttoned up my coat.

Two weeks later I received the letter with the authorization for the X-ray. To say I was surprised would be an understatement, as the NHS was not renowned for speed. The appointment was for the following Tuesday.

And that brings us back to the beginning, the part where things could, or could not, get rather interesting.

Six-fifty. Still Tuesday. I think. Letchy bloke had gone, and the waiting room was beginning to look a little bigger than it had. Maybe because there was only me still there, and because the air was definitely a little sweeter. At least if I did have to take my clothes off, there would be no one there to get a glimpse of my arse. Bonus.

"Mrs Hughes?"

I looked around the waiting room and then realised the nurse was talking to me. Hughes, yes, but Mrs? Was this like the old-fashioned family planning clinics where everyone was addressed as if they were married?

"Mrs Gemma Hughes?" She was staring at me intently by now, knowing full well, as did I, there was only her and me left, and I think she knew her own name. Unlike me, as it appeared.

Somewhere deep inside me, I dragged up a grin and nodded, wincing straight afterwards. "That'd be me." No shit! "But I'm—"

"Pop in there and slip out of your top." She shoved a hospital gown into my hands. "Put this on, and then bring everything with you to the room at the end of the corridor." Then she was gone, and without a broomstick, either.

After a struggle, I managed to get my top off and the gown in place. Why do people insist on putting the ties at the back? Even if I weren't lame (sympathy vote here), I would've found it impossible to do them up. With the thought of "Aw fuck it", I gathered my clothes in a one-armed grip and made my way down the ominous passage, looking like a pigeon flying home from the chippy.

All the time I was walking, I was dreaming up scenarios of huge holes appearing and gulping me down. But nothing. Then I went into *Silence of the Lambs* mode. You know— the bit where Jodie is walking past all the cells and they fire abuse at her (and other home grown ingredients), and for the life of me I wouldn't have been surprised if letchy bloke had appeared at the side, playing with his dingleling and chanting, "I can smell your fart."

Yep. My imagination always amazes me. I'm just surprised I haven't been banged up in a mental hospital before now.

"In here." Miss Personality of the Year was back and waiting for me to enter the examination room. "Give those to me."

I would have, too, if she hadn't snatched them out of my hands. The name I called her under my breath is not worth repeating, but I imagine you get the gist of it. I think she did too, as no sooner had the epithet left my tight lips than she turned back to me and gave me a look that would have frightened terrorists. Slam. Down went my clothes on the table near the door, and she was gone, and I was left sticking two fingers up behind her back.

"If you've quite finished."

The voice came from somewhere on the far side of the room. In retrospect, it was a very nice voice, but that's the hindsight of me talking. At the time I honestly believed I hated everyone in the vicinity and would be within my rights to give them a piece of my mind. Whether it was verbal, or in the shape of a well-drafted letter.

Walking farther into the room, I still couldn't see anyone there. Did the voice belong to a vertically challenged person? Was she hiding somewhere near the skirting boards, and for once in my life I was too tall to see her? Yes. Didn't I mention that before? The voice was definitely female. And if her voice was any indication, a very sexy female. Maybe this wouldn't be as bad as I—

"You need to actually be in the room before I can take an X-ray."

Scrap the last bit. She must have given the nurse training in rudeness. Trust me to get the Simon Cowells of the medical world. I can hear it now. Both of them looking at my X-rays, shaking their heads in unison (hers decidedly lower—'cos she's a midget) and saying, "That is absolutely dreadful."

"Well, if you actually told me where to stand, I might have a clue."

A tutting sound came from the back of the room, and I saw a shape appear. Talk about getting my facts wrong. If the shadow was any indication, this woman was a giant. Part of me wished I'd kept my mouth shut.

I quickly moved towards a machine that gave the impression it would be good for looking right through me and waited patiently, and worriedly, for the next set of orders. Unfortunately, as it turned out, I was facing the wrong way. I knew this for a number of reasons. One—I could read the instructions for the doctor. Two—my shoulder was nowhere near the machine. And finally, three—the huge sigh from behind me that indicated I was an idiot. It was at this point that I felt even more stupid than I had, which is an achievement in itself considering I was waltzing about with the back part of me on display to the world. I thought, "She is going to have a field day with this." Gritting my teeth, I was ready for her.

But no. That's not what happened at all.

Unexpectedly, she placed her hand on my shoulder with, if truth be told, the gentlest touch I believe I have ever experienced. Her warm hand landed on my semi-exposed back and stayed there, almost as if it was there to cure and guide. I waited for her to say something, but she didn't. I waited a little longer, then, before she had the chance to speak, I turned around, her hand staying on my skin and trailing around the overly sensitised flesh.

My eyes fluttered—I couldn't help it—as the sensation ripping through me made me forget why I was there in the first place. And though I was facing in her direction, I couldn't seem to raise my face to look into hers.

A white coat. That was the first thing I noticed about her. Such a clinically clean, white coat. The vee at the top exposed delicate flesh, smooth and slightly tanned. The hollow of her neck was pronounced and shapely and sitting snugly at the base of a soft neck. It wasn't until I noticed I was staring at her jaw line that my gaze had started to drift upwards, and part of me began to panic. Why? I don't know. Breathing started to become a problem. Maybe it was expectation. Or asthma. Or both.

"I'm sorry for being rude." Gentle breaths hit the top of my head. "A long day, I suppose." The voice was even more magical from up close and definitely not what I was expecting...that is, if I had been expecting anything in the first place. "Here. Face this way." Fingers slipped underneath my chin and lifted my face higher.

And as my face went higher, the picture of the woman became all too clear. It wasn't her mouth that captivated me, sitting there curled in a half smile encased by red, nor was it the wonderfully straight nose. It turned out to be the epitome of everything you honestly believe can swallow you whole in one perfect moment: her eyes.

Those eyes. God, those eyes. Have you ever looked into eyes that seemed to know you? Read you? Digest you? Looked into eyes so clear and honest that you believe they will never hurt you? Lie to you? Or cheat you? Eyes that were as blue as the clearest of skies in the middle of a summer's day? So much so, you almost believe you can smell the newly cut grass? The same eyes that were now widening in surprise, as they looked straight back into my own startled green ones.

"I'm not married." What the fuck? Where did that come from? "I...I mean...*erm*...the nurse...*erm*...Mrs." I sounded as if my voice box was deliberately shutting off the volume or completely missing the words out for a prank. I sounded like an idiot; I looked like an idiot; I *was* an idiot. It was those eyes, you see? They made me react in a way I didn't know I could. Her fingers were still tucked underneath my jaw, as if they, too, were in on the act. We were a tableau, and I believe if the nurse hadn't come back in at that very moment, we would still be standing there today.

"Ready to shoot?"

I think that had already been done, as I could definitely feel something lodged underneath my breast bone.

"Dr Moran? Are we ready?"

Dr Moran. That was her name. Dr Moran. Perfect. I just wished I knew her first name so I could rattle that around in my head too.

"Sorry...I...yes." Dr Moran pulled her fingers away, and I felt their absence acutely. Next step was her moving backwards and away from me, and all I wanted to do was relive the moment, catch those fingers and put them back. It was amazing to realise that all the time she had been touching me, captivating me with her blue, blue eyes, I hadn't felt any pain in my shoulder or neck. But the further away from me she moved, the more intense the ache became. Funny thing was, it seemed to be coming from somewhere inside my chest.

Watching her trying to collect herself should have been amusing, but it was anything but. Slender fingers brushed the front of her immaculate white coat, as if she was trying to smooth out non-existent wrinkles. She swallowed once, twice, three times before she directed her questions at me.

"Neck and shoulder, yes?"

All I could do was nod, as my voice box appeared to have given up completely.

"Anywhere else?"

A slight shake—both of my head and, if I'm not mistaken, her voice, too. I wanted to show her I was in control, but I couldn't. It seemed as if everything had either shut down or closed off...everything apart from my intense fascination for the woman standing in front of me. Did she feel something too?

"How did you do it?"

I didn't do anything. It just happened as soon as you looked at me.

"Did you lift something heavy?"

Apart from my jaw off the floor, no. Obviously, I didn't say that, I just shrugged my shoulders and then winced.

"Looks painful. You have no idea at all how you did that?"

It was at that moment when I knew I could have impressed her. Any story I wanted to spin was there on the tip of my tongue, as the truth was a little more embarrassing. Could I stand there and admit I had been clicking off my computer when I pulled something? No way. "I just turned off my computer and something clicked." Why did it have to be at that precise moment that my voice decided to come back from the Land of the Mute? Why couldn't it have stayed there for a little while longer? You know— grabbed a cocktail...stood at the bar of the resort...maybe lounged about in a deckchair... But no. The truth decided it was too big to be contained, and it didn't stop there. "I'd been sitting in front of the screen for hours and when I finished, I thought I would save electricity." So, now I am officially an idiot *and* a tight arsed git.

"You'd be surprised how many people come in with exactly the same complaint." At this point she turned to pick up her clipboard. "Do you play games?"

Huh? Like what?

"Online games...Mrs...Mrs..." Her eyes were glued to the sheet in front of her, and I wondered why she couldn't say my name. "Mrs Hughes?"

Was it my imagination, or did she look disappointed?

"No. I'm not one for games." That should have come out as light-hearted, but it sounded as if the statement I had spoken held the meaning of life. "And it's Miss." She mustn't have heard me announce I wasn't married before.

"Excuse me?" And it looked as if she hadn't heard me again.

"Miss." Fuck the games. "As I said, I'm not married." I wanted to say "*Or in any kind of relationship, either*", but how would I explain that? "Or in any kind of relationship, either." What was the matter with me? Can't I have an internal monologue without it turning into a dramatic monologue? An audible dramatic monologue, at that.

Looking up from the clipboard, she seemed to absorb what I had said before she nodded curtly and crossed something out.

Slipping the board on the desk, she slowly walked over to me.

All the moisture collected in my mouth before being loudly swallowed. This woman was too beautiful, too beautiful for mere words. She was tall, but not in a giantess kind of way—more like an Amazon. Black hair was tied back into a ponytail and collected rays of light before dispersing them back into the atmosphere. A slight smile played along her lips, and I wanted to ask her what she was thinking. Thankfully, the mechanism for voicing my thoughts aloud decided to keep quiet. For a change. Inwardly, I sighed.

"We need to take a couple of shots from different perspectives."

Dr Moran was in front of me now, and I could feel the jittering of butterflies dancing inside my gut.

"And if you don't mind waiting..."

For you to finish work? Not at all.

"...so I can check that everything's as it should be, and we have a clear shot of what's going on inside you."

I hope they didn't get a clear shot of what was happening inside me; how would I explain that one away? I had no computer to blame this time.

"Here. Just move..." As she was telling me where to stand, she placed her hands on my shoulders and gently manoeuvred me into position, and I moved like a lamb. "There you go."

She was at the side of me now, and I couldn't help but turn my face to hers once again.

Freeze. We were back to the statue pose of minutes before. What was happening? Why was it that every time we made eye contact, we both stood frozen like rabbits in the headlights? I could sense something moving rapidly somewhere below her face, and it was an effort to drag my eyes away. But there it was.

Her chest was heaving as if she was having difficulty catching her breath.

It was at this moment that I realised I had been holding mine.

"Dr Moran?"

Why couldn't the nurse just fuck off back to her coven?

"We need to get the shots down to the lab before they close."

My gaze moved back up to her face, and at that instant I saw her click off the fascination and replace it with professionalism. Disappointment flooded through me.

"Okay. *Miss* Hughes, I will be just in there, if you need me..."

As her words trailed off, a little voice inside me, deep down inside me, whispered, "*I* do *need you*", and I involuntarily shuddered it away. Was I cracking up? Was this the after-effects of a lack of sleep? Before I had a chance to answer her, she was gone. Back to the darkroom with the first witch from Macbeth.

I didn't hear anything else, probably because I was too caught up in my own mental musings to pay attention. The machine had performed its function, and it was completely pain free. Thankfully. Because if anything would have happened, anything else unexpected, I don't know how I could have handled it. All the time she had been in the back room, I had watched her, watched her fiddling with the controls I didn't understand until just before she pressed something. As she did it, she stopped and stared at me, her face showing a definite confusion, the same confusion I was feeling inside. What was going on here? Why did I seem to feel a connection with a woman I had just met? Especially when all I knew was her surname?

As the questions were rattling around inside my head, I saw her move towards the doorway again. Her actions were slow, and this enabled me to capture everything about her—the grace of her movements, the way her ponytail bounced slightly with the momentum of each step, the way the smile began to curl itself around her mouth and finally settled into some divine pose as she stood in front of me.

A small laugh delicately slipped from her lips before she said, "You can move now; the first one is out of the way."

But didn't she realise I wasn't staying still because of the X-ray? The reason why I was stationary was because physically I couldn't do anything else?

"Right. You have to turn slightly more to the side, the injured shoulder facing the panel."

An easy set of instructions to follow, but I couldn't seem to move. Still.

"Here. Let me help you."

Maybe it was the anticipation of her hands touching me again that had made me reticent about moving in the first place.

Strong, yet delicate hands cupped my shoulders and turned me away from her.

I could feel her standing against my back, my bareness exposing me more than I ever imagined it could.

A soft breath was next to my ear and her words drizzled down onto my skin. "Did you know you're not fastened at the back?"

I nodded, gulped, and then whispered a "yes."

"Seems stupid to fasten you up when you'll be taking this off in a minute."

At that, my heart seemed to kick start again. I knew it wasn't what it sounded like, but you can't blame a girl for having an overactive imagination...when it's not thinking about *Silence of the Lambs*, that is.

"Okay. We're set."

I felt her move away, and once again I missed the contact. The situation was surreal, to say the least. Considering I had dreaded this moment ever since I had received the letter, I can honestly say this was not panning out the way I had foreseen.

Standing there on my own, a myriad of emotions rushed through me...and thoughts, too. Can't leave out those little snippets, can I? Fear, anticipation, elation, anxiety, confusion... Do I have to list them all? I think you understand this was a weird moment, one of the weirdest I think I have ever experienced. Why was I being attracted to someone so quickly? Nothing like this had happened to me before, so why now? And what was I going to do about it? Nothing, I should imagine. What could I do? Tell her that I thought her touch divine, her eyes magical, and how I wouldn't want these newly found sensations raging through me to ever stop? It was not just about the doctor-patient relationship, although that was a factor; it was the insecurity of not knowing why I was feeling like this in the first place. Was it lack of sleep? Pain? The onset of madness?

As these thoughts were presenting themselves for inspection, I hadn't noticed where the doctor had gone. I couldn't see her from the position I was standing, mainly because I was facing the other side of the room.

"All done."

Strangely enough, it wasn't just her voice that told me she was back. A sensation I can only liken to a jolt of electricity raced through me just before she spoke. Was it the residual effect of radiation? That would just be my luck: I come in with a bad shoulder and leave with a third eye or an extra nipple.

"Are you okay?" The voice was soft and situated to my right side.

A slow turn of the head and there she was standing there in resplendent glory, blue eyes half closed and taking me in.

"Huh?" Sometimes it is good to act stupid; whilst at others to have some semblance of an IQ could be highly recommended. This was not that time. Regrettably. "Done?"

"And dusted. We're just checking that the pictures came out clearly. It saves time in the long run." A slight pause. "That way we don't have to call you back and do it all over again."

I wouldn't mind. If it helps. Helps what? My libido? It didn't need any help—especially since ten minutes ago, *that* I could guarantee.

"I doubt you would be happy traipsing all the way back here, would you?"

My lips moved, but that's all they did. Nothing came out. I looked like a ventriloquist's dummy without the ventriloquist.

"So..." Her eyes left mine briefly and searched in the air for something. "Did you come straight from work?"

Was she trying to make small talk, or was she interested?

"Traffic must've been bad at this hour."

"Not bad." The ventriloquist was back! Hallelujah!

"What do you do? Computers?"

Is this a boring conversation, or is it me? I wanted to spice things up and answer "What would you like me to do, baby?" But...nah...that isn't me. "I teach. English."

"Sorry."

"I teach. English."

"No. I heard you. I'm just sorry." One eyebrow rose, and her face showed a hint of challenge before breaking into a grin. "Couldn't resist. That's a difficult job. What age?"

In truth I was still a little shocked by her response and attempt—I stress the word *attempt* —at humour, to answer straight away.

"Teens?" Why did I say it like a question? Was I turning into an Australian, or worse, a pupil?

She opened her mouth as if to speak, but she didn't have the chance. The Worst Witch was back, and I wanted to tell her that the next Harry Potter book needed an evil character, but as you can guess, I said nothing.

"Everything is fine. That's it for the day."

But instead of buggering off, the nurse stood there and waited. Was she expecting a tip? *Don't polish brown shoes with black shoe polish. Look both ways before you cross the road. Don't overstay your welcome.* Yes. The last one fit nicely.

"Do you need me for anything else?"

Did I need you in the first place?

"No. You go. I'll finish here."

Without another word, she was gone.

Dr Moran turned to me, her face apologetic. "Sorry about that. She's a good nurse, but rather brusque sometimes. I like to tidy up everything after she has gone. Makes me feel like it's all done the way I want it."

Brusque? Spiky, more like. Nurse Porcupine, in the flesh.

"Now, let's sort out your clothes."

Huh?

"Are you okay getting dressed behind the screen? I can help you if you wish."

What an offer. Her and me behind the screen, me coming to grips with my clothes and her coming to grips with...

"I'm a doctor, after all"

...my medical notes.

"That's okay; I'll manage." Turning around I saw the screen in the corner of the room. So the other people hadn't fallen down a huge hole. Shame really. The NHS really does need the money. When I turned back to her, I was certain that I saw disappointment on her face, but her expression changed so quickly into a grin, I couldn't stake my life on it.

"I'll just be in the back, okay?" With that, she was gone, and I was left standing there with my gown flapping and my jaw hanging slightly.

In a matter of minutes I was behind the screen with my clothes, the hospital gown hanging in my hands. Funny things, hospital gowns. When I first realised I would have to wear one, I was mortified, but now it looked so innocent. Green and floppy; used and abused; worn once and thrown aside. Apart from the green bit, it was a little how I was feeling. Why? Fuck knows, but that was the truth of it.

Getting dressed was a little more difficult than I had thought it would be, mainly because the space behind the screen was even smaller than the fart-sized changing room in the waiting room. Grunts and groans came out as I lifted my arm to slip my top on, and anyone listening would have thought I was masturbating. As if. If I didn't have the strength to write the date on the board in my classroom, self-love was definitely out the window. More's the pity. It was like the pleasure/pain theory...being there, I mean. On one hand (the one attached to the sore shoulder—well, separated by an arm. Thought I should clarify in case you had the idea I had a hand sticking out of my armpit), I was not a happy bunny. Sitting in the tiniest room known to man for the best part of an hour and a half, then getting undressed in a shoebox, followed by a meeting with the Cowell twins (okay, okay—I know the doc wasn't a Simon wannabe, but the nurse...definitely), who provided an in-depth insight into hospital staff cuts, naturally keeping the ones that should have been sacked. That was not the way I wanted to spend my evening. But—and this is a big "but"—on the other hand, meeting the woman who was by now turning off everything in her office and wishing I would get my arse into gear and leave, was a definite bonus. Can I have three hands? We could put it down to overexposure to the radiation if we have to. The pleasure part did have a fault. After I dressed and bade her adieu, I knew it would be the last time I would see her.

Or I could ask her to go for a coffee. Couldn't I? There was no law against asking. Just one cup. Maybe talk about things other than X-rays and school. Get to know each other a little better...maybe even ask if she would like to meet up another time.

Whoa! What was I doing? Just because I was a lezza didn't mean every other woman in existence was one too. Ignore Freud, or whoever said we all had the tendency to be attracted to people of the same sex. If, and I mean IF, she said yes to a coffee, that didn't mean she would fall for my charms and fall into my arms. For a start, I was injured, and would most likely drop her, just before she metaphorically dropped me.

"Are you okay in there?"

Apart from having an internal debate, yes. "Yes!" A little high pitched, even if I do say so myself.

Five minutes later I was ready. Stepping out from behind the curtain, I had the sudden urge to catch my breath, maybe because that way she wouldn't realise I was there.

Dr Moran was leaning against a table and reading the chart on the wall. Her body was relaxed, yet not. Her elbows were supporting her and her chest was pushed out, her head slightly tipped back.

What an image! It was like she was absorbing everything, yet allowing nothing to penetrate. I just stood there and watched her adjust herself slightly, like she was getting comfortable as she waited. The white coat was gone, and she was wearing a brown leather jacket that hung loosely over dark trousers. A firm breast was peeking through and that's where I was staring as she turned to me. Even though I wasn't looking at her face, I knew she was looking at me. I could feel it...just before I felt the hot blush skim from the base of my neck and glow all over my face. I shot a quick look at her before looking away, embarrassed.

"Ready?"

Didn't she notice? Why didn't she say something? Glancing back at her, I saw the vestiges of a grin on her face before it was completely gone and the professional face took over.

"Would you mind if I walked down with you? It would be nice to have a little company for a change."

"Y-yes. Yes."

She cocked her head to one side, and I realised that I had actually refused her offer.

"I mean, no, not at all."

The grin was back and I couldn't help joining her.

As she pushed herself up from the table in one fluid movement, I couldn't seem to tear my eyes away. If I had felt something more than a doctor-patient connection beforehand, now was a new ball game. She was beautiful, even more so than I had previously thought. Her hair was freed from the ponytail, and it came just below her shoulders, framing the elegant face in the process. Blue eyes watched me, but I couldn't move. It felt as if pixies had sneaked in and stapled my feet to the floor.

"Are you okay? You seem a little...erm...out of it."

One nod, that's all I could muster. Maybe the X-ray had buggered about with my chemical balance. Worth a shot.

Before I knew it, she was in front of me, her hand touching my forehead. "You seem hot and sweaty. Maybe you need something to eat or drink." After a pause, she added, "Have you eaten today?"

Loads, actually, as I had remembered to take my own lunch rather than risk poisoning from the school canteen. I nodded slowly. Well, I couldn't lie, could I?

"But I am thirsty, now you come to mention it." Should I say that I was worried I might pass out if I went to the cafeteria all by myself? And if I did say that, would she escort me like my own personal medical guard? Nah.

However much I wanted her to accompany me, I wouldn't stoop to feigning illness to get her alone for a little while longer. I wasn't ill—just caught red handed staring at her tits.

"Maybe I should take you to the cafeteria and make sure you're okay." That capable hand was now on my cheek. "If...if you don't mind, that is?"

I shook my head slowly, as if any more effort would see me off. Talk about a drama queen. I even wheezed out a "thank you" with what sounded as if it could have been my dying breath.

"That's settled then. Would you like me to get a porter to wheel you down in a wheelchair?"

What the fuck? As if she would be enamoured by my charms if I was being wheeled along in a wheelchair to the café, not that there was anything wrong with being in a wheelchair... Aw fuck. I was racing down a one-way street the wrong way with no brakes. I couldn't take this illness thing too far or else I would shoot myself in the foot and end up in a wheelchair anyway. And it is amazing that from one moment to another, I had changed my mind about using illness as an excuse to get her on her own. Shallow. That's what I was. But needs must.

"I think I can manage walking. Maybe if I feel a little woozy..." (who the fuck uses woozy?) "...I could hold on to you?"

"Here. Grab my arm; I don't want you going down on me."

Not the response I was looking for, but I slipped my good arm through hers and allowed her to lead the way.

Being with her seemed the most natural thing in the world. Allowing her to support me all the way to the cafeteria also seemed to be one of those situations where it was the thing to do. Dr Moran may have thought she was helping a sickly woman, but I had other thoughts racing through my head. Linking arms with her was not done in the way of a person that was just about to keel over. Nope. It was like we were out on a date. My arm through hers felt perfect. Our connection was as if I had ordered it and we fit like a hand in a glove. That wasn't all of it, though. All the time she was linked with me, little shocks of delight kept racing along my skin. If this was what it was like to touch this woman when all we were doing was linking arms with our clothes on, imagine what it would be like if—

"Here we are. You sit here and I'll grab us both a drink. Coffee? Tea?"

You. No sugar. "Tea, please. No sugar."

Then she was gone and I was left grinning like an idiot, all by myself at the table. I felt good. Alive. Pain free. *Huh? Pain free?* A quick jiggle of my arm and shoulder... nothing. No pain, no cramping, no nothing. Another wiggle and stretch. Nothing. The pain had gone. Kaput. Disappeared into the walls of the hospital. How on earth had that happened? Ten minutes ago I could barely move because of the nearly constant pain, but now...

I felt like a fraud. I had made that poor gorgeous woman help me down to the café when all I was suffering from was a bad case of Caughtmeitus. Who would have guessed that staring at someone's boobs would have qualified as a disease? I looked over at where she was standing and, bugger me, she was staring right back at me. Was it contagious? Like in *Outbreak*? Or had she seen that I was waving my arm around like a mad woman without the usual signs of any pain? Should I go for the pain-filled look now, just to cover my back? Grip my shoulder and scrunch up my face in agony?

No. What I did do was grab my handbag and rummage around for too bloody long as if I was valiantly searching for something—like a misplaced pulled muscle, or even the ever faithful "trapped nerve" who was probably down at the bottom, encased by fluff and fighting for its life.

"There you go." She was back. And with a huge mug of steaming tea. "Thought you might want a cake, too. Help with the sugar levels."

How thoughtful. I could manage a cake; I could always manage a cake of some description.

Dr Moran pulled the chair out opposite mine, the legs screeching in defiance over the tiled flooring. "I'm starving. Been a long day."

My heretofore injured arm was outstretched at this point and grabbing for the plate which held the little brown pocket of delight, when I realised I wasn't making any agonised face pulls. Therefore, the face I did pull was one of surprise, and she noticed.

"Hey."

Fuck.

"You shouldn't be doing that. Let me."

Considering she was a doctor, I thought she would have realised that my arm seemed a damn sight better than it had.

"You'll knock your tea over."

Maybe she had noticed my miraculous recovery. *Bugger.* And why couldn't I make up my mind if I wanted to go for sickly or bodybuilder?

"I'm fine. Look." With that, I lifted my hand over my head and waved wildly. The look of shock on her face was priceless, and I wanted to continue with a one-armed handstand, just to nail the point home. "My shoulder...and neck...they're okay." At this point, someone on the far side of the café waved back. *Bollocks.*

"I can see that." Dr Moran leaned over the table and her eyes narrowed. "But what I don't understand is why? You couldn't even fasten your blouse up a few minutes ago."

I looked down and, sure enough, my blouse was buttoned up all wrong. But then again, it would have been more unusual if I had done it up right. I wasn't going to tell her that. My mouth opened and I mentally checked what was going to come out of it before continuing. "I don't know what happened. As soon as I sat down, it seemed to just...erm...just go."

"That's usually the way. Injuries like that usually go as quickly and silently as they appeared." A soft smile was forming along her lips, then it slipped away and I was left wanting more. "But that doesn't mean your shoulder is okay. You still need to go and visit your GP and get the results of the X-rays." Leaning back into her chair, I saw the professional come back. "If the injury is left untreated, you could end up with a lifetime of X-rays."

Well, that didn't sound so bad. As long as they were with her.

"And physiotherapy."

Maybe that was going a little too far. It would be easier to just do what the doctor ordered after all.

"Or it could have gone."

Had she seen the flash of thoughts skid across my face?

"You won't know until I get the results back to your doctor in about five days...maybe a little longer because of the weekend."

Her hand came out and she lifted the cake nearest to her, and with a swoop she had bitten off a good quarter. A muffled "good" came out and she closed her eyes briefly to savour the sweetness. Then another bite, and I was so mesmerised by the contentment on her face, my hand hovered over the remaining treat. Dr Moran's chewing slowed as the desired effect took over, and I could actually see her energy levels increase as the sugar hit home. Swallowing, she focused her attention back on me, and I witnessed an idea take shape in her mind, just before a smile flitted on and off her face. "Or, you could just call the ward if you want. I could give you the results quicker, if you're interested." Blue eyes waited for my answer, and I don't know if it was me, but there seemed to be a little bit more than "getting test results" being offered with that phone call.

It was so quiet in that cafeteria, so bloody quiet, though there were quite a few people around—including the person who thought they must know me. Were they, like her, waiting for my answer? Shit. She *was* waiting for my answer.

"Yes!" Why did it sound so loud? Was it because I half screamed, half squawked it? "Yes...that would be great." A lot better, and a lot quieter. "Would save me the trip to the doc's, at any rate." Was I fucking things up? "You know… parking and all that." Yes. I was. I could tell by the way she looked down at her half eaten cake, and then looked back at me with a look of resignation at my stupidity. "I mean… erm…that would be great." Would I ever learn?

Placing the cake gently back onto the plate, she leaned down and lifted her bag off the floor. After a minute of rummaging, she plucked out a piece of paper and a pen. Magical, eh? Was I expecting flowers? Probably. Thirty seconds later she was offering me the aforementioned piece of paper with her number on it. Small, neat writing sat pride of place on the once pristine whiteness, her name glaring out above everything else. I didn't even read the rest.

Dr Maria Moran.

Maria. MM. If you said her initials it summed her up completely…mmmmmm. It could almost feel like a kiss, if performed correctly. A smacking of the lips; a readiness for something tasty…

"You okay?"

Was I moving my lips in a cannibalistic fashion? Knowing me, yes.

"Miss Hughes?"

"Gemma. Call me Gemma." Better than the "call me anytime," which I was thankful didn't come out instead.

"Okay." A full out grin.

Why were there butterflies flapping their brightly coloured wings in my belly?

"As long as you call me Maria." The last part was spoken in a normal voice, but for some reason it seemed to resonate everywhere.

Now, stop me if I'm wrong. How often do you go to see a doctor and she walks you down to the cafeteria, buys you cake and tea, gives you her phone number, and finally, tells you to call her by her first name? I don't know about you, but this was definitely a first for me. And I wouldn't care if it was the last time either—in a good way, of course.

"So...Gemma..."

Just the sound of my name on her lips was stirring up the beast within me. That and the delectable smile she favoured me with as the word popped out, I should say.

"...how are you feeling now?"

Like I am in a dream. In heaven. In my own romantic novel and not wanting it to end.

Lifting the cake from the plate, I took a huge bite and chewed dramatically. After swallowing, I grinned, and I'm sure I had bits of it jammed in my teeth, but I didn't care. "A lot better. Thank you, Doc...erm...Maria."

She grinned full out and grabbed the remaining half of her cake, raised it up in salutation, and then started to eat again.

It was comfortable. The silence, I mean. Even though we were eating and people usually don't talk when their mouths are full, it didn't seem weird that I was there with her in the first place. Actually, it seemed the perfect place to be, as if we had known each other for a lot longer than an hour. When the cake was gone, we still sat quietly, sipping tea and looking around the now emptying café. Now and again, we would catch each other's eye and smile. I felt like a teenage girl out on a first date, you know, that sensation where you are not too sure what is expected from you. Then I received a text message from my brain.

"*y dnt u spk 2 her?*"

"I'm good." Shit. I said mine aloud. Why couldn't I select "reply to message" and conjure up my own cyber speak like "I'm gud"? Probably because I was crap with mobiles.

Maria was looking straight at me by this stage. "Good for what?"

Nothing? Anything? Erm...*something*? I cleared my throat and hoped the words would present themselves as I opened my lips, words I actually wanted to be there. "I'm feeling a lot better. Must have needed sugar, like you said." At this point I realised my brain had sent another text and I was stubbornly trying to ignore the beeping noise. "So... you worked here long?" It was a start; however weak, a start nevertheless.

"Just over three months. I moved here from Cambridge." And that was it. Conversation flowed between us so easily it made the point about feeling I was in the most natural place on earth seem even more apt.

An hour later we were still gabbing about anything and everything, and I came to the conclusion that she wasn't just gorgeous, but a wonderful person, too. I also knew that I should let her get home; she looked tired. One of the very first things she had said to me was that it had been a long day, and there I was taking up her spare time. The next thing I said was the most difficult thing I had ever said in my life, as there was no way I wanted our time together to end. "I suppose I should let you go. You've had a long day."

In the blink of an eye, her face changed from the smiling one to a brief look of disappointment.

"Do you need a lift? I can drop you anywhere, I'm easy." And by the looks of it, I was. But not in the taxi driver way, unless you count Robert DeNiro's role, although I wasn't going to exclaim *"Are you looking at me?"* Or was I? Anything was possible this late in the evening, especially with the way I had been acting up until now.

"You're okay. I'm parked just out the front." Maria slipped her mug back onto the table and then lifted her jacket from the back of the chair.

Cleaners were working their way over to us in the hope we were at last pissing off and letting them close up for the night.

"Right. Want to walk out the front with me?" Maria asked.

I want to walk anywhere you want me to walk to, as long as I'm with you. I think I was in danger of turning into one of those blokes with cheesy lines, but thankfully, most of mine stayed inside my head. Most.

Within five minutes we were standing in the brisk February air in the parking lot of the Norfolk and Norwich University Hospital, and I knew that in another five, I would be saying goodbye to the only person I had felt any kind of connection with for years. Or ever, if truth be known. I'm not saying I hadn't dated, just saying that I wanted the kind of connection I had felt with Maria to continue, as part of me was scared stiff that I would never feel this again.

"I'm over there."

Turning, I saw where she was pointing and my heart dipped a little lower. My car was on the other side of the parking lot, clocking up time on the parking meter. The sigh I had stuck in my throat was insistently begging to release itself into the air and become mist, and it tried every way to stop me speaking. It nearly succeeded, too.

Maria faced me fully and looked down into my eyes, and I believe I was mesmerised again.

"You should wear a hat in this weather." A hand shot out and flicked my blonde hair off my shoulder, then a laugh popped out of her mouth. "Sorry...just the doctor in me."

Wish there was one in me.

"Look. You've got the piece of paper I gave you, the one with my numbers on it?"

I patted my handbag and gave her a smug look.

"You can call me whenever." Maria stopped abruptly. "I mean...about the...erm...results."

"When can I call? Erm...I mean...when will they be ready?" No. That's not what I meant at all. What I meant was: "When can I call and ask to see you again?" But that wasn't the done thing, was it? Well, it was the done thing, but not with your doctor. Part of me wanted to bite the bullet and just ask her out. I didn't know whether she was gay or not, and I wouldn't know unless I asked her out. And even then I wouldn't know if she was gay, unless I told her I was and wanted to see her on a more personal level. That did it. There was no way I would be outing myself in the car park of the hospital. I was way too cowardly for that.

But I wanted to. Ask her, I mean. My mouth tried to move into the position of saying "I like you..." but that lump of sigh was battling against the admission. Therefore, the only thing I could do was watch the air collect into mist and float away, just like my hopes of ever seeing her again.

"Friday or Thursday. Just give me a bell and I will let you know if we have the results back."

That seemed such a long time away. At least two days before I could speak to her again, hear that beautiful voice again.

"Or you could just go to your doctor's next week."

I could ask him what my future held, have him read my tea leaves, tell me if I was going to ever again meet the tall, dark, gorgeous woman who had been a stranger until six fifty-five tonight.

But what did I do? I thanked her. Thanked her for her time, her skill, her patience, her hospitality. Thanked her for the tea, cake, conversation. Then thanked her for walking me to the car park. How twattish. And all the time I was thanking her, I could see she was becoming more and more embarrassed, and that made me gush even more. Eventually, after realising I was getting on my own tits too, I stuck out my hand in farewell. Slowly, gently, she took mine within hers, and I had the most electrifying experience I had ever had. Literally. Sparks shot up my arm and dispersed themselves around inside my chest. I quickly looked into her face in the hopes that she had felt something too, and by the looks of it, she had. Were we standing on lay lines? Did the connection between two people have special powers and that's why they built the hospital there? There was nothing else to do but pump her arm up and down like a maniac and grasp it as if I was clinging onto the side of a cliff.

"My...you have one hell of a grip on you there." Her laugh rang through the air as clear as crystal being chimed. "And it's your bad one, too." More laughter, but this time joined with my own. "But don't overdo it. Remember what I said."

I will remember everything, Maria. Everything.

"Now, unfortunately, I will have to let you go."

And I, you, it appears. I let go of her hand, and I felt empty. Again.

"It has been lovely meeting you, Gemma. Just a shame it wasn't under different circumstances."

I nodded and whispered, "Same here."

She turned slightly away before turning back, licking her lips and repeating, "Just give me a bell and I will let you know if we have the results back. Thursday, okay?"

"Okay." And then she was gone. Striding over the tarmac, she was moving away from me, whilst my voice was begging me to call her back and my brain was texting me like crazy. It wasn't until she was out of sight that I turned and made my way to my car, the same car whose windscreen was frosted up by now, and I didn't have any de-icer.

By the time the windscreen had cleared, I was feeling totally dejected. It wasn't just the fact that the only woman I felt something for had just walked away; it was because I hadn't even made the effort to ask her out. Story of my life, really. Good ideas, but shite at putting anything into practice.

Slipping my car into gear, I eased out of the space, eased out the car park, and eased out of her life.

Waiting until Thursday was torture. Too many times I had taken the once white and neat piece of paper out of the compartment of my purse and just looked at it. All it had on there was her name, the number and extension of the Radiology Department, and another number. It was the other number that intrigued me. It appeared to be a mobile number, but I wasn't sure. Maybe it was a pager number. Doctors had pagers, didn't they? The thoughts of her giving me a direct line to reach her were quashed. If it was her pager number after all, I would look even more idiotic than usual if I called her on Wednesday.

So, Thursday it was.

All day at work I found opportunities to lift the phone and start to dial: before registration of my manic tutor group; during break, even though I should have been monitoring the playground. Lunch time saw me slipping out of GCSE revision group to lift the phone again. Even at the end of the day, I sidled into the staff room to attempt to dial the number again. Someone came in as I was halfway through it, and I put the slim white receiver sharply into its cradle. I would just call her when I got home. At least I wouldn't have the school listening in.

That decided, I made my way home. Sounds easy, doesn't it: "made my way home". It should have been too, if the traffic hadn't decided to go all frenzied. By the time I pulled up at home, parked, and got inside, the hallway clock read six-thirty-one. She would still be there, wouldn't she? It had been later than that when I had gotten in to see her. It must've been the knowledge that time was of the essence that made me actually dial all the numbers and then ask to put through to extension 137. The phone rang about four times before I heard it clang against a head.

"Radiology."

I knew that voice. God, did I know that voice. It was the nurse. Bollocks.

"Could I speak to Dr Moran, please?" I was crossing my fingers that the nurse didn't go all doctor's receptionist on me and start asking a million and one questions before telling me that—

"She's not here. Can I help you at all?"

That would be a first. I wanted to ask if the doctor had just popped out, ask if I should call back. But no. "It's Miss Gemma Hughes here. I was just calling to ask about my X-ray results from Tuesday's examination."

"Sorry. I can't divulge that information on the phone. You will have to make an appointment with your GP."

Was that because she wasn't a doctor? Or didn't they usually give out that kind of information over the radio waves? And if that was the case, why had Maria asked me to call?

I didn't ask her why not, or tell her I had been told to call. "Okay. Thank you." I just hung up the phone and stared at it for what seemed like too bloody long. Turning away, I leaned against the wall. Fuck it. Dr "I See All" it was then.

Not until I was lounging in the bath did it hit me, something Maria had said when I had seen her on the Tuesday. The nurse had just come in and said that everything was done, and Maria told her to go, then apologised to me for her being brusque. But it wasn't that bit that made me sit up sharply in the bubbly water and splash all over the floor. It was what she had said after. Remember? "I like to tidy up everything after she has gone. Makes me feel like it's all done the way I want it"—that bit. The nurse was still there, and by the good doctor's own account, the nurse always went home first. What was going on? Had the nurse purposely lied to me? Or had Maria gone? Or, worse still, told the nurse to lie to me? And was I turning into Jessica Fletcher from *Murder She Wrote*? Part of me felt hurt, part of me felt angry, but the biggest part of me felt miserable. I knew now that the call was nothing more than a getting of results, even though I had wanted so much more.

Sighing, I leaned back into the water, hoping the aroma from the bath salts would soothe me. Closing my eyes, there was only one thing I could see...blue eyes twinkling. Another sigh, this one voicing the disappointment I was feeling. Well, there was nothing I could do about it now, the hour was late, and I knew that tomorrow I wouldn't do anything about it either. It was over before it had begun.

Chapter 3

One Week Later

THE WEEK HADN'T BEEN A good one, to say the least. Work was a bitch, and so was I. But most importantly, I couldn't seem to shake off the image of Maria's smiling face. It was as if she was haunting me, sneaking into my head and haunting every thought I had. Asleep, awake, daydreaming, in mid sentence, there she would pop, and I was captivated all over again. Not the best scenario when you have thirty teenagers waiting for you to continue speaking and you are standing at the front of the room with your mouth hanging open.

Saturday night saw me at The Castle Pub, hoping to get to grips with a poor unsuspecting female who might help dispel the demon that tormented me. But I couldn't even do that right. Every woman who came over, I rebuffed. Every drink bought for me, I left untouched. I wasn't in the mood for anything, or should I say anyone, but her. I was home by ten-thirty.

All the next week I promised myself I would go and see the stargazer and find out my results, but as I said—work was a bitch.

It wasn't until Wednesday evening when I received a message on my answering machine from the local surgery that I should make that appointment. I stopped feeling sorry for myself and began to panic instead. All it said was that my results were back and I needed to make an appointment. They might as well have said, "You are going to die. Painfully," because that's how the message made me feel.

Thursday morning saw me making a call and fixing a date with Destiny. Five-forty. I smiled when the investigator, I mean receptionist, pronounced the time.

Obviously I was early. Who wouldn't be if you thought your ticket was up? I wanted my last hours on this earth to be memorable, so the sooner I found out, the better. Of course, just because I was early, that didn't mean they would be early, too, or even on time, and I had digested three copies of *Woman's Own* before I heard my name being called. Amazing to read your star signs from different years, too. It beats me why they couldn't bin all the ones that were three years out of date. So, I wasn't expecting a windfall after all, or meeting with a blast from the past. Just my luck.

Less than five minutes later, I was on my way out again. No near death experience, no tidings of bad news, just a clear result. The X-ray had come back to say there was nothing wrong with my shoulder, well, nothing I should get my knickers in a twist about. I don't know why I had been twisting them in the first place, because I hadn't had any pain since the moment I had been with Maria—Dr Moran, I should say, now that there wasn't a cat in hell's chance of being anything more than a memory for her—in the cafeteria.

That made me stop next to my car, the keys dangling loosely from my hand. This was the time when I should put all the memories of her to one side, maybe out of my head for good, and start over again. But just as that thought came into my head, another one took control. It was of her standing in front of me, her hand on my cheek, her face impossibly close to mine and leaning in closer. It felt so real, the kiss she delivered, so soft and real, so perfect and real, so much so I felt my legs give slightly and felt my body lean against the car door. Even the coldness of the metal didn't deter me. It was all so real, you see; the kiss, I mean.

However, real life has a way of forcing its way in to bite you on the arse, and this came in the voice of a bloke who must have been just getting into his car. "You okay, luv?"

My eyes fluttered open and I saw him moving in my direction, evidently concerned that I was going to flake out in the car park of the local GP's office. "Need any help?"

"No... No... I'm fine. I was just..." What? Daydreaming about snogging a doctor? Falling for the charms of my imagination? Humping the side of my Seat Ibiza? "I was just getting my keys out." As if! It looked no way like I was getting my keys out, and I could tell he wasn't convinced either. But, he seemed to get the message that I wasn't going to tell him anything else. Therefore, he did the totally British thing—didn't get involved—and left me to get on with opening my car door.

It was when I was settled in my seat that I noticed something on my windscreen, something rectangular, something dark, something that resembled a letter. *Don't tell me I got a parking ticket for being made to wait for my appointment.* I thought my stars said I was going to have a windfall, not line the pockets of the local council.

Stepping out of my car, I leaned over and snatched the envelope from behind the windscreen wiper. Small, neat handwriting was centred on the front, and part of my brain sparked up. I knew that handwriting, knew it as well as I knew my own, though I had only seen it once. Rummaging in my bag, I pulled out my purse and dived straight into the compartment at the side. There it was. The week and two days old piece of paper. Sure enough, the same hand had written both.

"Miss Gemma Hughes." And it was for me too. Added bonus.

Ripping open the envelope—well, actually, not exactly ripping; more like carefully peeling back the flap to make sure I didn't destroy anything—I pulled out the card. A hand drawn teddy sat on the front, a rose in one hand and a tag around his neck which read "Would you be my Valentine?" Valentine? It was Valentine's Day? Fuck. No wonder I had spent all day stopping kids from kissing, breaking up scraps, and also using a whole box of tissues in one morning. I should have guessed, like when I had written the date on the board. That should have been a huge clue, shouldn't it? February 14th, with sobbing coming from one of the students behind me.

Opening the card was a task in itself, as my hands were shaking. My brain was chanting, "*Please don't let me be wrong. Let it be from Maria and not the bloke who is staring at me from his Skoda."*

"Gemma,
Well. Will you?"

A question mark and kiss finished the note, and I was half filled with happiness, but also half filled with something that seemed like despair. What should I do now? I didn't have any way of contacting her, apart from the numbers she had given me. But then I would have to get past the nurse and her clipboard. I could drive to the hospital and see if she was still there; hang about a bit until she had finished; look casual instead of desperate, like usual.

Hang on. The card had been slipped underneath my windshield, and if my knowledge of the Royal Mail was up to scratch, didn't they usually put the mail through your letterbox? That would mean only one thing. She had to be around somewhere. Head up, eyes engaged, night vision on, and I was searching. Every corner of the car park was scanned, and I believe if I had had a heat detector on me at the time, I would have used it. But there was nothing there. Even Skoda man had gone and left me alone in my mental breakdown.

I looked back at the card in the hope that there would be some secret message written at the bottom ... but no. The message stayed the same; it was only me that was changing into a madwoman. Although the situation of not knowing how to contact her was still paramount, I couldn't resist the rush of joy that raced through me, and I pumped my arm up and down whilst shouting "Yes!" into the air. Whatever I had to do, I would let this woman know that I wanted her to be my valentine, wanted her to be more than my valentine, or for her to give me the opportunity to be both, or one... And I'm rambling.

"Good. I was hoping you would say that."

Maria. She was here! Or was I hallucinating?

"And you shouldn't do that with your injured arm."

She was here. She must be. Shooting around, I looked to the place where I thought the voice was coming from. But nothing.

"And what did I tell you about wearing a hat?"

Turning back to face my car, I looked straight into blue eyes. How on earth had she sneaked up so quietly? And did I care?

For once in my life I didn't think about the consequences of my actions; for once in my life I went on gut instinct. For once in my life I did the only thing that mattered at that moment in time. Blame it on excitement, on expectation, you could even blame it on relief. But I knew the blame wasn't really blame at all. It was want that made me do the next thing I did.

No thoughts, just actions. Act don't react, as they say. And I did. Seeing her standing there in front of me was like a gift, and I for once wasn't going to make the same mistake as I had done the last time I had seen her. I had to show her that I wanted her. Grabbing her face between my hands, I pulled her to me. I hesitated briefly to look into her eyes before I kissed her mouth ardently, trying to press home everything I was feeling onto those startled lips. All the daydreaming I'd had about kissing her paled in comparison to the real thing. Her lips were softer, harder, more delicate, more delicious than I could ever have imagined. And the best thing was they were kissing me right back. God. Could this get any better? Could I feel more than I was feeling at that precise moment?

Her hands were on my face, in my hair, over my skin, down my back. And yes...I could feel more. Lips were leaving my mouth, kissing my cheeks, my eyelids, my neck... So again, yes, I could feel more. I didn't even feel her turning me; didn't feel the coldness of the car touching my back. All I could feel was her body over mine; her hips between my legs, her hands on my hips and pulling me into her. All I could feel was the growing wetness between my legs, the growing need in my heart, belly, and core that was screaming to be satisfied. Grabbing her hips, I pulled her against me more fully, the crux of her pelvis hitting the spot where I needed her. Maria pulled away, and I wanted to pull her back again, but I didn't have to. She pushed back and hit the spot all over again, and then again, and again, and I thought I would cum just from her kisses, her touches, her presence.

But that was something I didn't want to happen, not this soon, not in the car park of a doctor's surgery. And definitely not before we had even had a first date, although I hated to be the one who broke the news to my rampant libido. However, I didn't have to say anything. The kisses slowed down; the pressing against me became less frantic and more gentle; the caresses became almost reverent.

Lifting her face away from mine, I looked into those eyes that had followed my every move for the last nine days, both awake and asleep. I watched, enraptured, as she licked her lips slowly and then moved her mouth as if to speak.

"Did you know you have the most amazing green eyes I have ever seen?"

Was she reading my mind?

"I have done nothing but think about them ever since I met you."

She could! She could read minds! Now all I had to do was to think of something I wanted to tell her and maybe she could see right through me and save me the embarrassment of actually saying anything.

"Fancy a coffee?"

Well, that wasn't what I was thinking, but it was a start.

"And maybe we could get to know each other better."

That was more like it. I was beginning to worry that she couldn't read my mind after all. "I'd love to." And I would. I couldn't wait to get to know the woman standing in front of me, and part of me was waking up to the realisation of what had transpired moments before. For the life of me I couldn't understand why I had tried to jump her bones in the middle of the car park. I couldn't work out why I had pounced on her the way I had. Never in my life had I kissed someone so rapaciously after only knowing them a matter of hours. Shaking my head, I saw Maria look questioningly at me. "Name your place."

The confused look disappeared and she leaned forward, her face coming closer.

I couldn't resist her, and all internal admonishments evaporated as we kissed gently again before making arrangements to meet at the café two roads away. And as she pulled away in her car, the thought popped into my head. *How on earth did she know where to find me?* With a grin, I said aloud, "I can just ask her." Yes. I liked the sound of that.

Turning the key in the ignition, I felt my future come alive again. What a day! Clean bill of health followed by the reason to live at all. What more could a woman want? And that was a loaded question. It was when I walked into the café, saw her look up from the menu and smile at me, that I knew the answer.

Dr Maria Moran. That's all I needed. All I would ever need. It was her eyes, you see. Her eyes. Looking into them I could see everything, see right inside her as she had looked right inside me.

Now I want you to imagine something. If it was like this after meeting each other twice, what would it be like when we actually got to know each other? And to tell you the truth, I couldn't wait to find out. Now was the time to start knowing, to start building on what we already had. It wasn't much, but actually, I felt it was everything at that precise moment. Only time would tell if we had a future, and the future I wanted was looking at me expectantly from the table, a delectable smile on her lips, a gleam in her eye, and me finally finding the momentum to move forward and join her.

Chapter 4

UNNY THING WAS, SITTING WITH her after the
snogging session in the car park seemed a little
unnerving. I am not usually the kind of person
who would take the bull by the horns and act on impulse.
All the time we were chatting, my traitorous brain was
replaying images of what had transpired between us, and
I felt a glow rush up my neck and spread all over my face
like a spilt strawberry milkshake.

"Are you okay? You seem to be sweating?"

Too bloody right I was. What kind of person did
she think I was? A slapper? A "loose" woman, whatever
the fuck that meant. Was it something like—I needed a
good screw to tighten up my loose bits? And why hadn't I
answered her?

"I'm fine. Just a little warm." I nodded towards the lone
candle glimmering weakly on the table, as if to blame my
condition on its inferno heat.

Maria looked at the candle also, her eyebrows
scrunching together.

"Must be coming in from the cold, and then getting
hot..." in more ways than one "that has made me flush."
Not a bad excuse, but I knew for a fact she hadn't bought
it. Mercifully, she didn't push the matter.

Silence. Golden silence. Golden silence that was panning out to be more than silence: it was almost echoey, well apart from all the other people's voices ringing in my head. I wanted to stop the silence, shoot it down with words, but, alas, the words were nowhere near ready to come out. So, silence continued. Where were all the thoughts I had thought when I had entered this dimly lit café? Starting to know, starting to build, starting to fuck things up big time, more like.

"Look...Gemma...I..."

I stopped twatting about with the napkin and looked up into her face. Those blue eyes had somehow managed to capture the feeble light clambering from the puny candle and bring it to life. Was she going to tell me that she'd made a mistake after all? My heart and stomach worked together in capturing my breath, readying me for the one hour relationship knock back.

"I'm sorry."

Thought so. Should I save her the trouble, the embarrassment of telling me that she thought I was a little forward and would rather not take this any further? Nope. My body had made the decision to wait it out, as it believed I hadn't suffered enough humiliation in my lifetime.

"About what happened in the car park."

See? I should join forces with Dr Horoscope, change my wardrobe to pink, and have done with it.

"If I moved too fast, I'm sorry."

Sorry?

"I'm not usually so forward...erm...and I think you are embarrassed."

Once again I sat and stared, and if sitting and staring had been a sport, I could have been an Olympic champion.

Maria leaned over the table, dodging Mr Candle on the way. "What I am trying to say is...shall we take things a little slower?"

Is this the new way of saying, "You're a minger, now fuck off"?

"I like you."

Maybe not, if the grin that slipped effortlessly over my face was any indication. She liked me. Me. Yes...*me*. And here I was doing a wonderful impression of the purrrfect Cheshire Cat and looking even more stupid than usual. If that was at all possible.

"And I like you, Maria." Not that difficult, was it? Just a bundle of sounds assembling together and pretending they were cool and collected.

It was her turn to smile, and as she did so, she leaned back in her chair and sighed.

What a beautiful sight; she was so bloody beautiful. And I think you are getting tired of me repeating this over and over again, but if you could have seen her, you would have said the exact same thing.

"So, does this mean we should start from the beginning?" Her head was tilted to one side.

I could tell she was waiting for my answer. A thought popped into my head, and I returned the smile she had given me. "Do I have to act all injured?"

Maria scrunched her eyes up, the smile still there, but looking a little more confused.

"You know...hold my arm and say 'ouch' on occasion?" She was still confused, and I was as clear as fog. "You said 'start from the beginning,' and our beginning was when you X-rayed me."

A light clicked on behind her eyes and I knew that the penny had finally dropped. But instead of laughter, the smile slipped slightly. Maria stretched her hand out and grasped her coffee cup, slowly lifting it to her mouth and taking a huge sip. "We could do that, I suppose."

Yes, we could. Easily, as it happens.

"But..."

Was she looking uncomfortable?

"That wouldn't be quite accurate."

Now it was my turn to look confused. She cleared her throat, and so did I. So, she cleared hers again. I didn't quite know what to expect, and I could feel a tension creeping up my body, but for the life of me, I couldn't tell you why. Because I'm thick, I suppose.

"I've seen you before."

"Eh?" Woman of many insightful words. No wonder I teach English.

"I said... I've seen you before last Tuesday. A few times actually."

Where? When? How? And finally... *What the fuck?*

"The first time was about two months ago...not long after I moved to Norwich, actually."

And she remembered me? Back to the "How?" and for good measure, "Why?"

It might have been the incredulous look on my face that made her falter and take another gulp of her coffee, but wouldn't you look a tad intrigued? "I was in The Castle."

"Norwich Castle?" I hadn't been to Norwich Castle since the History Department made me go two years ago.

She must have been mistaken. I was just on the verge of putting her straight, when she stopped me.

"The Castle Pub. Off Kett's Hill."

Ah... The Castle Pub, just off Kett's Hill...that one. The gay one.

"You were...erm...you were dancing on the stage."

Aw fuck. I should've known it would have been that night. It had to be *that* night didn't it? I told my mate Colin I didn't want to go on the stage, but he insisted, told me in his pissed up way to show them how much they wanted me. And like a git, after too many sniffs at the alcohol, I had joined in. Briefly. It hadn't been the best experience of my life, not by a long shot. And here was the woman I wanted to only ever think of me in a perfect way telling me the first time she had clapped her eyes on me I had been dancing like a Muppet. Could this get any worse?

"I saw you from where I was standing at the bar, and before I knew it, I was wading my way through the crowds toward you, as part of me wanted to say hello." Another gulp and her coffee was finished. She paused in her embarrassing recollection of my "Hot Gossip (the shite dancing group on Top of the Pops) on crack" to gesture to the waitress she would like another one.

I was waiting *almost* patiently for her to continue, but when I saw the grimace flash across her face, I wanted to change the subject. "Someone threw her knickers at you and they stuck to your face..."

Did I actually ask if things could get any worse before? "and..."

Please, don't continue...

"you went crackers."

Wouldn't you? Some tit-head had the gall to throw underwear at me—underwear that could stick to skin—and I was supposed to act all understanding and calm? I was pissed up, but not comatose.

"Actually, the way you threw your arms around, I did wonder if that's how you got the arm injury."

This was the point where I was glad the candle was so crap. In fact, I could have blown the fucker out and lit the whole café with the glow coming off my face. The images of that night came flooding back into my head, and I remembered it vividly. It was Colin's fault. Just because we were celebrating him getting a promotion, I had allowed my usual "stick up my arse" to be removed for one night only. As if by the magic of memory, I felt a stiffness cover my cheek, and my hand swiped at the spot where the knickers had jammed themselves to my horrified flesh. I can't believe I had forgotten about it until she had mentioned it. Must have been the trauma.

A waitress came over and plunked two more coffees in front of us and collected the dirty cups. We both sat in silence and waited for her to shift. Part of me wanted her to take her time, as I still hadn't thought of a response. But no. She must have been the quickest waitress in Norfolk. Just my luck. Before I could say Jack Robinson, or any other epithet of useless intent, she was gone, the cups clinking together like a Town Crier's bell. I had to say something, anything, to get myself out the feeling of utter dickheaddom into which I had been propelled.

"What made you not speak to me then?" Wherever that had come from, it should have stayed. It was the most stupid question I think I could have asked. I mean, why would she speak to me after that manic performance? And me asking! Would you speak to someone who looked as if they were being stung repeatedly by a swarm of killer bees, flapping her arms around, and even smacking the bloke next to her in the face in the process? Although Colin did deserve it. Then rush off into the loos to scrub her burning skin? Shall we agree that the question I asked her was rhetorical?

"I was going to, but you ran away."

Fuck. She saw that bit too, although I doubted many people missed it that night, as I did scream and wave my arms around like a maniac.

"And before I knew what was happening, I got kicked in the face."

Kicked in the... Aw double fuck. That was Colin AGAIN. He had gotten a second wind after my hasty departure, and also commented that the thwack I had given him had incited his creativity. Hence, my friend, soon to be ex-friend, had jumped up and grabbed the rafters, and swung his legs up and out into the crowd. Next thing he knew, he was being pulled outside by the bouncers who informed him that the lesbians were complaining after one had been kicked in the head and that he had to calm things down. No swinging from the rafters, leave the lesbians alone, and put his knickers away.

"I went home not long after that, as I had a black eye."

Shit. Colin was going to pay for this. Dearly. On top of making me cleanse and tone for a month, he had given her a shiner. How do you top that? What do you say? Sorry? It wasn't me? Colin has been committed? Considering what she had seen and experienced, none of them seemed worthy of even a half arsed attempt to get off the hook.

"But," she paused and waited for me to make eye contact, "you know what the most painful thing was about that night?"

My dancing? I shook my head and began to worry about what other moronic thing I could have done that could be more painful than everything she had already told me.

"I never got to speak to you. I didn't even find out the name of the woman who had made me walk across a packed dance floor just in the hope of hearing her voice."

That wasn't what I was expecting, not by a long shot. And all the tension seemed to melt away as I looked into those blue eyes, blue eyes that looked at me so openly and with such honesty. If it had been anyone else I would have told them that it was the corniest line I had ever heard, but not her. From those perfect lips it seemed as if the last thing she had said had taken a thousand lifetimes to create. I could feel myself turning into a ball of mush in front of her, and I had to force myself to sit erect.

"Really?" This should have been spoken in a suggestive way, a sensual and alluring way, but instead it came out accusatory. So I tried again. "You really thought that?" Did that sound any better? Or did it sound like I didn't believe her times two?

"Yes...*really*." Thankfully she appeared to have overlooked my social faux pas and allowed my inability to question with tact to slip by unnoticed. "But I must admit, it was worth the wait."

I wanted to say "really?" again, this time with a dreamy tone, but I just grinned stupidly before realising I had to snap out of the haze that was drifting over me. This woman was a charmer of the highest order, and for once in my life I was loving it. I wanted to fall for her charm, fall for her one-liners, and then fall into her arms to rest my head against her chest and stay there. Part of me thought I was jumping the gun a little. A lot, actually. In fact, I was halfway around the track and the bloke who was supposed to start the race hadn't lifted the gun yet. Time to go back to the start line and try to keep track of the proper proceedings, or, more succinctly, the correct protocol for first dates.

First dates. Fuck. This was a first date, wasn't it? She had sent me a valentine's card and then we had met for coffee, not forgetting the snogging session in the car park. At this point, I felt exposed again. Thoughts of Colin and his size thirteen feet aside—even the sticking knickers taking a back seat, however hard they had been to shake off—this was me and the doctor out for coffee, and maybe the chance for something more. And that final word was the one that grabbed my attention the most. More. Even "something more". I did want something more, but I didn't want it to be just something I did once and then told myself I wasn't dreaming. I wanted to get to know the woman who was by now leaning forward and looking concerned, and not just know her in the Biblical sense.

And now, in the words of Monty Python, time for something completely different. Have you ever had a panic attack? I haven't, but the feeling welling up inside my chest, the one sneaking up my throat, the tightness of my skin and the inability to breathe properly gave me an indication that I would be soon having the hands-on experience of what one would feel like. Either that, or I was having a heart attack. And why? Because this woman was too beautiful for me, too perfect, too out of my league, and my body, brain, heart, and soul knew it. Therefore they would have to rebel, stop the consummation of the "something more". Destroy any chance I had with this woman before it began.

"So..." I was surprised she didn't ask me what the matter was, because I was sure the beads of sweat would be glowing like pound coins all over my face by this point. "Can we take things more slowly?"

And just by her repeating the question she had asked me before, it felt as if an invisible paper bag had been placed over my mouth and nostrils. Instead of answering her straight away, I did the next best thing a person could do when they had an imaginary paper bag on her face. I slipped my hand in hers and squeezed her fingers. Such long capable fingers—warm, too. Safe, secure fingers. Fingers that made the bag disappear completely.

"I would like that, Maria." Within a few minutes I had gone from looking like a twat to being a twat, a twat who nearly embarrassed herself fully, to a woman who would take whatever came her way. If she found out that I wasn't the person she thought I might be as she struggled across the dance floor to get a kick in the face for her efforts, so be it. I, for one, wasn't going to miss the opportunity of getting to know her, being with her, maybe building this night in a café into something more, something lasting. I would have been a fool to, wouldn't I?

But even as the tension shifted and the ambience of the dimly lit café reasserted itself, there was a burning question at the back of my mind. That question that we ask ourselves so many times a day with the knowledge that it will never come to anything, the same one we know is a rhetorical question after all. The one that begins with the ever elusive "What if..."

And why did this innocent, usually rhetorical question have the quality of becoming a non-rhetorical question? Fuck knows, but it was there all the same. I'd better get a stock of imaginary paper bags ready.

It was over too quickly. The night in the café, I mean. After we had revisited the escapade of Colin and his acrobatic skills, the conversation changed. I don't know why, it just did. I didn't even bring up the other times she had mentioned she had seen me, just in case they were as bad as the first. But that didn't stop me from wondering about them.

By the time we reached the car park, I was a bag of nerves. What if (See? Here already.) she didn't ask to see me again? I know. I could've just asked her if she wanted to do something over the weekend, but there was a part of me that was still in denial. Sometimes I wish I could just take the initiative. I know I had done previously, but those occasions came few and far between. Each step I took towards my car seemed like a step away from everything I wanted. Freaky, I can tell you, because Maria was right next to me. It might have been metaphoric, although I don't think my panicked brain could've conjured up anything that had such a posh word to back it up. It was taking all its time telling my legs to move one in front of the other. Shakily.

Standing next to my car, I turned to her, a part of me wanting the night to never end. Maria was close to me, but there was still a safe distance between us. Maybe she thought I would jump her bones again.

"So..." Why did I stop speaking? That's easy. I wasn't sure what to say. I wanted to tell her I had a wonderful night...tell her I wanted this to continue, but nothing came out. I think it was her face that dried up my words. No. It wasn't like she was grimacing, or showing signs of inner prayer; it was the expectation. Funny thing was, my brain was still on leg duty, and therefore the only thing that sprouted from my mouth was the question I had been avoiding all night. "Tell me—where else have you seen me then?"

In a flash the expectation was gone, and I am definite I saw embarrassment take its place. Crap-itty crap. What else had I done? Kicked a puppy? Walked into her house on Christmas Day and pissed on her kids? I know, I would never, and I repeat *never* kick a puppy. And whilst I was having the demons of forgotten memories whirl around my head, I didn't even notice that her face was back to normal again. It wasn't until she said my name and touched my arm that I came back to the land of the here and now.

"Tell you what?"

What? You can't get my pee stains out of your carpet?

"I'll tell you when you agree to come out with me again. How does that sound?"

Does the word "perfect" sum it up? Do I need something more Latinate? Regal? Ostentatious? "Perfect." Nope. "Perfect" was fine, if her face was any indication.

"Are you free on Saturday?"

And that was it. Saturday would be the time I would see her again, as she was going to pick me up from my house at seven-thirty. That is to say, she would be there if she could understand my hastily drawn map. It is hard to draw a map on a scrap of paper, leaning on the bonnet of your car, being watched by the most gorgeous woman you have ever seen, and your hand shaking like a shitting dog.

When I offered her the map, her hand hovered slightly before taking the scrap of paper and slipping it into the inside pocket of her leather jacket, the same leather jacket she had been wearing the last time I had seen her. Part of me, a bloody big part, wanted to stroke the softness of it, but for once my body did as it was told.

"Okay then, Saturday night it is." She paused. "Is there anything you would like to do, or should I just surprise you?"

Even more so than you have already? I mean, you sent me a Valentine's card, came out of the blackness of the night like a dream, swept me off my feet, and have asked me out again. "I'm easy." Why do I always go red when I say that? I meant "easy" as in "easily pleased"...and I'm bollocking things up again.

"There's something I want to do before I let you go."

Red alert! Red alert! She was going to kiss me...see if the easy I had said I was, was the kind of easy that would make me a loose woman. *Bugger.* And there was the loose woman again. And yes; I was panicking. I thought we were going to take things slowly; where had *slowly* gone? I missed *slowly,* as I wasn't ready to show her just how much I wanted her at that precise moment. But her hand was coming toward me, and I was trying to swallow my heart back down and into my chest. My mouth was losing all moisture, and my stomach was performing some kind of acrobatic swan dive. I could feel her hand on my hip and the heat began to burn through the layers I was wearing. Then it was gone. Had she noticed I was in the state that precedes a faint?

"Let me..." her arms were above me now, "put..." and they were coming down, "your hat on. You'll catch your death. Look. You're shivering." The woollen material slipped effortlessly over my unruly hair and clamped itself to my head. "Come on. You get in your car and get warm." Quick as a flash, Maria kissed my cheek. "See you Saturday, Gem."

Gem? Gem? She called me Gem. I liked Gem. And I was standing "shivering" in front of my car, and she was looking at me. Why was she looking at me in the way people do when they are waiting for you to do something? Probably because she was waiting for me to get my lardy arse into gear and get into my bloody car and let her go home. See? It doesn't take a genius to work that out. Even I cracked the code eventually.

A smile shot onto my face as it dawned on me that at that moment in time I would only have less than forty-eight hours before I could see her again. I couldn't help the next thing I did. It was automatic. It was as if I jumped forward to kiss her, the excitement making me lose all reservations. One set of lips meeting another, warmer set of lips, and as quickly as they hit their mark, they were separate again. The crazy thing was that even though I pulled away rapidly, I could still feel them. Soft. Warm. And slightly parted. I wanted to do it again, take the initiative again, and the few and far between times I seemed to take it were rapidly becoming a thing of the past, as part of me was becoming an initiative junkie, but I controlled myself.

"See you Saturday, Maria."

She waited for me to start my engine and pull away, but as I reached the exit of the car park, I stopped and looked into my rear view mirror. Maria was still standing there, her fingers on her mouth, her eyes closed. That's all I needed to know for sure. Dr Maria Moran wanted me, too. And that, I believe, was the best feeling I had ever had in my life.

Pulling out of the car park, I felt a jolt of happiness fly through my body. It had been too long since I had felt anything as exhilarating as that...if I had ever felt anything as wonderful as that in the first place. I couldn't wait until Saturday. Couldn't wait. But at least it gave me two days to get myself ready to see her again. Two days. I glanced at the clock in my car and quickly worked it out. Forty-four hours and twenty-three minutes until I could look into her eyes again, hear her voice again, just bask in her presence *again*.

What was the matter with me? I was acting like a teenager. A love struck teenager to boot. Thank God I didn't have acne. Now that would have been a little too much role playing, even for me. Here I was, a thirty-nine-year-old woman feeling as if she had just hit puberty and was having a rush of the hormonals. If this was what I was like now, God help Maria when Saturday came.

A grin sneaked over my face. Yes. God help her.

Chapter 5

RIDAY WAS A BITCH. A total bitch. The kids were like fleas on a rice pudding, and each and every lesson crawled by as if it was a tortoise on downers. It could have been that I was waiting for the next day to arrive more quickly, or it could have been that the kids were affected by the wind outside. Who am I kidding? It was because I was seeing Maria the next day. Obviously!

It didn't help that the tutor time at the end of the day focused on the sex education class I had taught the previous morning to my demented tutor group. Part of me wondered why on earth I had put a question box on my desk for the kids to write questions they might be too embarrassed to ask in front of others. Embarrassed my arse. Their main objective was to get me to say words like "penis" and "vagina" in front of thirty smug faces. I know they are only thirteen, but come on! They knew more than I did.

Sifting through the questions, I put them in rank order. The first one I picked up simply said "Will it hurt?" I smiled and wanted to say, "Imagine driving a nail through your nipple" or "shoving a cucumber up your nose" but I decided that the "Will it hurt?" didn't just mean life in general, so I kept that one on the top. I have never known my tutees to get back to tutor time so promptly; I was always left waiting at least five minutes for them to amble in as if they had all the time in the world. I didn't even have time to get the room ready before the last one was in the door.

After the first few explanations I gave, the class seemed to realise that I wasn't getting embarrassed after all. Some people think that talking to a bunch of kids about sex education is the most daunting thing to ever happen, but in all honesty it felt like an honour. Well, when I say "honour", I still had to get through the stupid questions, "How does a man who doesn't have a willy have sex?" With great difficulty, I should imagine. "If I masturbate and then finger the girl, can I get her pregnant?" Wash your hands...and not just when you are playing with bits and pieces. Wash your hands, with soap. It's amazing to think the only time I saw my tutor group with clean hands was after they had made bread in cookery. No wonder I always refused their burnt offerings, even before the fingering/masturbating question. "Can you get pregnant if you don't have sex?" Yes. And then I sat back to watch them squirm for a few moments before explaining they had to do more than kiss with their clothes on. A beauty of a question came right near the end of the pile. "How do lesbians have sex?"

I had read it before but as soon as I lifted the question to read it aloud and then answer, Maria's face floated in front of my own. It wouldn't have been so bad if my imaginings had stayed on her face, but they didn't. Unfortunately. The image expanded to two bodies writhing in the midst of carnal infusion, and I felt the blush start to creep up from my neck. I couldn't answer this one yet; I knew it was too close to home. Looking up from the scabby piece of paper, my eyes met a class waiting for me to continue. So, I looked back at it again, then back up. Yep. They were still there. And so was the unanswered question.

"Could you give me a minute? I have to give something to Mrs Roland." Standing up quickly, I snatched a folder from my desk and marched out of the room as if the Hounds of Hell were chasing me. The next minute I was standing in the English office, clutching the folder to my chest. What was I doing? Why had I been able to talk about lack of willies, fingering, masturbation, and penetration, and not miss a beat? Maybe because none of that hit home as much as the last question, you know—lesbians performing the beast with two backs. And trust Maria to pop into my head at that precise moment. Bollocks. I couldn't just stand about for the remaining few minutes of the day and hide away; I had to get back and finish the session.

Walking over to the sink, I grabbed a glass and filled it with water. With one gulp it was gone, and I turned, breathed deeply, and made my way back to my tormentors.

Even before I reached the door, I could hear them whispering in their usual loud whispering way. One more deep breath and I was inside, shushing them before making my way to my seat.

"Where was I? Oh, yes..." Lifting the stack of papers off my desk, I slipped the lesbian question to the bottom. "Okay. If two fourteen-year-olds are caught having sex, can they get arrested?" I actually saw the kids look at each other, and I knew they had been discussing the reason why I had left the room.

"That isn't an embarrassing question. What is going on? We feel cheated."

I couldn't help but smile at them. A huge smile. A shit eating smile. And then I answered. And they still looked disappointed. Good.

"Can pregnancy tests be wrong? Cos my mate did one and it said she was, then she went to the doc's with her mum and she wasn't."

And then... "How do lesbians have sex?" I wanted to ask them if they would prefer a diagram, but I knew they would love it, so... "With each other, I suppose."

Brrrrrrrrrrrrrrrring! Saved by the bell, and I have never been so bloody happy to hear it. Not because I knew they were bursting for me to elaborate on the final answer, but because the sound of the bell meant it was only twenty-eight hours before I saw her again. Maybe she could answer the kids' question. She was a doctor, after all.

Friday night saw me getting lessons ready for Monday. Surprised? I was. My usual time for getting ready for the upcoming week was late Sunday, or even Monday morning, accompanied by frantic typing, racing to the print room, followed by my putting the last touches on my first lesson with Year 7 as they were lining up outside my room. But tonight was different. It wasn't a case of following my "after Christmas" pledge to always be prepared, it was more a case of trying to occupy myself for long enough so I didn't start the usual demon thought process I always ran through when I was worried. You know—the thoughts about how I was bound to fuck up big time as soon as I clapped eyes on Maria the following night...thoughts like, "She won't turn up anyway, so why are you worried about what you are going to do to fuck things up?"

It was gone two in the morning when I allowed myself to stop trying to nitpick the following Friday's lessons apart and finally decided it was time to get to bed. Thankfully. I slept the sleep of the dead and wasn't haunted by dreams, although the covers on my bed would say otherwise.

Saturday morning came along in her cheerful way, and I was up, fed, and showered well before ten. Sitting alone at the kitchen table, I deliberated how I was going to spend the rest of my day. Work was sorted. I didn't need groceries. The house was tidy, for a change. I had been sitting staring out of the kitchen window for God knows how long when the phone shrilled its existence. My first thought was it was her, cancelling, and when I heard the cheery male voice on the line, I was momentarily taken aback.

"Morning, sunshine! Up for lunch?"

Col. The one person I wasn't expecting to be up early at the weekend.

"You there?"

I grunted a response, a response that was enough for him to blabber on and on about something that for the life of me I couldn't tell you what. All I knew was it ended with "So...you up for lunch? My treat?" Funny how thought processes go, isn't it. Col's voice...thinking of him singing...thinking of him drunk...thinking of him paying for lunch...moving on to—he has more money...

promotion...pissed...kicking the lesbian in the head... Maria's head, to be exact.

"That would be great, Col."

After putting the phone down, I realised I wasn't nervous about how the evening would pan out; I had more important things to do. The first one was to bollock my friend about his behaviour, although if my memory served me right, he always behaved like that. So why did this time make a difference? Was this maturity kicking in? (Excuse the pun on kicking. It wasn't intended.) Was this fate that he should ring on the day I was to meet with his Doc Marten victim? Would he remember the events of the night and say "Look, Gem, don't go near that woman. She is a fruitcake...believe me. She leapt into my boot and then tried to get me evicted." Who am I kidding? He couldn't remember his name by the end of that night, never mind anything else.

Two hours later I was slipping into a seat opposite my overly excited friend. I knew he was overly excited because as I was sitting down, he lunged forward and tried to give me an excessively zealous kiss on the cheek. However, it didn't go as he, or I, for that matter, planned. Instead of an air kiss of welcome, he gave me a head butt right on my nose. I heard the crack, and then felt myself slump back on the chair, lights beginning to sparkle and swirl around me. I think there were a few birds flying around, too. Through tear-stained eyes, I saw that Col was back in his seat now, the grin splitting his face...for a moment, that is, and it wasn't because I was trying to gather my thoughts together so I could give him a sample of them, none of them what he would be expecting. It was more like he was just about to pass out that made the smile slip from his lips. Lifting my hand, I guided my fingers to pinch the bridge of my nose to try and click it back into place, but the sudden change in his appearance stopped me.

"You okay, Col?"

His mouth was moving, but the words he wanted to say seemed to be stuck.

"You okay?" Did he look okay? Did he? Bollocks. He looked as if his fake tan was slipping down his neck, as the colour had all gone by now. A solitary hand stretched forward and he pointed at my face, words still having difficulty making an entrance. "You're freaking me out now. What is it? You need help?" I needed help. My nose was aching like a bitch by this stage, and all I wanted to do was to give it a sharp push so it would feel normal again.

"Blood."

Blood? What was this? Was he pissed again?

"Blood. There."

Blood? Where?

"Face. Bleeding."

No it wasn't. His face was anything but bleeding. White. That's what it was. Not even a Dulux rose white, just white. Then I tasted it. That iron taste that comes with blood. My blood, to be exact. My blood trickling down my face and into my mouth. Swiping my hand across my lips I saw it. Glistening. Scarlet. Fresh. Mine. *Fuck.*

"Nose."

"For fuck's sake, Col!" By this stage I was rummaging around in my bag, trying to hunt out a tissue. "My nose is bleeding. I get it. Get over it."

"Nose...your nose..."

He must've hit his head harder than I realised. If the pain racing though my face was any indication, I already knew he'd given his head a good whack.

Click.

Well, when I say "click", what I actually meant to say was "CLICK!" My nose, that was pissing blood like a soda siphon, had decided it was time to go back into place. Honestly. I'm going to plead my case to you, as I think you might believe me more than all the other customers in the café at the time. When I shouted, *"Fucking hell! Fuck fuck fucking hell!"* it was out of pain alone, and not because I wanted to kill Colin. That came later. Three hours later, in fact. Most of which was spent waiting in Accident and Emergency to see a doctor, who promptly informed me that my nose was broken, broken and bruised. And the bruising was making its way around my eyes. The same eyes that had a date with a beautiful woman in four hours, the same two black eyes that would be accompanied by a broken nose *and* a criminal record, if the way I felt about Colin bore the fruit of action.

Colin couldn't apologise enough. Too bloody right. He couldn't apologise enough to make me feel better. What was I going to do? I was supposed to be going out on a date with Maria, but how could I when I either looked like an extra from *The Munsters*, or worse still (as if it could get any worse), Chi Chi the panda. No wonder pandas were becoming extinct. Two black-rimmed eyes were not sexy in my book, and by the looks of the panda population, not in theirs either.

Throughout the journey home, I spent my time glaring out of the window, cringing every time I caught my reflection. It wasn't until Col's car came to a halt outside my house that I could bear to face him.

His hands gripping the steering wheel, he was looking forlornly at the dashboard.

There was still a part of me that wanted to grab the back of his head and bang it repeatedly onto the solid plastic disc, but there was also a bigger part that felt a hint of sympathy. I could tell that he was sorry, although sorry didn't butter my bread at the moment, but what else could I do? I know—I could break his nose and give him two shiners to match mine, or I could reach out.

"Hey." I saw his eyes flutter, and I spotted the tears welling there. "Come on, Col. It's not that bad." Over the tears went, making their way down his face in a bid to flee the scene, a bit like I think he was feeling at the moment. "The bruising will go."

At that, he lifted his eyes and looked me squarely in the face, the first time since the incident in the café.

Even when I was ranting and raving at him, he had avoided looking at me. I knew it was because he was feeling guilty. It didn't take a rocket scientist to work out that if he hadn't tried to kiss me, my nose would be as straight as it always was rather than looking like it had been battered with a cricket bat. With that thought, I remembered that he had seemed a little too excited about just seeing me. There must have been something he wanted to share, but by the looks of him now, all of his excitement had disappeared.

"Gemma...I...I..." Tears stopped him from continuing.

"It's no big deal, Col. The bruising will go." *But not before tonight.* That I knew for a fact. There was no way I would tell Col about my date with Maria as he was upset enough already, and if he knew that he had buggered up my chances of being with the gorgeous doctor... Aah, let's just say it would tip him over the edge. He had been waiting for far too long for me to get my act together and find someone. Seemed quite ironic, really. Swallowing the disappointment, I leaned over and took his clammy hand in mine. "It was an accident...and you know why they are called accidents?"

He sniffed and shook his head.

"Because you didn't mean to do it. You were only trying to give me a kiss...say hello...show you were pleased to see me."

"I was..." Col swallowed again, "pleased to see you... and not just because I had news to tell you." Even though his face was streaked with tears, I spied a glimmer of a smile playing around his mouth.

"What news?"

Turning to me, Col's smile spread out fully, before he remembered that this was not the time to be grinning. "It doesn't matter now. Let's get you inside and settled."

"You're not getting away that easily, Col. Spill." I knew he was going to refuse me again, so I grabbed his jaw and pulled him toward me. "You've broken my nose, so the least you could do is tell me what you were grinning about." His eyes widened just an instant before he let out a laugh, my hand leaving his face in the process. Swiping the errant tears from his cheeks, he nodded.

"Okay, Hughes. Let me make you a coffee and I'll tell you."

I gave him the one raised eyebrow look.

"Without the head butt greeting."

When I laughed, I felt the pain shoot up my nose and through my cheeks, making me wince.

"And maybe get you an ice pack for those eyes."

With that, we got out of the car and made our way into my humble abode.

Ten minutes later we were in the lounge, both on the sofa with our feet on the coffee table, steaming mugs in our hands. Stuff the ice pack. I had gone way past saving my peepers from growing blacker by the minute. Apart from the pain in my face and the worry about meeting Maria looking like death, I was pretty chilled out. Then it dawned on me that Col hadn't told his all. "I'm waiting."

I felt him shift next to me, and I knew he was plunking his cup down. Turning my head, I saw that he was staring at me sporting the look of an excited eight-year-old boy. "I hope he's worth it."

His look changed quickly, and he scrunched up his face as if to say, "How did you know?"

I grinned at him. "For God's sake, Col, you're so transparent."

The grin was back on his face.

Leaning forward, Col shuffled into narrative position. You know the one. It's the one where you make sure the person who is listening to you is in fact listening and not checking out the wallpaper behind your head. "I met him on the night we last went to the Castle."

Castle? I hadn't been to the Castle with Colin. The last time I had been to Norwich Cas...

"The night I nearly got evicted."

That Castle. The gay Castle. Why did I always think of that bloody history trip? It wasn't as if it was that interesting. Well, admittedly the dungeons were pretty coo—

"His name is Trevor."

I didn't remember a Trevor. Although, up until I'd had a coffee with Maria, I hadn't really remembered anything about that night.

"He's a doctor."

That made me sit up, spilling the remaining bit of my coffee all over me.

Without flinching, Col snatched a handful of tissues from the box on the table and started to wipe me down. "I know! A doctor."

This seemed a little too coincidental. I mean, two doctors on one night? One hitting their target whilst the other was the target being hit seemed too perfect—well, apart from Maria being my prototype, as she only got one shiner from Colin.

"After you ran off screaming to the loos, he came up to me to ask if you were okay." He laughed at that, but I just waited for him to get over himself. "Remember me telling you about swinging from the rafters?"

"Kind of." Or I remembered Maria telling me, more like.

"And I kicked someone in the head?" He looked so happy. *Git.*

"Kind of." *Did I growl that one out?*

"He was the one who grassed me up to the bouncers."

So why was he grinning like he'd lost a penny and found a wallet full of tenners? The bloke he seemed to have fallen for was the one who told the door men that Col was swinging from the rafters and had kicked someone in the head, and nearly got him evicted.

"Well, he wasn't the one who actually told them. He went to do it, but someone beat him to it."

I wished it had been me.

"But after I'd been outside being told off, he came to tell me off, too."

Was I hearing this right? Had the blow to my face knocked all sense of reality out of me?

"We got chatting—after I calmed him down, that is. You left not long after you came out of the loos, and told me in no uncertain terms that you would prefer me to stay."

Wouldn't you? I was concerned with what trouble he would get me into on the way home, and thought it would be wiser to let him stay where he was.

"He left not long after too, but not before I got his number." The grin was back in full force by now. "We've been seeing each other for nearly two months now...and, Gem?"

I couldn't even respond; I was too bloody stunned.

"I love him."

Being stunned evaporated as the weight of his words hit home. Colin had never admitted to being in love with anyone before, and I had known him for years. Lust, yes; craving and fascination, once a month at least. But love? Nope. This was a first. Colin was too much of a free spirit, to use a crappy expression. He liked to be able to make his own choices, and that didn't include the words "I love him."

Colin didn't even notice that my mouth was open, or if he did, it didn't stop him from continuing. "I wanted to see you today to ask if you would come out tonight...meet him. I've told him all about you."

"I can't."

"Look. Don't worry about your black eyes. For one thing, he wouldn't be interested in your looks, with or without the shiners." I think he knew the statement wasn't welcome, and the laugh he emitted died halfway out of his mouth. "Sorry, Gem. I'm acting like a twat."

Yes, you are.

"I just wanted the most important person in my world to meet the other most important person in my world." He slumped back on the seat as his effervescent bubble popped in front of my eyes. "And all I ever seem to do is bugger things up." Puppy dog eyes looked my way. "If I hadn't given you two black eyes, would you have come?"

"No." I think my answer surprised him as much as when he had inadvertently cracked me in the face. "Nothing personal, Col. It's just...just..." I hesitated and then finished, "I have a date tonight. Or I did."

"Did?"

"How can I go and meet her when I look like this?" I waved my hand in front of my face in a gesture that encompassed it all. "One look at me and it'll be 'Cheque, please!'"

Colin leaned back toward me, his face serious. "If she is put off by a couple of black eyes, she is not worth bothering about anyway."

True.

"You have more beauty in your little finger than most people see in a lifetime."

What a lovely thing to say. Sometimes Colin surprised me...not often, but sometimes.

"And even if she was put off, the condition is not permanent. You'll be back to being a stunner in no time."

Sentimental moment over.

"So...who is she? What does she do? Is she a fox?"

At that point I could have gone crackers, or cried, but I thought I would just bear it. I wanted to talk it over with someone, and Colin was my best option. For all his faults, I loved him, trusted him, and relied on him to tell me straight if I was doing the right thing.

"Her name is Maria. And she's a doctor too."

"You are winding me up!"

"Nope. Dr Maria Moran." Slapping him on the knee, I stood up. "And yes...fox is an understatement." With that I stood up and left the room. At least I had given him something to think about. I could hear him calling after me as I climbed the stairs and I couldn't help the painful smile that filled my face. His voice started to get nearer and I knew he was following me. Like a kid I started to giggle and run up the stairs, taking two at a time. Colin was right behind me, trying to grab my ankle, but I beat him to the bathroom and slammed the door in his face.

"Let me in! Let me in, you git!" Bam! Bam! Bam! "I don't want to have to break the door down!"

That made me laugh. Colin breaking the door down? As if!

"I can hear you laughing. I will break it down." Thud. "Ow!" Thud. "OW!"

Quiet.

Thud. "For fuck's sake, Gem, are you trying to injure me? Let me in. Please! I promise to be good."

Another thud. Then silence. And more silence. Part of me wondered if he had knocked himself out.

A few minutes passed and Colin hadn't made a sound. Part of me believed he was trying to trick me, but another part of me started to worry. What if he was lying in a pool of his own blood? Most accidents happen in the home, don't they? I touched my nose and cringed. Look how quickly I had gone from normal to freak. It had been just an ordinary thing to do to lean over and give someone a kiss, and look what that had gotten me—two black eyes and a broken nose. And by the sound of Colin thumping on the door... *Jesus.* Panic was definitely setting in now. "Col?" Nothing. "Col? You okay?" Still nothing. I touched the bolt tentatively. Cold metal greeted my fingers. "Are you okay?" Still nothing.

I opened the door slowly and, right enough, there was Colin lying on the floor. *Fuck!* He'd whacked himself too hard and flaked out. It wasn't until I was on my knees beside him that I realised I'd been had.

Two hands grabbed my waist and pulled me down. "Gotcha."

Relief, and pain in my nose from being pulled down, flooded through me, although I should've been angry.

"And you're not going anywhere until you tell me everything."

So, I did. It was weird enough actually telling someone all about how I had been feeling about Maria, even though I hadn't known her for all that long. When I told Col the part about The Castle and it being her he kicked in the head, his eyes widened an instant before a guffaw shot out his mouth. I joined him. How could I not? Here we were, after he had broken my nose, on the floor, me on top of him, talking about him kicking the woman I was enamoured with in the head. It must have been nerves, or something just as fucked up.

Half an hour later, Col rose to go, but not before he pulled me into a hug and whispered in my ear, "You'll be fine tonight, Gem. You'll blow her away."

"Even looking like the losing opponent?"

Drawing back, his dark grey eyes looked squarely into my green ones. "You could never be a loser, Gem. Never. Your heart is too pure for you to lose." A kiss landed on my cheek. "And if Doctor Maria can't see that...she's not the one." With that he was gone, and I was left standing in the doorway, watching my best friend climb into his car and pull away.

But I wanted her to be the one, wanted it so much. Inside I honestly believed that I knew she was the one. I could only hope that deep inside her, Maria knew it too.

Closing the door, I turned and saw my reflection in the hallway mirror. How on earth could I meet her looking like this? But then again, how did I get out of it? I didn't have her phone number, well, apart from her work phone, and she wouldn't be there. Hesitantly I ran my fingers over the bruised flesh, gliding over the bump in my nose where it had swollen. Colin's words came back to me, *"You'll blow her away."* More like make her run for the hills screaming. *"If she is put off by that, then she's not worth bothering about anyway."* Easy for him to say. If it had happened to Colin, he wouldn't have left the house, so why on earth was I even contemplating meeting Maria?

Because I needed to. Not just wanted to, *needed* to.

Decision made, I turned away from my reflection and dragged myself up the stairs. It was too early to start getting ready, but with my face the way it was, I needed all the extra time I had.

Chapter 6

*D*ING DONG. SEVEN-THIRTY ON THE nose—
excuse the pun—Maria was standing at my
doorstep waiting for me to get up the courage
to open the door. Pushing my sunglasses into place, I
twisted the lock, pushed the door open, and felt the cool
air hit my skin.

"Hey—Jesus! What happened to you?" Maria didn't
even wait for me to answer before she was inside the house,
her hands on my face. Sunglasses were carefully slipped
away, and concerned blue eyes stared into my own. "You've
broken your nose."

"No wonder you're a doctor." The words came out
quickly, followed by a nervous laugh.

"All part of the training." A small smile flitted over her
mouth, and then she was back to being professional again.
"When did you do that? How did it happen? Have you had
it checked out? Wh—"

Gripping her hand, I moved it away from the swollen
flesh and waited for her attention. "If you give me a chance
to answer, I'll tell you all about it." Tilting my head to
the side, I smiled, and although it made my face ache, the

smile she gave me in return was worth it. "Come in, and let me shut the door."

Inside, I led her to the living room and gestured for her to sit on the sofa. "Do you fancy a drink before we go out?"

She was just settling herself down, but she stopped short and looked up at me.

"What? Did you think a couple of black eyes and a broken nose would keep me from wanting to go out with you?" Blue eyes widened and I knew that was exactly what she had been thinking. "Don't you want to be seen in public with Uncle Fester?" I meant it as a jest, but I don't think she quite had the hang of my sense of humour. That is, if her darting back up from the sofa and racing around the coffee table to stand in front of me was any indication that she hadn't gotten the joke, I don't know what it was. Maybe because deep down, although I had tried to make it sound as if I was joking, I was in fact hoping that she would respond exactly this. I know. Just like a woman.

"I don't care if you have a busted nose...or black eyes; it's you I want to be with." Once again she gently cupped my chin and tipped my head up to meet hers. "I am more concerned about concussion—bright lights affecting you, headaches, the feeling of being uncomfortable out in the open air."

Concussion? Had I missed that bit at the hospital? No one had mentioned I could have concussion. *Bollocks.* And when you realise that you could actually be on death's door, that exactly how you respond, isn't it? Like the energy has been sucked from you.

With that realisation I felt my legs wobble slightly, and I leaned forward heavily into her hands, honestly believing that if she hadn't been gripping my chin, it would have been the floor for me. Maria didn't flinch. One minute I was being supported by my head, the next I was lying on the sofa. Had I blacked out? Erm…no… I had just gone all Emma Thompson and swan dived to Oscar winning status. Fluttering my eyes open, I saw Maria leaning over me.

"Did they tell you whether you had a concussion when you got it checked out? You did get it checked out, didn't you?"

I was thankful Col had insisted he take me to the hospital. God only knows how she would've reacted if I had squeaked out a "no". "No…I…they… I don't think they did."

Maria was rummaging inside her leather jacket, and for a minute I thought she was going to ring an ambulance. Could things get any more embarrassing? "I'm okay. I think I had a head rush or something." Her hand appeared and I spotted a small cylindrical object there. That wasn't a phone, was it? Fuck that was small.

"Lean your head back and open your eyes."

Was she going to jab me? Knock me out? Was I becoming hysterical? You bet. I hate, and I repeat *hate*, anything to do with eye exams, and part of me believed that she was going to be sticking that cylindrical object— the one I previously thought to be small but now perceived as the size of a cricket bat—into my eyes. My heart was racing, but it still wasn't getting me anywhere fast. If I hadn't been dying of concussion, I would've made a run for it.

"Relax, Gem. This won't hurt."

That's what they all say, isn't it? It won't hurt...much... and then it stings like a bitch.

"I just want to look into your eyes and check your pupils. See if they are dilating properly."

Bright light glared into my startled eyes; even though she had said that was what she was going to do, I still wasn't expecting it. First one, then the next, then back, and then over again to the other still smarting orb.

"Slightly."

Slightly what, freaked?

"Your left pupil is taking slightly longer to respond to the light. It's not bad, but something I should keep a close watch on."

If it wasn't that bad, why did she have to watch over me? Closely. Watching over someone closely usually meant there was something to watch out for...like imminent death.

"How did it happen?"

What? My rapid decline?

"The broken nose. How did it happen?"

Who cares? The nose was nothing in comparison to my brain shutting down. *STOP!* For fuck's sake! I had a concussion, not a terminal illness. Why should I even be complaining about the most gorgeous woman I had ever met looking me over in a way that should have been setting my heart aflame, rather than believing it was gradually coming to a halt. Inwardly, I bollocked myself, before sitting up quickly and holding back an expression of pain the movement had caused. "It was an accident."

"I'm glad to hear it." She grinned at me. "Otherwise it would mean you purposely gave yourself an injury..." stray fingers stroked my bangs away from my eyes, "...and that would be worrying."

I wasn't really listening; her fingers were so soft, and the sensation was too perfect.

"So, what happened?" Little joyful shocks were making their way down my face and trickling along my neck, the throbbing sensation from my nose taking a back seat. This was the life: glorious attention from the gorgeous doctor. If I had thought it through earlier—properly, I mean, instead of just worrying myself stupid—I would have come up with this scenario.

"Gem? What happened?"

I mean, not every woman gets her own doctor, does she? Someone to flash her light in your eyes anytime she wants to...stroke away the pain...cause a fluttering that should just be focused in the injured area, but was decidedly lower.

"GEM!"

Shit. She had been waiting for me to answer. "Sorry. I...I..." was drifting off in a state of BUPA healthcare with benefits and didn't feel like stopping my examination. "I was just..." thinking up a lie to cover the fact that I couldn't tell her that I was daydreaming about having her as my personal slave/doctor? "...thinking how it all came about. It was so sudden." And now I'd indicated that the story I was going to tell was going to be as interesting as the ones I thought of telling her when I fucked up my arm and shoulder. Saving kids was always a winner, although I did have a leaning toward saving a dog from a vicious owner who was kicking it and I stepped in and put him in his place, thus saving the dog...nah...*puppy*...from a fate worse than death. "My friend head butted me in the face."

She was looking at me with such trust, there was no way I could lie about it.

But that trusting face turned into something more like shock as she nearly choked out, "*Friend?*"

I nodded.

"Your *friend* head butted you in the face?" And then the inevitable, "Why?"

Sitting up, I grabbed her hand, which was by this stage suspended in front of me. "I've already told you. It was an accident."

Maria looked at our hands and then back at me.

"I met Col for a coffee today and he leaned in to kiss me a little too eagerly..." And on my story went. I don't have to repeat it to you, as you already know all the gory details. By the time I had finished, Maria was trying her hardest to laugh along with me. Amazing to think that before she came around, I had found it difficult to laugh about it too. Strange that. Not.

Before we knew it, an hour had glided by, and we were just too damn comfy to move. It wasn't just me that thought so. By the looks of Maria, she was as content as I was to just sit and chat. Who needed to go out? At least it would save all the staring that was bound to happen. In the end, we decided to watch a film. Turning the lights low, we settled onto the sofa. It wasn't long before my sitting bolt upright turned into a slouch, and when I felt her arm slip along my shoulder as the opening credits ended, I didn't resist, just relaxed onto her chest. A soft kiss landed in my hair, and I stopped myself from looking up at her, mainly because if I did and she had been looking back, I doubt we would have seen any of the film.

I love *Rebecca*. Not generally a woman named Rebecca, but the film. I know Olivier seems rather camp, but didn't the majority of the actors of that time look as if they were chasing the lavender bus? I love the atmosphere of it: so depressing, so dark and mysterious, so long and dramatic. The last few times I had watched it, all of which were by myself, there always seemed to be a point where I would feel my eyes becoming heavy. Mentally, I believe my brain processed the part at the ball when the second Mrs DeWinter comes down in fancy dress and her hubby (Liberace) bollocks her in front of the strongest man and the whore Heidi. Okay, okay. They weren't really the strong man and Heidi, but I'm not going into detail (not much, says you, through gritted teeth). Then the lids flutter, boom of cannons (you are intrigued now, aren't you), and then the fuzz turn up, growling, "'Allo, 'allo 'allo...an' wat doo we 'ave 'ere then?" I usually wake up as the end credits are shakily jittering their way up the screen and curse myself for nodding off again.

This time was no exception. Well, apart from the waking up at the end credits, that is. I had slept way past that point, by about three hours if the hands on the lounge clock were right. The TV showed the menu screen of the DVD player, and for a moment I was a little disoriented. What was that very soft, yet firm object underneath me? I pushed my head into the softness, and it felt good. And that sound... like breathing? I held my breath. It was still there, the breathing, I mean. My eyes opened wide and a sharp pain sped along my cheeks. I felt the glow of embarrassment. *Shit.* I'd fallen asleep on Maria. What bloody hostess falls asleep on their guest? Me, as it happens. I just hoped I hadn't dribbled on her top. That would undoubtedly be the finish of anything that could ever have come to pass between us. With a swipe, and a satisfied smile, I relaxed a little. Spit free. One thing to feel relieved about. But that didn't change the fact that I had nodded off on a first date, did it? What was I to do? Say? How was I to act? Wasn't this kind of situation reserved for at least date number five? Should I wake her? Apologise? Sit up and wait for her to open her eyes?

Asleep. Thank fuck for small mercies. She was asleep also. A feeling of power came over me as I thought I had the situation in the palm of my hand. She didn't know I'd slept for as long as I had, as she was in the Land of Nod too. I could use this to my advantage, couldn't I? No. I'm too much of a lady to do anything underhanded, but looking at her wasn't wrong, was it? Looking at her when she was asleep, I mean.

With great care, I lifted myself up and above her. The light from the lamp was just enough for me to make out the contours of her face. And what a face. What a beautiful face. This woman was a vision, awake or asleep, a vision. A finely chiselled jaw line, high cheekbones, beautifully shaped eyebrows, a straight nose (unlike mine), perfectly shaped lips that were slightly parted, a strong chin, a slender neck touching a divine collarbone. My fingers lifted of their own volition, and it was an effort not to trail just one of them along the inviting skin. Then the movement of her chest as she breathed caught my attention. Up—hold—down—hold—up—hold—down—hold. It was almost hypnotic, and almost my undoing. I couldn't seem to stop staring, couldn't seem to stop wondering what lay underneath her shirt, although I had a pretty good idea. At that thought, I felt the saliva build to such an extent in my mouth, I had to swallow, and having swallowed, I had to lick my lips to restore some of the moisture.

Tearing my eyes away, I moved my attention slowly back up to her face, part of me feeling a sense of guilt about what I had done, whereas another, bigger part of me was wondering why someone as beautiful as Dr Maria Moran was asleep on my sofa in the first place.

She had such blue eyes, such gorgeous, mind blowing, captivating, and wonderful blue eyes. A person could drown in those eyes and feel honoured. *Just a minute. Blue. Eyes.* If I was considering the blueness of her eyes, that could only mean one thing.

"Gem?"

Although she only whispered my name, it seemed to my shocked ears that she had screamed out, "What are you looking at, you dirty little creep!" Therefore, the only thing I could do was to jump backwards, catch the back of my leg on the coffee table, and hit the floor like a bag of spanners. Maria tried to save me, but I think my rapid movement had surprised her, too. As a result, it was me meeting strip wood flooring at speed.

"Gem? You okay?"

Such a sweet trusting voice; and there I was lying on the floor, exposed as a nocturnal fiddler.

I wanted to say I was fine, but I couldn't get the words to leave my lips. It seemed to me that if I opened my mouth to speak at that precise moment, I would blurt out a pile of incomprehensible shite. Even more than usual, that is.

"Is it your head?" Genuine concern there, folks, genuine concern, which left me feeling even more of a twat than I was already feeling. "Here, let me check your pupils again." With the speed and dexterity of a cheetah on the hunt, the torch was back in her hand.

Where on earth had she put that? I hadn't felt it when I was lying up against her.

Flick. Flick. Flick. "Your left pupil is responding fine now, Gem."

Her face was in deep thought, and I knew she was thinking that if I wasn't confused or disoriented because of concussion, why had I fallen off the sofa? And if she was thinking about why I had fallen off the sofa, then she hadn't seen me eyeing up her chest.

"I'm such a klutz..." Pause for effect. "I tried to get up more quickly than my body was ready for. Must've been laying watching the film in one position for all that time." As an excuse, it wasn't bad, if I do say so myself.

Maria laughed and held out her hand, as if to help me to my feet. "Watching the film, eh? Can I ask you something, Gem?"

I nodded, although the rational part of me wanted to say no.

"Do you always snort when you are watching a film?"

What? Fuck! No! Snort? Me? Crap. And yes. One word epithets were the only thing I could muster after I found out that Maria had been listening to me whistle through my nostrils for God knew how long. This was not turning out to be a dream date, was it? For her, at least. Let me get one thing straight. I do not snore. It was because my nose was poorly, that's all. And if you've ever had the misfortune to have a broken nose, you might know what I'm going on about.

"And no saying it's because you have a broken nose, lady."

Could she read minds, too? Because if she could, then I thought I'd try her out with something else.

"Would it be okay if I stayed here tonight? I don't fancy driving home at this hour. And that way I can keep an eye on you."

How did she do that? I hadn't even had the opportunity to think about it, never mind let her read it from inside my jumbled grey matter.

"I don't mind sleeping on the sofa. As it happens, I like sofas."

"I can't have you sleeping on the sofa when I have a perfectly good bed upstairs."

Maria's eyebrow lifted slightly, and I began to blush.

"A spare bed...in a spare room." In a spare house on a spare hill. Yes. The way I had responded was slightly emphatic on the "spare" bit, as if I was too frigid to sleep in the same room as the gorgeous doctor without the fear of her forcing herself on my virgin bones. Chance would be a fine thing. I had only ever seen her once when I was perfectly fit and well. With the thought of only seeing her once when all my body parts were working properly, I suddenly remembered she had said about having seen me before. "Where else have you seen me?"

Although Maria pretended she didn't understand what I was talking about, as if it wasn't in some kind of context (you know, and I know, that it was perfectly placed), I knew she had a very good idea what I was referring to.

However, to save her the embarrassment of me going on about when and how and why and every other device known to journalism, I just said, "You mentioned you had seen me a few times before I came to the hospital. I know of one; how many other times have there been?" I wanted to add, "I hope they were less horrific," but the sticky feeling gathering on the skin of my cheek with the memory of the underwear (underwear sponsored by Prixstick) stopped me.

A smile was dodging around her mouth, and I wanted even more strongly to know now. Had I been doing something I shouldn't? Should I have kept my big fat mouth shut? What if it was when I was in Tesco's arguing about the minging oranges I had bought? Or the time when I cut the bloke up near the electrical shop and he had slowed his car down to have a go, and me being me and nearly ripped his head off, although that was mainly down to PMS. There had been numerous occasions when I thought it would have been for the best if someone I knew hadn't witnessed me making a total tit out of myself. I was living proof that agoraphobia can, in fact, be a blessing.

"Tomorrow." Maria leaned back and stretched, and for a minute I was too put off by the glimpse of the toned muscle of her stomach to argue my point. The stomach had me, and I wasn't sure that I was really prepared for what she might say. "I'll tell you tomorrow, I promise."

"Okay, Doc. Tomorrow." That would give me time to go over all the other scenarios I had involved myself in that she might have witnessed. Even in the short while Maria had been in Norwich, there were quite a few.

After sorting through my drawers—not those ones, the ones I keep clothes in—I eventually found something she could sleep in. God bless T-shirts, that's all I can say, because there was no way any of my sweat pants or pyjama bottoms would have fitted her. Well, they would have, but they would have also been half mast. I could have sorted out a pair of shorts, but what was the point? The T-shirt covered the main bits, or so I thought.

It wasn't until I saw her coming out of the bedroom as I was leaving the bathroom that I realised two things. One: I am exceptionally short-bodied compared to Maria. Two: wow; those legs, so long, so toned, so exposed! I felt moisture forming in my mouth and I'm sure I was beginning to sweat, but there was nothing I could do except just stare. And stare. And then stare some more for good measure. Even when she spoke and I answered, I didn't look at her face. How could I? How could anyone when they were privy to such wonder?

"So, have you? A toothbrush I can use?"

I grunted. Grunted! Can you believe my Avril Lavigne response? I was turning Emo. The next thing I would do would be to sit in the corner and cry, saying, "The world doesn't understand me." With the growing realisation that the world could actually do without another "grunter", as there were enough teens to go around, I finally dragged my gaze up to her face, a face that was grinning in a *knowing* grinning way.

"Seen enough?"

Her voice was light and I knew she was only poking fun, but that didn't stop me from becoming flustered. Turning sharply, I nearly smacked into the doorjamb, and it was only the deft movement of my hand pushing me away from the wooden frame that saved my nose from taking another battering. I looked as if I was pissed, as my movements were slightly off kilter and I was definitely staggering.

"Here. Let me help you." With that, Maria was behind me, very closely behind me...close enough that I could feel her breath on my back. Then not just her breath, but a hand, followed by another hand. Slowly they slipped down my sides and rested on my hips, and I knew if I turned around at that moment I would kiss her. That was the main thought racing around my head...bugger the toothbrush. A gentle squeeze on my hips, and then the sensation of her mouth next to my ear, "Where do you keep them?"

Keep what?

"Are they in the drawer or in the bottom cabinet?"

Is what in the drawer or bottom cabinet? My brain? My sense of rationality? One thing I knew for sure that wasn't in those drawers or cupboard was my libido. That little tyke was well and truly with me at that very moment.

"Cupboard." *Was that so difficult?* "At the back." *Well done, Hughes. Your first speaking part.*

A soft kiss landed on the top of my ear, and she moved me out of the way.

It was a good job she did, because if it were left up to me, I think we would still be standing there. It was the feeling of loss that made me snap out of it, the loss of her breath on my skin, the loss of her hands on my hips, but mainly the loss of a missed opportunity. She had gently kissed me, and I had been contemplating kissing her, but alas, once again I had regressed into "Woman of Stunted Impulses". Maria was in front now, bending over, and I could clearly see my reflection in the mirror in front of me now she wasn't blocking my way. Unfortunately. Jesus! Did my face really look as bad as that? It had been hideous at the start of the evening, but falling asleep had done me no favours. Sleeping Beauty? Bah. Whoever has tried to sell the notion that sleep helps to rejuvenate and refresh has never taken a blow to the face and then fallen asleep on it. Or they had, and had said this as they were in the "I'm going to hit the floor" stage.

"Here it is!" She sounded as if she had just found Captain Flint's treasure instead of a new toothbrush. And considering she had found it with no help from me, I stepped away in order to leave her to her ablutions. Honestly. That is exactly what I intended to do, up until I spotted her bending over, that is. The T-shirt had slipped up her back, and my God, I think those feet-nailing pixies had returned. There was no way I could move my size sixes, or the legs attached to them. Funnily enough, I couldn't quite remember if I even tried. And who cared? Seeing Maria in that position was worth a slap around the face, a social faux pas, and a broken nose—all rolled into one. I'm not saying she was naked underneath the tee, but the panties she was wearing were the smallest, most delicate garment I think I have ever seen. The thong portion allowed the curves of her buttocks to delight and enthral, and I was obediently delighted and enthralled. I knew if I just stretched out my arm, my hand would make glorious contact with the toned flesh and I would be transported to another time and dimension.

"Your eyes look all glassy."

And you are breathtaking.

"Are you feeling okay? Do you want me to check your pupils again?"

Snap. That was the sound my brain made as I popped back into reality and found myself standing with my arm outstretched like I was communicating with ET. "I was just pointing to where I thought the toothbrush would be." And pigs fly, thus making the price of bacon soar.

"Really?"

Why couldn't I say "really" the way she did? And why was she moving closer to me?

"That's strange."

Strange?

"Because...to me..." she was in front of me now, very closely in front of me, and looking down into my eyes, "I could have sworn you were just about to..."

Faint?

"Touch me."

Just like her fingers were touching me—softly, reverently, trailing down my throat and along my collarbone...eliciting small murmurs from the back of my throat. Flick. They were gone.

"Or maybe not...maybe you were only...*pointing.*"

I couldn't help it; I swear. It was because she was just so close, so beautiful and so close. And her eyes had captivated me, drawn me in, pulled me closer until my lips brushed hers. Once, twice, then third time lucky. Soft lips covered mine, and I was lost.

Arms wrapped around my waist and pulled me closer, whilst my hands slipped up her chest and captured her face. Deeper, and then deeper still, the kiss was moving from innocent to something more carnal, something unrestrained. Nothing else mattered—nothing but the feel of her mouth moving against mine, nothing but the sensation of her body pushing into me. I was moving backwards, Maria still holding me, me still holding her. Coldness hit my back as I leaned against the wall, but I didn't care. The heat coming from her was enough, and my body was acting like a heat seeking missile. Pressing myself against her, I slipped my thigh between her legs, legs that were naked; legs that were long and toned, and separating to allow me to get closer. A groan slipped from her mouth and into mine, evoking a groan from me in response. Lips parted and disconnected, and air rushed around the wetness on my mouth. Maria tipped her head and began to nuzzle my throat and my eyes fluttered with the sensation, making the room seem to blur. Softly, her teeth began to nip my skin, and jolts of expectation raced from the spot to gather and float around in my gut before continuing their journey to somewhere more southern. Another push, and I felt her breasts pressing against mine; soft, firm orbs demanding contact, and mine willingly complying. My hands moved down and fingers met the hem of her T-shirt, toying with it for a second.

Inside. Those renegade fingers slipped inside and up along the taut skin of her ass. I felt her push back to increase the contact, before I gripped onto it and pulled her back into me. Lifting her head, blue eyes looked deeply into mine; blue eyes that were full of want, the same want I was feeling. Then those eyes changed their expression. The once blue wanting turned into something I didn't want to see, didn't want to happen. That want seemed to fade, and I felt a jolt of panic shoot through me. I was dying inside—dying for the touch of her mouth, dying for the touch of her hands on me, dying of need for this woman, dying to claw back that look she had given me a few seconds before she decided that I wasn't what she wanted after all.

Maria's eyes closed briefly, opened again, and then shut once more. When they reopened, I knew there was no way anything else was going to happen between us, because the desire that had been so apparent before had been replaced by concern. Her tongue came out of her mouth and swiped along her lips, and I wanted that tongue, those lips, back on mine.

"I think we'd better stop, don't you?"

No. Actually I didn't.

"Your face looks so sore...and..."

"I'm fine. Honestly." Was that a pleading tone?

Maria sighed and I wasn't too sure why. Everything had been going so well, hadn't it? We'd kissed, we'd touched, we'd pressed against each other as if our lives depended on it. What had changed? I knew it wasn't me.

"I want you."

And I want you...so what's wrong?

"But not now."

Why?

"I thought we were going to take things slowly. I...I... don't want..." She pulled away from me and turned away.

Part of me felt a growing anger. I hadn't been the one to initiate this; it had been her. And now she was backing out? I opened my mouth to tell her just that, but she beat me to it.

"I don't want this to be something we rush into. I want something more for me...for *us*."

How could I be angry? She wanted what I wanted. I, too, wanted an *"us"*, and not just a memory of a brief encounter.

When she turned to face me, I swear I could see tears glistening in her eyes. Why was she on the verge of crying? And as I stepped forward to tell her and show her it was okay, that I would wait for the right time, she lifted her hand as if to stop me, but changed her mind, and moved her hand to cover her eyes.

Standing in front of her, I placed my hand on her forearm. "Hey...Maria, look at me."

She sucked in a breath, held it, and released it noisily into the air.

"Please, look at me." My voice was gentle; I made sure it was.

Her hand slowly moved away from her eyes, and those blue eyes looked back into mine.

"I really like you. And I want something more for us, too." Lifting my hand, I stroked away the stray locks of hair from her face. "Come on. Brush your teeth and get into bed." Bringing my fingers to my lips, I placed a kiss on them before transferring it to her mouth, "I'll see you in the morning, okay?"

I had just made it to the doorway when I heard her call my name. When I looked back, she was still in the exact position I had left her.

"Thank you. And sleep well."

I didn't ask her to elaborate on the thank you part, as it was pretty obvious why. "Sleep tight, Maria." I smiled at her. "And don't let the bed bugs bite." There it was... the grin that I had grown to know, and with that, I turned around and left her to ruminate over the last ten minutes... just like I was going to ruminate over them myself.

Lying in the dark, that's exactly what I did. Ruminated. Why had she come on so strongly only to get cold feet? What had happened between the kiss, me grabbing her backside, and the look into my eyes that made her change her mind? You won't believe how long I wracked my brains trying to work it all out, and it wasn't until I went to rub my hand over my face that I realised the answer. The reason for my realisation was that as soon as I started to rub my hand over my nose, the pain shot all over my head. And fuck, it hurt nearly as much as the realisation that Maria didn't want me because I looked like the runner-up in a World Featherweight boxing match. She had actually started to say it, the "your face looks so sore" part. But deep down I knew there was something else stopping her from continuing what she had started, something a little more dramatic than a broken nose and two black eyes. I also knew that logically it would be better for us to wait, for more than just that one reason. One, it wouldn't have been the most perfect scenario, would it? Our first time together and I wasn't up to my usual scratch. Two, I, for one, wasn't the kind of person who would sleep with someone on the first date, and by the looks of things, neither was she. Three, I hadn't really thought of a three, but I was sure there was one.

Thoughts over. Time for sleep. It was well past three in the morning, and even though I had grabbed a long nap, I was exhausted. Must've been all the mental meanderings. With that decision in the bag, I turned over and nestled the side of my head further into the pillow. Just as sleep was about to claim me, one last thought came tumbling in. Must've been number three. *"Instead of trying to work it out, ask her. Ask her first thing in the morning."*

"I will." And as those two words hit the air, I was away into sleep. The morning would come soon enough, and I, for one, wanted to be alert enough to actually ask why Dr Maria Moran was playing hot and cold, although I wouldn't say it in those exact words.

It was the sound of the shower that woke me. Initially I thought I was being burgled, but how many robbers do you know who shower whilst they are stripping you of all your valuables? It took a few moments before I realised that it was Maria taking a quick wash before I got up and claimed the bathroom for myself. Stretching in my bed, I let out a grunt of satisfaction. There's nothing like a good old-fashioned stretch to get the blood pumping around first thing in the morning.

Slipping my robe on, I opened the bedroom door, just in time to see the bathroom door open and a very wet, very flushed doctor emerging wrapped in a towel.

For a moment we both just stopped and sized each other up, and then a grin broke out on her face. "Good morning."

What a voice. If I hadn't stubbed my toe on the bedstead when I'd gotten out of bed, and hopped around a bit in pain, I would have believed I was still dreaming.

"Hope you don't mind." She flicked her hand over her shoulder to indicate the bathroom, before saying, "I felt all grubby this morning," then promptly went beetroot. "I mean…you know…"

I did know what she meant, but I wasn't going to tell her that. "No worries. And good morning to you, too. Sleep well?" I walked towards her as I was speaking, and when I got next to her, I could smell the body wash I always used. It always amazes me that scents smell so different on different people. I could still smell her smell, even though it should all have been washed away. "I'm just going to shower myself. Why don't you grab yourself a coffee and something to eat?" And keep the towel. It suits you.

She nodded, and started to move away.

I entered the doorway, stopped, and turned back to her. "And then I think we need to chat."

Maria stopped suddenly, and I knew she wanted to turn back to me, but she didn't. She didn't even question what I wanted to chat about, just answered with a quiet "okay".

Closing the door, I felt a weight I didn't even know was there lift from me. What did I want to chat about? Why she didn't find me as attractive as she had last week? Well, kind of. But I would have to think about it more fully before I started the conversation.

Thirty minutes later, I was washed and dressed and heading for the kitchen. Smells of coffee were wafting out, and I needed a cup. Badly.

Maria was sitting at the table, and she looked over the rim of her cup as I slipped into the seat opposite. "Coffee?"

I nodded. It was good having someone make me a coffee in the morning; usually I had to make my own. The next words to leave my mouth surprised even me. "Why are you playing hot and cold?" *Shit.* I had practised what I was going to say when I was in the bathroom, and this was not what I had come up with. In those minutes in front of the mirror I had been thoughtful and eloquent, yet direct. This direct was a little too direct, even for my tactless ass. I knew I was being tactless when I heard the mug she had been filling with coffee hit the counter with a bang, spilling coffee everywhere.

"Shit!"

Not me this time, and by the jump she did, I think the boiling hot coffee had splattered all over her. In a flash, I was up and at her side, trying to mop up the flowing stream of hot brown liquid, which was racing across and over the countertop like it had been given a five second start to run for freedom.

"Let me." I slapped a kitchen towel over the mess and the coffee halted in its tracks. Turning to Maria, I scanned her face. She wasn't just startled by the coffee; on closer inspection, she hadn't gotten any on her. Therefore, the look was because of what I had said. "Hey. What's the matter?" As if I didn't know. "Come. Sit down."

She went to the table and sat heavily on the seat.

I turned away to finish clearing up the mess and make myself another cup.

"I'm sorry, Gem." Her voice was so low, I only just heard it.

"It's only coffee. It will clean up." I picked up the tissues and threw them in the bin at the side.

"Not about the coffee...although, yeah, that too."

Coffee in hand, I returned to the table, sitting next to her rather than opposite. In my mind it seemed less threatening. I know—I'm a dick head.

"I like you so much; I just don't want to blow it."

That's the bit I didn't understand. How could she blow it by kissing me in the bathroom? It wasn't as if anything else had taken place. Chance had been a fine thing.

"Look, I understand, Maria. I'm not the kind of person who puts out on a first date either." I saw the colour literally drain from her face when I said that, and I was beginning to wonder whether I should keep my big mouth shut. But no; I had to carry on. "I want to wait, just like you do. All I wondered was why you gave me the green light and then changed your mind. Is it because of my face?"

That seemed to snap her out of herself, and she spun her head round and boomed out, "No! God no! You're perfect."

That made me feel a little better, although I knew I wasn't perfect, far from it, in fact.

"It's just...just...if I tell you I'm scared, you'll think differently of me."

Why? And more importantly, how could I think of her differently?

"You're thinking—how could anything I tell you make you feel differently, aren't you?"

This woman was unnerving. How did she do that?

"You're a good woman, Gem. I can see that. But...but... I need to tell you something, and I don't want you to think it's any reflection on you."

I thought it safer to just nod, as what came out of my mouth was usually not what I intended.

"Okay. Here goes everything." And she told me. Told me the reason why she just couldn't take our encounter in the bathroom any further than we had. Told me about her past, about something that had happened to her, something that filled me with anger, with disgust, with a longing to get in my car and drive to Addenbrookes Hospital in Cambridge and hunt down Dr Jennifer Fielding and give her a piece of my mind and maybe a smack in the face. And do you know why I felt all these things? I'll tell you why. Dr Jennifer Fielding used to be Maria's mentor, used to be the person Maria looked up to, used to be the woman that Maria had a crush on for the last year and a half. Until Dr Fielding decided that it would be a good idea to take Maria out, get her pissed, shag her, and then dump her right after. And then brag to all her colleagues about Maria being an easy lay.

"I couldn't bear being in the department anymore, to be in Cambridge full stop. It wasn't just me she hurt..." Maria began to fidget with the outside of the cup, sliding her finger up and down the outside of the mug. I watched as the demons from her past reared up and taunted her. I don't know why, but there seemed to be something else, but for the life of me I didn't know what, and asking was not the "done" thing. Was it? Then she seemed to snap herself out of it. "When the job came up in Norwich, I took it. Didn't even come for an interview...just accepted their offer on the phone." At that point, she stopped, grabbed her cup, and finished off her coffee.

I knew she didn't want to continue, mainly because I could see the tears collecting in her eyes. I could feel my anger bubbling, trying to escape and pepper the air with coloured vocabulary, but how would that help her?

"Hey, come here." Wrapping my arms around her, I expected her to cry, but she didn't. In fact I could feel her mouth getting closer to my ear, the breath tickling the skin on my cheek.

"Just think." A soft kiss landed on the outside of my ear. "If that hadn't happened, I never would have met you."

Leaning back, I looked into her eyes. There was no jesting behind what she had said; she had meant it. She had gone through all that humiliation, left her home and friends, moved to Norwich to a job she hadn't even checked out, and she still could find a positive amongst it all. What a woman. What...a...woman. If she could see something good from all that shit, then I could push down the anger I had towards her former mentor in Cambridge.

"You are amazing." The words blurted from my mouth, and Maria snorted as she laughed. "You *are*." I moved closer to her, my fingers trailing down the side of her cheek. "I won't do anything to make you uncomfortable, I promise." And with every fibre of my being, I meant every word. I wouldn't push this relationship. I would take things slowly, or at any pace she wanted it to go at. I didn't want her to feel uncomfortable, ever. And there was no way I wanted to hurt her in any way, shape, or form.

It was after the internal promise and the shuffling of my chair to be closer to her, that I noticed that her face was beetroot. *Fuck.* I hadn't meant to make her feel like a twat. Where had the "I didn't want her to feel uncomfortable" part disappeared to?

"Thank you, Gem. I know you won't."

So why are you still glowing?

"Could you do something for me?"

If it would stop you being luminous, yes.

"Could you take your chair leg off my foot?"

Huh? Chair leg? And why I looked at the chair leg rather than moving it off her foot, I'll never know. Realising that I was in fact imprisoning her foot under the solid pointiness of my chair, and with the weight of my ass, I did the only thing I could do. I shot up. And in shooting up, I also chinned her with my left hand. Could things get any worse? With me about? More than likely.

I think it was the feel of her teeth along my knuckles that made me not want to look at her. But before I could die of embarrassment, I heard her laugh. What a sweet sound...a glorious sound, and not just because I thought I had knocked her front teeth out, either.

"Are you trying to give me a matching broken nose?"

Before I could respond—and thinking about it now, I doubt I could have come up with a response anyway—Maria grabbed my hands and pulled me to her. I was standing above her, and those blue eyes were looking straight into mine, even straight through me. I felt open and on display for her eyes only, and for once in my life I didn't care. I wanted her to see that I felt more for her than a brief fling. Wanted her to know that I was mesmerised by her beauty, and not just the physical beauty that flowed so easily from every pore of her, but that inner beauty that so few people have.

Before I realised what I was doing, I had tilted my face down to be mere centimetres away from hers, and it wasn't long before she closed the gap. A soft kiss ensued, and before I knew it, we were physically separate but very much joined at the same time.

Breakfast carried on. This time with food. This time without the pouring out of past imperfections or the crippling chair manoeuvre. And over breakfast, we discussed what we were going to do for the rest of the day. Maria decided that considering we hadn't had the opportunity to go out and paint the town red the night before, we would go to Hemsby on Sea, a small seaside resort not far away, full of penny arcades, grabbing machines, junk food, and teenagers. I hoped that it was open, as the half term break didn't happen until the following week.

Pots cleared and washed, the kitchen tidied, and we were off to her house so she could get a change of clothes. Before we left my house, Maria gave my eyes the once over again to make sure the concussion had well and truly gone, her little torch nearly blinding me once again.

"I'll drive, okay? Give those eyes a rest for a while."

Good job too, as I was still seeing little floating balls of light hovering in front of me. Imagine crashing the car on our first day out. I know I am not the most graceful being under the sun, but I doubted I could live with that.

When we got to her house, I think I stood outside with my mouth open for a little while before I could move my legs in the direction of her front door.

"I should warn you. I don't live alone."

Shit. She didn't still live with her parents, did she?

"I rent a room to a bloke I used to go to uni with. Well, I say 'rent a room,' what I mean to say is that he shares the house with me."

No wonder she could afford to live in a house as big as this. It was huge! The driveway was bigger than both my front and back gardens combined. And even though there was a little red sports car already parked there, her car fit in with room to spare.

"Looks like Trevor is still here."

Trevor?

"I thought he was out with his other half last night."

As her key hovered over the lock, she stopped, turned, and looked me straight in the eye. "Unless he is not alone."

"Haven't you met his girlfriend?" Seemed like a logical question, and I was a little surprised when she started to laugh. "What's funny about that?" I know the tone I used was a little sharp; I knew it as soon as the words came out, but it didn't deter her. So, I went for the "actions speak louder than words" scenario. I shoved my sunglasses firmly up my face, and then squealed as the pain shot through my nose and eyes. At least it shut her up.

"Careful. You'll make it worse."

And how's that? I already looked like I should be laid out in a morgue.

"Sorry for giggling, but...you see...Trevor hasn't got a girlfriend. I don't think he's ever had one and isn't likely to get one."

Call me thick, but I didn't get it, and my expression told her as much.

"Trevor is gay."

And why did it have to be spelled out to me? Had the blow to my face made me even more of an idiot than I thought I was already?

"And I haven't met his boyfriend yet."

"Maybe it's time that you did." I grinned, winked, and nodded at her, all at the same time. Good job I didn't have to think about it, as I believe I would have bollocked it up.

The grin she flashed back showed me what she undoubtedly looked like as a mischievous child.

It wasn't until she actually opened the door and was part way inside that she stopped. I could see the deliberation on her face, and pushed her forward. I was just as intrigued as she was, even though I had never met Trevor, and up until three minutes ago, I hadn't known of his existence. Call it the woman in me.

"Maybe now's not the right time." She was backing up, pushing me backwards with her.

"I thought you wanted to—"

"I'm good, honestly. I've showered this morning; I'll be fine in last night's clothes."

"But—"

"Trust me, Hemsby will make us feel dirty however many times we get changed before we go."

I shrugged, nodded, and was preparing to turn and leave, her hands on my waist almost pushing me out.

"Is that you, Maria?" A voice floated down from the top of the stairs, and part of me believed it was familiar, but for the life of me I couldn't place it. If only I could get a good look at the man who was beginning to descend the stairs. "Wait just a minute. There's someone here you—"

"Can't stop now, Trev. Speak later, okay?"

And that was it. Before I had a good look at the bloke with the hairy legs, I was outside, the door firmly closed behind me.

"Quick. Let's get going." Maria grabbed my hand and began dragging me towards the car.

I could hear the door clasp move, but that's all that happened. No one came out, maybe because we were in the car so bloody quickly. Slam. Slam. Both doors shut, and she had the engine started before I had a chance to say Jack Robinson.

"Sorry, Gem. But if he had collared us, we would have been there for hours."

Strangely enough, I believed her. There was nothing to say that I shouldn't. Or was I being thick again?

Chapter 7

HEMSBY WAS COLD. BLOODY COLD. And the grains of sand whipping around us made seeing a tad difficult. Even as we stepped out of the car, the itty bitty pieces of gold were jamming themselves unceremoniously into every exposed orifice. The sunglasses I was sporting tried valiantly to deter the wannabe glass particles, but to no avail. And another thing—Hemsby was nearly closed.

When I say "nearly", what I mean to say is there were about three arcades and one beverage stand open. It would have been better if it had been shut completely, then we could have gone somewhere else, somewhere where the elements weren't attacking us from all directions. At least it wasn't raining, not at first. That waited until we were about four minutes away from the car, and there is one titbit of advice I would like to give you at this point: avoid running in sunglasses when it is raining. Simple as that. The reason? Simple again. You end up running into anything and everything. Even some poor unsuspecting sod in a wheelchair ended up with me half sprawled over his knee.

I could tell by his expression he was more surprised at my blackened face than me straddling his legs, and for a minute he was just as speechless as I was. Until he looked past me, trying to see who I was with. "I know it's not my business, luv, but I'd leave him if I were you," he muttered conspiratorially.

"But...I—" I didn't have a chance to finish; two strong hands grabbed my waist and yanked me up and off the bloke. Stumbling back, I landed with an oof against Maria's chest.

"Monster! If I wasn't in this chair, I'd give you a taste of your own medicine."

"But...I..." It was Maria's turn to sound half-witted.

Thankfully the bloke started to move away.

"Did I miss something?" This was directed to both his retreating back, and then at me, the same me who was grinning as the rain flowed down our faces.

"Beats me."

There was a muffled, "Well, leave him then," from the bloke in the chair.

I couldn't help a giggle popping out. "He thinks you're a woman beater."

Maria looked confused.

"My face?"

She still looked confused, so I pulled my sunglasses off and glared at her. "He told me to leave you." And then in my best Gingerbread Man impression from Shrek, I added, *"You're a monster."* She was either playing thick or the rain had done something to her brain cells, as she didn't move, smile, or respond in any way. "Come on, Tyson. Win me a teddy."

Grabbing her hand, I dragged her to the nearest brightly lit arcade and then promptly left her. We were both soaked through by now, and I believe we would have been even if we hadn't had a run-in with the mobile anti-wife beating corps.

Within five minutes I had changed a tenner into a pocketful of ten and twenty pence pieces, and was on my way to the brightly lit, garishly coloured, music pumping, wage guzzling, teddy grabbing machine. And you know what I saw when I got there? Maria, winning a huge pink pig. Can you believe it? She won! There was no way on earth that anyone ever won on those things, unless they were willing to part with the best part of twenty quid.

When she turned to me, she was beaming. "Must be my medical training."

Or sheer luck.

"That's the second one I've grabbed since you left me."

Second?

"Look." And she bent down and retrieved another fluffy toy from between her feet. "I've only spent forty pence."

The change in my pocket was beginning to burn; I wanted to win one too. It's funny that when you see someone winning something so easily, you think you can do the same. And whilst I was thinking about the weight and heat of the change burning a hole in my pocket, Maria won another one.

Turning to face me, she grinned before saying, "I've never tried one of these things before. They're fun."

Not to be outdone, I sidled up to the machine next to hers and checked for my stuffed victim. Scanning the selections, I ignored the sound of her winning yet another teddy and focused on my upcoming victory.

In went the coin, and down when the button. Steady. Steady. Drop. Grab. I snatched the ugliest teddy known to man, and watched with joy as it swung precariously in the air. Just as it approached the hole... Flick. The grabbing hooks opened slightly and Ugly Bear went slamming back onto her bed of polystyrene chips. *Bastard.* And the worst thing was I knew Maria had stopped playing herself to watch me. Another coin. Another grab. Another flick and drop onto the chips. And then again. And again. And obviously I was getting pissed off, as I could see from the corner of my eye that Maria had five teddies sitting on the top of the machine and was once again watching me pump money in hand over fist.

"Do you want me to have a go?"

Why did I have the urge to growl and blurt out profanities?

"I think you should grab it just—"

Turning sharply, I glared at her, and even felt some hot air escape from my nostrils before I said, even though it was through gritted teeth, "It's just for fun. I didn't want it anyway." I even managed a laugh. "I mean, have you seen it? Talk about a face only a mother could love." As I turned back, I caught my reflection. Talk about the pot calling the kettle black. So why did I put in another three quid? Empathy?

By the time I had given up trying to get Ugly Bear, Maria had toddled off on her own, probably to win the jackpot from some poor unsuspecting fruit machine with ten pence. I wandered around the machines but couldn't see her anywhere, and when I spotted the shooting machine, I couldn't resist. Now, don't get me wrong, I am not an advocate of violence or guns, but I loved trying to aim those pink or blue plastic guns at the flying bullseyes. What I failed to remember was that my vision wasn't up to scratch. This I found out after my fourth go, and I had eventually made it into the machine's Hall of Fame. I was twenty-seventh on the list. It must've been the woman in me that made me scroll up to see who had bagged the number one spot, and what their score was. Imagine my surprise when I saw "MariaM" with a number I would never get even if my vision ever returned to twenty-twenty.

"Hey, there you are."

She was behind me, and I was valiantly trying to ungrit my teeth so I could turn around and smile at her.

"I've had a go on that. Never done it before, either." Her voice sounded innocent enough, but part of me was beginning to believe otherwise.

That was it. I spun around, ready to be totally unreasonable, but when I saw her standing there looking for all the world like an angel sent down to earth (a very jammy angel, with an excellent shooting eye and amazing grabbing abilities), the anger melted away.

"Look what I've got."

The most amazing lips in the world? The most gorgeous blue eyes? A smile to die for? All three?

"Close your eyes. Go on; close them tightly."

How could I resist? So, for her, I closed my tender eyes, even if it meant not seeing her for a matter of seconds.

"Open them."

And when I did, there, clutched proudly in her hand, was Ugly Bear.

"I knew you wanted her, so I had a go."

Not even a smidgeon of me felt envious that she had succeeded where I had failed so miserably. How could I? She had spent at least twenty pence on winning that just for me. But as they say, "It's not the cost of something; it's the thought behind it." And this was a definite example of someone wanting me to be happy. Part of me began to melt, again.

"You were right, though; she was difficult to get," Maria said.

And this was getting better. It wasn't just me who couldn't get the teddy. It was jinxed after all.

"It took me two attempts, but finally I nailed her."

Maybe not.

However, I didn't go all moody. How could I? She had, after all, gone back to the grabber and freed Ugly from a life of ups and downs just for me.

I tentatively held out my hand and curled my fingers around the crusty fur of the teddy. Before I pulled the bear to me, I looked straight into blue eyes and said, "Thank you, Maria. I think this has to be the nicest thing anyone has ever done for me." As the words came out, I thought she might think I was a bit of a saddo, as who on earth would admit to that?

Nevertheless, she didn't laugh, or sneer, she just blushed beautifully, her lips trying to form a response.

And when I placed a well aimed kiss on her cheek, I could feel the heat absorb into my lips. "You are an angel."

Was that my breathy voice? The same breathy voice that was flirting, in public, outrageously with the good doctor?

"That's okay. I...I... Well, I'm glad you...erm...like it."

Looking at her now, I couldn't place the woman I had first met, the woman who seemed rather brusque when I had entered the hospital X-ray department. This woman seemed to be seventeen years old and out on a first date. I liked that. And you know why I liked that? Easy. The reason I liked it was because I was feeling exactly the same way.

You know the even weirder part to this situation? It wasn't that I had found someone who could win from the grabbing machines and was an excellent shot at the arcade games, it wasn't even finding out she had purposely gone back to win me something because she thought I wanted it. It was what I was feeling gurgling up inside my throat that was weird. Something I didn't know was there. Something like hope, or happiness, or elation. Something I thought existed only between the pages of a trashy romance novel. Something I never truly believed I would ever feel for someone else. It wasn't love. There was no way it could be, as I, in truth, didn't know enough about Maria to fall in love with her. All I knew was that I wanted this to continue, this feeling I had when I looked at her, or when I sensed she was near me. And this feeling was wonderful. Light, airy, free, yet not wanting to be free. I would even go so far as to say this felt right. Right for me. Two weeks ago I didn't know Maria existed, and at this precise moment I didn't know what I would do with my life if she didn't. What if she didn't feel the same way? What would I do?

You guessed it. All my mental meanderings were hastily racing to the end of the track, or should I say, the part of the track where everything turns to shit again. Was it some kind of human trait to think of the positives and rapidly turn them into negatives? Why couldn't I dwell on the highs instead of expecting the relationship to fall and shatter? Is this some kind of brainwashing we receive as we are growing up? "Don't press the red button or else you will eliminate human kind as we know it." And you spend your life staring at that same red button, your palms sweating.

I'm not making any sense, am I? And as I was standing in front of the most beautiful woman I had ever met, I knew I wasn't making sense, although deep inside a tiny voice was saying that what I was feeling for Maria was the truest feeling I had ever had in my life. Fuck being sensible.

This is exhausting. It seems I am running around in circles like a woman with one foot nailed to the floor. It was nothing to do with the pixies now; I had nothing to blame but my own insecurities and the growing feeling of want flooding through me.

"What would you like to do now?" she asked.

Ah, Maria, that is the question. But, obviously, the answer I wanted to spill delicately from my lips, the one that announced I wanted to stay with her and ignore the red button, was not the actual answer I gave.

"I'm easy." Before promptly going red again.

Unfortunately, the day was over before I knew it, and it seemed like mere seconds after standing there holding Ubie (ugly bear's God given name) and trying to collect the world and her mysteries into a single thought. Maria drove me home, and as we sat in her car, I had this urge to ask her to come in and have a coffee before she left me to contemplate further on my "red button" status. Call me an idiot—you have probably done that a fair few times up to now—but I just couldn't seem to pluck up the courage to say those innocent-yet-definitely-guilty-of-wanting-more little words that invite one person to partake of a beverage of their choice. Instead I sat like a lemon, waiting for Maria to invite herself in. Which she didn't.

I sighed a few times, and then a few more for good measure, before thanking her for a wonderful day and grabbing the door handle.

"What? Not even a peck on the cheek?"

I am so glad I was looking away from her, because it gave me the opportunity to mouth a "yes!" before turning innocently back. Leaning over, I placed a kiss on her cheek, paused, then kissed the other cheek. As I did, I noticed that as my lips touched her skin her eyelids seemed to flutter. So I kissed the first cheek again to see if she would repeat the action. There it was. Only slight, but definitely a flutter.

"Goodnight, Doc." Another kiss. "Thank you for a wonderful day." At that point, I was looking straight in her face, and with all the grace I could muster, I brushed my lips across hers. Once, twice, three times, before pulling back and waiting for her to open her eyes again.

Her lips were moving as if she was savouring the taste of my lips, and mine began to mimic the action. I couldn't resist kissing her once more. A brush, again, until her hand slipped behind my head and pulled me closer into her. Lips locked onto lips, and as if we were connected by more than our mouths, the kiss developed. Mouths opened to allow tongues to tantalise, as fingers caressed hair and faces. The world was fading, everything was fading, as the kiss became more ardent, but I didn't care. What could hurt me? I had her here and that's all that mattered. Nothing could harm me when I was with her. Nothing.

I didn't even notice I had pushed her backwards, until I felt something jam into my thigh. Initially I tried to ignore it, and I would have succeeded, too, if I hadn't leant on the horn. As the blast echoed through my neighbourhood, I had the distinct impression that the street became lighter. I am not sure to this day if it was me coming back into the real world, or the fact that the majority of my neighbours had flicked on their lights and opened their curtains. To be perfectly honest, I didn't care which it was. What mattered was the very next thing she said. "Can I see you again?"

And that's when I kissed her again.

Chapter 8

I WASN'T GOING TO SEE MARIA until Thursday, but I wasn't worried. And why did I write "worried" just there? Fuck knows. Anyway... where was I? Thursday. That was it. And the reason it wasn't going to be until Thursday was because that was the day neither of us was busy doing something else. Monday I had a department meeting, Tuesday she had a department meeting, Wednesday I had Parents Evening, so...that left Thursday.

Amazing to think I have filled a whole paragraph about a day of the week, and then another one—albeit short—commenting about it.

Right. I should give you a little taste of what my week was made up of until I could see her again. It is called filling out a character, I believe. Here goes.

Monday. Rechristened "Day from Hell". Getting my arse out of bed was a chore in itself, but it didn't top the feeling of looking in the mirror and realising I would have to face a myriad of staring, curious eyes, and that was only the staff. The kids were a little less tactful; they just asked who had clocked me one. Each time I replied it had been an accident, I was given a look that suggested I was either ashamed of the truth or I was just an out and out liar. By the time I reached the end of the day, I was already at the end of my tether. Then came the meeting.

Jesus and the Mary Chain. The department in which I work has four other members: the Head, the "drama" teacher, and two elves. As you may gather, the two elves are not my favourite fairytale characters. This is due to many factors. One, they both think they know everything, but in fact all they know is words. Two, they are lazy, and a stick of dynamite up their arses couldn't get them to volunteer to do anything they deem to be "not in my contract", even when it actually is and they skim round the details. Three, one has a wart the size of a third world debt on her nose, and this made my attention waver from serious to intrigued, thus ending up volunteering for jobs my HOD (Head of Department) wanted them to do. Fourth, and yes, my math gene is being exercised, the other one talks *at* me rather than *to* me.

Okay, okay, I will stop with the bitching. But all I wanted to do was get out of work and check whether I had any messages on my phone, and instead I had to be with them, listening to the wonderful world of Ms MacDouglas. This is the sans wart teacher, by the way, the "I'm talking about myself, and how brilliant I am; you MUST listen" one. I had been sitting there for what seemed like at least an hour and a half before we moved on to item three. Item three! After glancing down the agenda and realising we had eight items to discuss in total, I was on the verge of suicide, homicide, or maiming.

Eventually I got out of work at six-twenty-four, after even the caretaker told us to leave. Ms Mac was still yammering on as I was getting into my car. I did have a brief feeling of guilt wash over me as I slammed my car door and then mouthed, "I can't hear you, sorry." As if! I would have been sorrier if she hadn't taken the hint and pissed off.

Why am I telling you all this? Yep. I thought I would read your thoughts. I'm telling you this so you have some insight into my sad little world. The same sad little world that I worked in with no complaints until I realised that time could be spent in a more enjoyable way than listening to ideas about the new curriculum turn into "Me and My Hysterectomy".

Tuesday wasn't any better, although I did manage to get out of work earlier. But alas, this was the night I couldn't see the delectable doctor. At least on Tuesday she did send me a text message, so I didn't have to wear out the buttons on my phone to see if it was malfunctioning like I had the previous evening. And the best thing was, unlike my brain, Maria actually used proper English rather than the abbreviated slang that was becoming all too common. Don't get me wrong, I totally believe that language should be fluid and ever changing, but come on! When I mark the kids' essays, I can barely understand half of the terms they used.

But I doubt you want to hear about that, do you? I didn't think so. You are more interested in what Maria had to say than in how she said it. Well, in the text message, I mean. Okay. I can easily tell you what the message said; I read it so many times I still know it by heart. It read:

"Hey, you. How has your day been? Are we still good for Thursday? Take care. TMBx"

The "TMB" confused me. They weren't her initials... her initials were MM. Maria Moran. All night I sat and stared at the message, making special note of the "x" at the end and wishing above all things that the "x" had been delivered in person. I didn't like to text her back, just in case she was sitting there with all those other doctors and planning how to save lives when my message announced its arrival at full volume. Therefore, I thought it best to wait. To wait and wonder. Bloody Parents Evening! If it hadn't been that I had to see the parents of Year 10, I would have been able to see her the next day instead of wondering why she had signed the message with initials that were not her own.

Getting out my phone—again—I looked at the keypad. Maybe she had written something else but the prescriptive text had gone tits up. The "T" could have been either a T, U, or V...the "M" an M, N, or O...and finally, the "B" could have been an A, B, or C. Bollocks. What if I included the "x?" Although I really wanted the "x" to actually be used for the symbol of a soft kiss. W, X, Y, and Z. I still couldn't make it out, and put it down to a typing error.

Until the next day. The Wednesday. The night before I would see her again. The day after receiving Maria's message with the code at the end, the code that one of my tutor group deciphered for me in a flash, although when I say flash, I mean in the sense of flash as applied by teens who are ready to fuck you off big time, in other words, as slowly as possible. And if I hadn't been on the verge of confiscating her phone and spotting the "TMB" at the end of the message she was reading, I would probably still be in the dark today.

"Vicky, what does that mean?"

Vicky was not my friend at that moment and just grumbled out that it meant she wouldn't be seeing Daryl that night unless she replied.

"You know you're not allowed to use your phone during school hours."

Grunt.

"So, what does that mean at the end?"

It still amazes me how teenagers can sigh so heavily. Their lung capacity must be fantastic.

"I said—" Her eyes rolled around as if she was talking to an idiot. "If I don't..." why was she breaking up the words? "reply..." Sarcastic little... "back. Daryl..." Was she chewing gum? I was sure I could smell Juicy Fruit. "will take Nikki to the flicks instead of me."

Part of me wanted to tell her that if that was the case, Daryl wasn't worth the sms; another part wanted to check to see if she was chewing gum; but the biggest part of me still wanted to know what TMB meant.

"Look, Vicky, what does TMB mean?"

Did she growl? And then flick the gum to her left cheek?

"It means 'Text Me Back', Miss."

It was a good job Luke had walked in, as I think I would have still been interrogating Vicky and displaying a perfect exemplar of being as thick as shit.

"Empty your mouth, Vicky." And before she could deny it, I added, "Juicy Fruit. Top left hand corner." As she raised her eyes in surprise, I continued, "And go and wash that crap off your face. This is a school not a Mardi Gras." With that, I turned sharply and raced out of the door. In the staff room I grappled with the contents of my bag and eventually found my phone, which, I believe, was having a cyber rendezvous with my Personal Organiser.

Click. Click. Click. And there it was:

"Hey, you. How has your day been? Are we still good for Thursday? Take care. TMBx"

She had asked me a question (two, even) and I had been so busy being concerned about the bloody coded message and the "x". I had missed it. Missed it. Me! The one who is paid to teach kids how to access texts and explore their literal and metaphorical meaning. Me! Who spent four years at university learning how to read for depth and understanding; how to analyse, evaluate, decipher, extract; and here I was, missing the question, and the whole fucking point of the text message in the first place: Text Me Back!

Why is it always the way that when you want to use your phone, you get the annoying message from your phone company "Server busy," or the even more annoying one "Emergency only"? Didn't they understand this *was* an emergency? Not in the person-stuck-in-a-burning-building sense of an emergency, but an emergency nevertheless. Maria would probably think I was ignoring her, and didn't want to go out on our date. I am certain that at that point I started to sweat. Should I just call her? But what if she was working? In the lab with all that electrical stuff. I was sure people weren't allowed to keep their phones on in a hospital. There was only one thing for it...stuff the Parents Evening. Adam Clarins's parents would have to wait a couple of minutes. I was going out of the school gates to wave my arm around like a madwoman in the hopes that British Telecom would have pity on me and give me a signal.

That was why I looked like a castaway from *Lost* when I saw her drive up to the school gates. And the funny thing was, she waved back. Stunned is the word. Stunned and feeling slightly stupid. Why was Maria driving through the school gates? Why was Maria not at work at four in the afternoon? An awful feeling rushed through me, accompanied by the memory "I've seen you before." Was she a parent? Nah...I think I would have known if she had a child, wouldn't I? She would have said, wouldn't she? It would have come up in conversation, wouldn't it?

All this time I was standing there with my arm in the air, pixie feet-nailing moment again, the questions backlogging and totally fucking up my already muddled brain. I couldn't even remember why I was standing outside in the first place.

Even when she got out of her car and started moving towards me, I still stood rooted to the spot. At least I had the sense to lower my arm.

As she got closer, I could see a worried smile forming on her face. You know the ones...the ones that are trying to appear and stay, but are worried that they aren't welcome. But it was, and if I wasn't such a twat I would have raced over to her and made sure that smile stayed exactly where it was.

"Hey, you."

I think I said "hey" back but I couldn't stake my life on it.

"I hope you don't mind. I was passing…"

Passing? *Passing*? I worked over twenty-five miles from where she worked, so how on earth could she be just *passing*? And more to the point—where would she be passing to?

"If this is a bad time?"

Why were my lips moving, but no words coming out?

"I can always go."

"*NO!*" My voice came back with vengeance, and I swallowed before repeating, "No. Stay." Stay and do what? I was already late for Parents Evening. "Although I have to go inside in a minute." Should I invite her in to wait? Or even sit on the benches and watch me race through parents as if I was on speed? "You can come in if you like."

Then it went quiet. The kind of quiet where the birds have lost their voices and all traffic ceases. Had I said something wrong? Didn't she relish the thought of being surrounded by whining fourteen-year-olds who were on the receiving end of their parents' disappointment?

"Erm…" Maria paused.

Looked like a no.

"I have to…*erm*…get back to work."

So why had she driven all the way out here when she was supposed to be at work?

"I…*erm*…just wondered if we were still on for tomorrow night. You…*erm*…"

Was she blushing? She was! She was blushing…and the reason why she was rapidly turning the most adorable shade of crimson was because she felt stupid admitting she felt vulnerable. Then I remembered I hadn't replied to her message...and the reason why I hadn't replied to it. Then it was my turn to go red. Fuck. Why was being attracted to someone so damned embarrassing and exposing?

"That's what I was doing out here." I held up my phone. "See? I didn't know what TMB meant until about fifteen minutes ago." Shit. That part of my confession I had wanted to hold back. Trust that bloody voice box to decide that muteness followed by excessive volume wasn't enough, that saying my inner thoughts was also an excellent way of making me look like a dipshit. Both of us stood there glowing in the soft winter's evening, grinning stupidly.

"So, are we? Still on for tomorrow, that is?"

Checking over my shoulder, I made sure there was no one around before moving closer to her. A soft kiss landed on her lips before I said, "Tomorrow can't come soon enough."

Five minutes later, after I had walked her to her car, just in case she lost her way, I was back inside. It wasn't until Adam Clarins's mother sat in front of me that it hit me. How on earth did Maria know where I worked? She knew I was a teacher, but I hadn't told her where I tortured kids. That was something that had never come up in conversation.

"I've told Adam that English is important. He will never get a place at college without a C," Mrs Clarins stated.

Snapping out of the disturbing consideration of how Maria knew where I worked, I looked at Adam. The only way he would ever get a C in English was if he paid someone to do his exam for him.

"Even his dad has told him. He sent Adam a letter last week from prison saying for him to knuckle down and get some qualifications."

What to do? Not about Adam, about Maria. Was she a stalker? Would she know Adam's dad? Would I end up in a body bag at the bottom of the river?

Sighing, making the most of my last breaths on this earth before I was mutilated, I opened my mark book and began to deliver the bad news to Mrs Clarins. Adam was not going to be another Shakespeare, but he could get a D if he turned up more often, and when he turned up he didn't spend the lesson farting about. Thoughts about the gorgeous doctor would have to wait. I had all night to think about her and her ability to turn up unexpectedly; at that moment in time, I had a job to do.

Thinking things through would come later. Unfortunately, as I have said before, I have an overactive imagination, and this was its time to shine.

It was just gone nine o'clock when I turned the key in my front door. The evening was draining, to say the least, and even more so with the thoughts of being watched at every opportunity, not to mention having to explain why I looked like a battered piece of fruit to every set of parents. What I couldn't understand was that she looked so normal—Maria, that is. But they always say that about serial killers, don't they? Things like "He was such a quiet man...would do anything for anyone...kept himself to himself. We can't believe he would do such things to all those women."

After turning on every light in the house, I felt a little more relaxed, although the soak in the bath would have to wait as I didn't want to be vulnerable when the shit hit the fan. A shower would have to do. That way I had a better chance of running if the key scene from Hitchcock's *Psycho* decided to play itself out in my bathroom.

Oh for fuck's sake! Who was I kidding? Maria wasn't a stalker, well, a serial killer at any rate. Just because she had a fantastic ability to sniff me out didn't mean she was going to do me in. And, more to the point, why would she want bump me off? I wasn't anything special.

Or did I remind her of someone...like her mother...the mother who was evil and treated her badly? Or did I look like Dr Jennifer Fielding, the woman who had screwed her over? And I decided to stop that train of thought before it developed any further and I ended up thinking I was being dated by Myra Hindley wannabe (Myra/Maria? Stop it!). The best thing was to ask her...ask how she knew where I worked...how she knew I would be at the doctor's at that time. Ask her if she was going to cut me into tiny pieces after playing doctors and nurses with all my bits and bobs.

I should write thrillers, shouldn't I? Should write about bodice rippers and things that go bump in the night. I have the imagination, I think. The imagination that would scare the shit out of anyone who didn't usually get the shit scared out of them easily.

Picking up my phone, I decided this was not the time to text and say things along the lines of "Are you planning to kill me? TMBx." This was a job for the voice box, assisted, obviously, by the brain. Click. Call. Ringing... still ringing...*still* ringing...voicemail. Click. End call. I couldn't leave a message, could I? Something like "Hey, Maria. It's me, Gem. Your next victim..." And so on and so forth. I decided to have a shower and call her back.

Shower over—with the door locked—I picked up my trusty mobile and attempted to call her once again. Still no answer, but this time it went straight to the mailbox. Had she turned her phone off? Turned it off because she was, at this point, looking through my bedroom window, waiting for her opportunity to climb through and strangle me with my own tights. My mother had always told me that would happen one day if I wasn't a good girl, but I thought it was the same kind of story as Johnny Big Eyes...the bloke who ate naughty children. Although my mum was an angel, she also had a wicked sense of humour. Funnily enough, I wasn't laughing now; I was too busy shitting my pants. Part of me was regressing to childhood, and I had to resist the urge to call my mum and whimper down the phone "Is Johnny Big Eyes real, Mummy?" whilst hugging a teddy and peeing my drawers.

Sleep was erratic, as you can imagine. Every noise my house innocently made sounded like an axe wielding murderer coming up the stairs. Dreams were made up of Maria on the teddy grabbing machine, and I was the one on the polystyrene chips. And I don't even want to go into detail about the shooting game.

By the time morning came I was a bag of nerves, but the daylight seemed to make something click on inside my head. Grow up. Just the two words—"grow" and "up". I wished they were accompanied by the words: "She is not going to kill you; she is a lovely SANE woman." I think it all boiled down to not believing Maria would want me any other way than as a mad woman's prey. Talk about a low self-esteem. This would make a great special on Jerry Springer. "I think my gorgeous wannabe girlfriend wants to cut me into pieces. Please give me a makeover."

Funny to think that all week I had been anticipating the date with Maria, but now I was dreading being alone with her. It was at lunchtime that I had the brain wave. Call Colin. Colin will save you. Colin will protect you with his dying breath. And if all else fails, hide behind Colin; he owes you one. Thankfully he answered his phone straight away, something that surprised me. Another thing that surprised me was his willingness to come along with me on my date, although there was a catch. He was going to bring the man in his life with him. In retrospect, that seemed even more plausible. A double date. How quaint. And *two* people to hide behind. Now all I had to do was let Maria know we would not be on our own. I was so absorbed in my thoughts that I didn't hear what else Col had to say, just told him to be outside the Forum at eight and to not be late.

Now, back to telling Maria. I couldn't call her cell, I couldn't text her—she might not get the message—so I called the hospital and asked to be put through to extension 137.

For once in my life I was happy to talk to Nurse Sour Tits, although I doubt the feeling was mutual. When I asked her to pass the message to Dr Moran that we would be going out in a foursome, I definitely felt the ice charge down the line, especially when she said, "This is a hospital not a dating agency." I was just about to tell her that she should work on her bedside manner a little when I heard

Maria's voice in the background. At that moment I felt like a shit. How on earth could I ever have thought she was anything but a wonderful, intelligent, gorgeous woman? She wouldn't hurt me; she was a doctor for Christ's sake. The nurse was trying to fob me off, and Maria off, by telling her that it was a wrong number, and I wanted to shout down the phone that she was a twat. Good job I didn't, really, as the next voice I heard on the line was Maria's.

"Hello. Dr Moran here. Can I help you?"

"Hey, you. It's me. Gem." It seemed as soon as I heard that glorious voice, all my worry just evaporated. It was at that precise moment that I regretted calling Colin and getting him involved. "About tonight..."

"You're not cancelling are you?" The disappointment poured from her in those few words, and that made me feel even worse.

"No...I...*we* are going to have company." Did she sigh? Or was it just me hearing things that weren't there again? "Colin wants to meet you. He won't stay long."

"O...*kay*." Why did it sound as if she didn't believe me? Probably because I was telling porkies. Well, kind of.

"He's been pestering me for ages to meet his new bloke, and I thought it would be a great opportunity, you know, for all of us to meet at the same time." The lie rolled perfectly off my tongue; I even felt the burn after it hit the air. "Shall we say seven-thirty? Shall I pick you up?" *Good to have my own car...quick getaway.* Fuck. There I go again.

"O...*kay*."

Why did she still sound as if I was feeding her a pack of lies instead of just the one?

"When you pick me up, you can meet Trevor...my housemate. We could call it a night for introductions."

I am definite I heard a snigger, but I wouldn't stake my life on it.

"Or maybe surprises."

What the fu—

"See you at seven thirty, Gem. I'm looking forward to it."

Then she was gone and I was left holding the phone in my hand, listening to the sound of the disconnected tone. Surprises? Were they *nice* surprises, or the kind of surprises you heard about on BBC? Don't get me wrong, I love surprises, but they must be the ones you can eat, or drink, or watch, or any other thing that is deemed to be a pleasurable experience. Like breathing. And at that moment I was making the most of that little treasure.

At seven-twenty-six I was standing on her doorstep. My knees decided this was the moment when they would practice for a maraca competition, and I could hear them culminating in a Mexican crescendo as my finger poked out and pressed the doorbell. I don't know what I was expecting, but it definitely wasn't what I got, that's for sure.

Through the glass I could see the figure of a man standing there as if in conversation with someone else. So I waited, although I really wanted to press the doorbell again. Talk about being a big kid. I had spent at least thirty seconds staring at the outline of the man, so that when the door eventually opened I seemed to have zoned out a little. All I could see was pink, well, a pink covered chest to be exact.

"Hey there, Gemma. Come on in."

That voice. I knew that voice from somewhere, but couldn't place it. I had thought the same on Sunday when I had heard it, and I now knew this was Trevor.

"I'm Trevor, by the way."

Thank you. Although I had worked that one out on my own.

"Come in."

I was still staring at the huge pinkness of the man, and had to command my eyes to stop staring at the vee at the top of his shirt where all the manly little hairs poked through.

Up. Up. A little higher, girls. We were now on the chin. Up... Up...and eye contact. Eventually. And that's where my first surprise came about. I knew this man. Not personally, but I bloody knew him. He was my doctor...the horoscope doctor...the one who I had slagged off for being on the wrong end of the IQ scale. So, meeting a blast from the past had come true.

"Good to see you can button up your coat better now."

What the—

"Lovely to meet you on a personal level at last." His hand shot out, and for a split second I thought he was going to smack me one. "A little nervous, I think." The laugh he emitted after he said that nearly deafened me, but funnily enough I didn't get fucked off like usual. In fact, I laughed right along with him. Relief, I think, according to the pitch and delivery of it. And the reason why I laughed with something bordering on relief was because at least I had a vague understanding about how Maria knew I'd be at the doctor's.

"Come in and take a load off. Her ladyship is nearly ready."

I must have been inside the house for less than a minute, hadn't even had the opportunity to slip out of my coat, when the doorbell went again. Trevor's voice boomed out as he welcomed what must have been his bloke. Imagine my surprise when I turned around and saw Colin standing there. Colin. Standing. There. There. In Maria's house. Smiling. Or should I say, grinning like a twat? Yes. That sounds more like the description I would like to go with. Twat-like.

"I think you two are already acquainted. Drink anyone?"

I couldn't speak; I was saving all my energy for murder. Colin didn't seem fazed by the fact that I was standing in front of him in his boyfriend's house. Not a smidgeon of fazing, to be precise. More like smug. Smug and annoying. Smug, annoying, and soon to be bleeding—of my ex friend's face—if he didn't tell me what the bloody hell was going on.

"I'm good, thank you, Trev," Colin said.

You won't be in a minute.

"But I think Gem might need a stiff one."

As long as I can beat you to a pulp with it, then yes...make mine a double.

After Trevor disappeared into the back to what must've been the kitchen, I grabbed Colin by the shirt front, delighting in the sound of a couple of buttons popping loose and tapping their way across the floor.

"What the fuck is going on? Why didn't you tell me instead of making me look like an idiot?" Never mind Maria being a killer, I wanted to be one at that moment. "I spoke to you today...*to-day*, Col, and you never said a word."

Colin's eyes were getting wider, and his mouth was moving with the hope that the words he was thinking about would spring forth and save his hide.

"I asked him not to. Sorry." Maria's voice was behind me.

When I turned, she was standing about halfway down the stairs. God, that woman was breathtaking. And because she was breathtaking, I loosened my hold, enabling Col to slip out of my grip.

"It seems stupid now, but I thought you might think it was a little weird how this all came about. You know, Trevor seeing Colin...me seeing you. I... Well, it's all in the open now."

"And you were afraid that she would realize you've been stalking her," Trevor's voice boomed from the back, and Maria went scarlet, her mouth spluttering words of denial. He appeared in the doorway, a tray of drinks in his hand. "And don't even try to deny it, Moran. You've been hankering after this woman for months."

Now, do I feel honoured or shit scared? I should have been feeling the latter, especially after my thoughts of serial killers and certain death, but I didn't. I felt chuffed, actually. Maybe because the "stalking" activities here were not the same ones I had been conjuring up. These seemed like something one person would do in order to get to see another person she liked. I wished I'd thought of it. But that would make me a stalker too, wouldn't it?

"It wasn't like that and you know it." Maria was at the bottom of the stairs by now, blue eyes looking beseechingly at me. "I haven't been following you; I was just in the right place at the right time, that's all."

Both Trevor and Colin sniggered, and she glared in their direction, making them go silent. I would've too if she had directed that look at me. "I first saw you at The Castle. I told you that." She was back to looking straight at me by this point, and I could feel myself being drawn in. Trevor and Colin were becoming a distant presence. "I was there with Trevor when I first saw you. That's where he met Colin, straight after he had kicked me in the face."

I heard a "shit" uttered from behind me, and I knew that this topic had already been discussed.

"Neither of us knew who you were at that time, and when you disappeared, I thought that would be the last time I would see you. Trevor didn't know who you were, as he had only been practicing at that surgery for six months."

"Is anyone going to take their drink, or do I have to stand here looking like a waiter all night?" No one answered Trevor, although I heard Col chink a glass as he took his from the tray.

"Shall we sit down and I can tell you everything?" Maria took my hands in hers and raised them to her lips. A gentle kiss landed on each knuckle before she continued. "I wouldn't want you to think I was a psycho or a serial killer."

Snort. That was me, if you were wondering. "As if I would ever..." Colin tried to interrupt just then. Shall I stress "tried"? "Colin? Can I have a quick word?" I turned and glared at him, Maria's hands still firmly in mine. "Alone."

I looked back at Maria. "I'll meet you in a minute. Okay?" Why was my voice so light and sickly sweet, so angelic and pure? I'll tell you why. The reason it was so demure and genteel was because I was saving my aggressive tone and teeth clenching bit for when I got Colin on his own. I wanted to tell him in no uncertain terms that it must never come to light that I had nearly begged him to come out with us tonight. Unfortunately he had already told Trevor I had invited him. All I can say is that I think I learned a lesson from it all. The lesson being—don't be a twat.

It took less than thirty minutes for all the details to come to light. The upshot of the discussion was Maria wasn't a CNN headline wannabe, although when I kept seeing Colin's grinning face, I didn't mind the thought of becoming one myself. And it wasn't for the "Best Friend Award" either.

Here it is in a nutshell, coming from yours truly, the number one nut. And remember, I'm not the kind of woman who does "nutshell" well.

I had gone to the doctor's after turning my computer off, right? Remember that? The doctor was a pink wearing, horoscope reading, "I'll state the obvious" type, yeah? Well, the reason why he seemed so vacant was because he could have sworn he knew me from somewhere, but for the life of him he couldn't remember. Until he got home from work, that is, and saw his housemate. Obviously, he had to say he had seen the woman she fancied, but couldn't say any more because of the doctor-patient thing. This made it all the worse, as Maria thought he was just being a tight bastard by rubbing salt in the wound. So, he told her that she would be able to see for herself as he had sent a recommendation for me to have my injury looked at. Once again, he wouldn't tell her what was wrong, my name, or anything substantial. However, he did make sure that I got my appointment as soon as possible because he was fed up to the back teeth of Maria giving him stick every time he got home from work. And there was I thinking the NHS was actually getting its act together.

Are you keeping up? I wished I did when she was blurting it all out, because it seemed a little crazy to me. Two doctors having this kind of conversation...I didn't think doctors acted like normal people—you know, played with each other's mental state. I thought that would go against all they adhered to—creating mental stress and all that bollocks.

"I knew you were coming on the Tuesday, but that was it. I didn't know what time, or anything about you."

I was sitting next to her on the sofa by this stage; the boys had decided to go back into the kitchen.

"By the time I got to you I was shot to pieces. I thought you hadn't come, as a couple of women had failed to keep their appointments. I didn't expect a Mrs to come in and it to be you."

I remembered the scene well, as do you, I suppose. I thought she was quite blunt, and a midget. Then she seemed to change at the very moment I thought she was going to have a field day with me facing the wrong way.

But it was when she touched me, when her hand touched my exposed skin and made everything seem better.

"It wasn't until I got right up close to you that I realised who you were. I was so relieved you were facing the opposite direction. My face was burning and I found speaking difficult, especially when you told me you were in fact a Miss after all."

I remember waiting for her, waiting to hear what she would sound like up close and personal. Then I turned to see what she would look like, what this woman with the magical touch would actually look like.

"All I could do was apologise for my rudeness, and, to be perfectly honest, I can't really tell you what happened."

I blurted out I wasn't married.

"The next thing I remember was standing in the back room watching you as the X-ray was being taken."

I remembered. I could remember everything. The only thing spinning through my head was this need for her to come back into the room so I could fall into the spell of those blue eyes again, those same blue eyes which were now looking at me with such openness I wanted to fall into them.

"It was as if a spell had been cast. There you were and I was going to lose you again unless I thought of a way to keep you longer."

A small laugh escaped and for a moment the atmosphere in the room lifted and shifted and allowed me to relax just a fraction. I don't know why I was tense in the first place, but it seemed the right way to feel at this juncture, the juncture where everything moves and changes and allows life to become everything you ever hoped it would be. "If it makes you feel any better, I was thinking the exact same thing."

Maria laughed, and this time I joined in.

"After I made a complete ass out of myself by nearly coming behind the screen with you, I went in the back and gave myself a good talking to. It was now or never. If I didn't ask to see you again, I knew I never would." At this point, Maria looked down at our hands, at the fingers that were interlocked. "You could never understand how hard it was to come up with the 'Can I walk down with you?' Not for one minute did I think anything would ever come of it. If it had taken me the time for you to get changed to think of asking to walk downstairs with you, God only knows what I would've said next." She gave me one of her radiant smiles, then stopped, then smiled all the more. "That was one time in my life I was happy a patient nearly fainted on me."

This time it was me who was feeling the blush of exposure. That had been the time I had been checking her out and thought she had caught me. *Bollocks. Big ones. Hairy smelly ones. Should I tell her? Admit that I had been giving her the once over like a prize heifer?*

"Aren't you two finished yet? We've booked a table and we're starving," Colin was poking his head around the door, his face open and innocent.

I love you, Colin; I do. You may have broken my nose, kicked my girlfriend in the face, kept the truth back from me, but I can always rely on you to appear when I'm not expecting you.

Fortunately, he didn't ask "What's the matter with your face? You seem all flustered and you're blushing? Anything

I can embarrass you further with?" Instead he said, "We'll just be out here. Okay?" then left.

The room was quiet again and I waited for her to continue. I know I could've told her about me not really feeling faint, made her feel that this embarrassment was shared by the both of us and not just by her, but...

"I felt so nervous giving you that piece of paper with all my numbers on it. I thought you might have guessed that it was more than just me telling you to call to get your results."

Was it?

"I thought it would give me enough time to come up with something more original than grabbing a coffee." At this point she put her head down, and I felt a wave of sadness wash over her. "And then you didn't call."

"Yes, I did."

"You seemed so up for it by the time we were parting, that when you didn't... You called? When?"

After explaining to her I had spoken to the delightful nurse with the missing personality, a cloud seemed to settle over her and rest for a moment. I didn't like the expression on her face, not by a long shot. It was the kind of expression you see just before a dog attacks another dog. You know the ones. They are the ones that are full of venom and command fear; the ones that read their victim just before eating it alive. I didn't want to be eaten alive. Well, it would depend on what the "eating alive" bit consisted of. Sorry. I thought I would be truthful for a change, and if that meant exposing you to my lecherous thoughts, so be it.

"Are you okay? You seem upset." Why do I insist on calling a spade a spade? Well, except when I trip over one of course. Then it is called something completely different.

Maria blinked a few times before conjuring a smile from somewhere. "Nothing. It's okay. I was thinking I need to have a word with someone."

I wanted to ask who, but I think we all know who she was talking about. The next thing I wanted to ask was why. Why would the nurse do that? Maybe I'm a coward and didn't want to know why, just in case it turned out to be the nurse was an ex or something. Nah. There was no way Maria would be caught dead with such a vitriolic, spiteful cow, was there?

"Come on. Let's feed the boys."

Let them feed themselves. They are supposed to be hunter-gatherers, after all.

Looking behind me, I saw Trevor and Colin waiting in the doorway. Seeing them standing there together, I wanted to laugh at the thought I'd had. Hunter-gatherers? They were more likely the "Can you cut my meat up for me?" types. Just after I had this thought, Colin smiled sheepishly at me. Aww...he was a cutie. A gitful, secret hiding, nose breaking, face kicking cutie, but a cutie all the same. And my best friend to boot, if you excuse the pun—again.

Decision made to get going, I stood up. "Well, come on then. It's not only the boys who want feeding."

With that, the conversation was over, and it wasn't long before we were piling out of the house and towards hunger satisfaction. Everything else would have to wait.

Chapter 9

ONSIDERING I AM THE ONE who is writing this I have the power to skip forward, backward, change setting on a whim; I could even bring in new characters if I wanted to. But I don't think you would appreciate it if I suddenly moved all my characters forward in time and plunked them on another planet. Although not changing planets, I will be skipping forward a tad. Not too far, but enough to move things along a little. Let's say two, no, three months.

So, where are we now? The month of May? Yes...May. Let's rearrange our setting. We are no longer sitting in Maria's house, or just leaving to have dinner. We are now standing at my front door, or should I say *I* am standing at my front door. And what am I doing? Simple. I am reading a letter. A typed letter. A typed letter signed "A friend". So, who do you think the "friend" was? Colin? Nope. Maria? I very much doubt it. This "friend" was in fact not a friend at all. The reason for that observation was in the neatly printed contents of the letter. This letter. This missive of confidentiality. The very same letter I could feel scrunching in my hand.

You're confused, aren't you? So was I, to be frank. But I doubt our confusion stems from the same thing. I should go back to my original plan of continuing the story from where we were two months ago, but I've started at this point, and to tell you the truth, just like my hand on that now crumpled piece of paper, I am frozen in time. Maybe I should compromise, tell you facets of the interim period. Okay. Once again I will attempt to nutshell my life until the day that this tableau of me standing in my hallway holding a once crisp piece of whiteness appears again.

Maria. Just the one word. Maria. That's what summed up my life until that moment after the letterbox rattled. Our relationship had blossomed, to use a worn out cliché, and I was living on cloud nine...ten...eleven... Shall I go on? Don't get me wrong, we weren't in each other's pockets, and to be coarse, we weren't in each other's underwear either. But it was a good thing—honestly. I loved becoming close to her, getting to know her, making sure I didn't rush her, didn't go too far in case she would think I was like Dr Jennifer Fielding and would sleep with her and leave her. I didn't mind waiting; I would wait for her as long as she wanted me to. A smile from those gorgeous lips would be enough to keep me going until I could see her again.

That was another thing. When *could* I see her again? I don't mean from this point on, I meant in the last three months. That was the thing that would play on my mind the most—the fact I couldn't see her when I wanted to. Work kept us from meeting some times, but that just wasn't it. I can't explain what it was, it just was, if you know what I mean. I wanted to see her all of the time, but I had a feeling she wasn't the "I want to see you all of the time" kind of woman. I thought she might have been, especially when she used to appear from nowhere and I thought she was a stalker, but that turned out to be a case of who you know rather than "I am following your every move". Even down to her turning up at the school gates. That was Colin. He had told her that she shouldn't rely on me checking my phone messages and should just pop by and do it in person.

Now that would suggest she was into me, wouldn't it? That's exactly what I thought, and whenever I had these niggling doubts that she actually wasn't as "into me" as I was "into her" I would think about that. Truth is, I had fallen in love with her so bloody deeply it frightened me shitless. Maria had become the epicentre of my life, the nucleus around which my whole being orbited.

It was weird, though. Imagine finding out the actual reason for us not seeing each other on a daily basis on the very day before we were going to go away for the weekend together for the first time. And the reason was detailed in the letter that was in my hand. The typed one. The "from a friend" one. It was timed, I was sure of it. Whoever this "friend" was must have known that we were going away...going away and maybe something more. Maybe consummating this relationship that had enveloped my whole being and become my reason to breathe.

"Maria Moran has a girlfriend, and that girlfriend isn't you." That should have been enough to set the alarm bells ringing, but like a fool I read the rest. I won't bore you with all the details, or maybe I just find it difficult to write the details down, as each word seemed to stab a little bit deeper. All I can tell you is that this letter helped me see things more clearly than I had for quite a while, or so I thought at the time. In truth, that very letter was having the completely opposite effect, although I didn't know it at that moment. My judgment was well and truly clouded by the time I had read the letter through for the third time. It's amazing, though. Most people would have screwed the letter up, marched to wherever Maria was, and demanded an explanation. Or even called her. That would have been so easy. Lift up the receiver, punch in the numbers, ask for extension 137, wait again, then calmly ask Maria what the fuck was going on.

But no. I didn't march, didn't call. I just folded the piece of paper, slipped it back into the envelope, picked up my keys and handbag, and headed towards answers. I still cringe when I remember my decision; well, not so much my decision, but what came after it.

In all honesty, I can't remember driving to the Norfolk and Norwich University Hospital. Can't remember parking, walking towards the entrance. Nothing. Until I saw her standing outside, that is. It seemed at that precise moment the whole world came back into focus. The images were sharp, so sharp they hurt my eyes. There was Maria, standing outside and grinning. You may think that is a wonderful thing to see, the gorgeous doctor grinning in happiness because I had come to visit. So would I, if she had been grinning at me. But you see, she wasn't. She was grinning at someone else, someone who was blonde, good looking, touching her arm and leaning closer and whispering something to her—something funny, something sexy, something I couldn't hear, and probably wouldn't have heard if she had said it to my face. Then came the hug, the holding and squeezing, the pulling each other closer as if they wouldn't see each other for ages.

That's when I snapped out of it. Snapped out of the dream state I had allowed to cocoon me. We were supposed to be going away tomorrow for four days. Did that qualify for "ages"? Was she hugging and holding this woman because she couldn't see her for at least that length of time because she was going away with me?

Then I did the thing I never thought I would do. I retreated into myself, and more to the point, I retreated out of the picture, leaving them to hold and caress each other for as long as they wanted to. What else would you expect me to do? Make a scene? Storm up to them and demand to know what they were doing? What they were doing was obvious even to me. Tears were blinding my eyes, and I could feel myself stumbling away, pushing people aside as I blundered through.

Back in the car park, and back inside my car, I allowed it all to tumble out. Each sob that broke out seemed to rip me apart. Each exhalation of breath came out as a howl. All this time...all this time and I thought she was mine... mine... I thought she was mine. But like all fantasies, the real world bleeds back eventually. What on earth was I thinking? She would never look at me. I was just a bit on the side, a distraction of sorts. All the thoughts I'd had for the last three months popped up and jeered at me. All the times I had convinced myself that she did like me, did want me as much as I wanted her, seemed to flit across my mind until I ended up screaming "STOP!" to nothing but an empty car.

Is that why she hadn't slept with me? Because she was sleeping with someone else, I mean. Had I fallen for the story of her being the victim, of her being used when in fact she was the user? Did Dr Jennifer Fielding exist? More to the point, was the good looking blonde holding her outside the front entrance the former mentor herself? Questions, and then more questions. But no answers, it appeared. I had come there for answers and then had run away like a spineless twat and hid away inside my car, feeling sorry for myself.

No. I wasn't going to just slip away and forget her. I couldn't forget her; that was the problem. She was so far under my skin that in order to forget her I would have to strip off each layer before scrubbing her out. It wasn't the physical pain of stripping off those layers that scared me, though. It was the pain I knew would follow, the one that was beginning to squirm inside my chest in readiness of breaking out and breaking me apart.

I could feel the air on my face as I marched back towards the entrance, and it wasn't until my hand touched the cool door handle that I realised I was on my way to confront her. There was no more feeling sorry for myself. No. Now I was angry. Seething, in fact. I was not going to leave there until she admitted she had led me on.

As I marched up the stairs towards the X-ray department, two things kept plaguing me. One: why hadn't she screwed me if she just wanted a bit on the side? And two...this was Maria. Maria wouldn't do all the things my brain had conjured up in the last hour. How could the woman I had grown to know, grown to love, do this? Be with someone else, I mean, someone else behind my back, with someone who held the place I thought I held, the place I wanted to be.

Ward G. The waiting room. Empty. The corridor echoed each footstep I made, and it ricocheted off the walls like in a crappy scene from a 1950s B movie. What if she had left? I hadn't even checked the car park to see whether her car was still there before venturing inside. Maybe because I hadn't realised I was on my way to confront her until I was at the entrance to the building.

Outside the door to the X-ray room, I stopped, briefly, and swallowed hard. It was shit or bust, now or never, live and let die. And yes, there were more pithy epithets, but now was not the time to run through the whole of Brewer's *Phrase and Fable*. Now was Confrontation Time.

A light was on in the back room and I could see the shadow of someone in the corner. It looked as if the person was preparing to close up. Maria—by her own admission— was always the last to leave. In retrospect, I should have shouted out her name before I spoke.

"So, who's the blonde?" A little louder... "No wonder you didn't want to fuck me!" The shadow stopped, and I knew she was listening. "Why did you lead me on, Maria? What were you hoping to get?" The shadow started to move in my direction, and, weirdly enough, I had the urge to run the other way. I even stepped back as I repeated, "Why, Maria? Why?"

And then I heard what I can only describe as a snigger. Fuck. If I had been feeling angry before, it was nothing to how I was feeling after I heard the snort. This was not the woman I had fallen for. This was not the Maria I knew and had fallen in love with. This was not Maria. Literally.

It wasn't Maria. And I believe you know who it was even before I tell you. It was the nurse.

"So. You've eventually cottoned on, have you?"

She knew. That fucking cow *knew*!

"I was wondering how long it would take you."

She was in the room with me now, and the only thing I was scared of doing wasn't hitting her, it was not being able to stop hitting her if I started.

"I did try to warn you. Well, put you off."

How? I hadn't spoken to her since I had called the last time, and that was months ago—the time I had called about the foursome. The time she had tried to fob me off and pretend I was a wrong number.

"Dr Moran has a thing about blondes, you see. As soon as I saw you, I knew she would make a move."

I tried to answer but it came out as a splutter. What could I say? What possible comeback could I deliver to this grinning woman? How many other people knew that Maria had been using me?

"It always ends up like this." She was standing right in front of me. "The good doctor always leaves me to tidy up her mess."

Tears were slipping out of the corners of my eyes and burning my cheeks, but still I couldn't speak.

The nurse pulled a face which attempted to show sympathy, but most closely resembled a mocking expression. "You poor thing."

As her hand came up to stroke the side of my face, I flinched away. There was no way I wanted her hands on my skin.

A laugh shot out before she lowered her arm. "As usual, she's not here. But I could give her a message..." With that she turned away from me and began to walk towards the room at the back. Just before she got there, she turned to face me, her head tilted to one side as if she honestly expected me to say something. It seemed as if the silence between us lasted forever before she broke it. "A piece of advice...you can take it or leave it, your call." A pause. "Dr Moran is bad news. Forget her. Leave here and forget her."

I wished I could.

"She'll try and talk her way out of it, and she always succeeds. Even her girlfriend believes her lies."

She knew she had a girlfriend too?

"The Doc has a way of making everyone believe *she* is a victim. Call it a talent."

At that point I knew I had to leave. I had to put as much distance between me and the nurse, me and Maria, as I could. Other than that I doubted I could perform any other action. My brain was sizzling and burring around and I was definite it would soon combust if I didn't just get the fuck away.

Everything was beginning to blur once again, and I wasn't sure if it was because of the tears or that I was going to faint. Parts of me felt numb, while other parts were filling with pain and revelling in the agony. My handbag slipped down my arm and I heard the crash of it on the tiles. I knew before looking down that all the contents would be spilled over the floor, just like I imagined my heart was feeling.

Slumping to my knees, I attempted to scoop everything up, but I couldn't seem to move properly. My arms were stiff and uncoordinated, and the smaller items were playing hide and seek, making it nearly impossible to gather them.

The next thing I knew, the nurse was crouched beside me, frantically collecting my things and unceremoniously throwing them into my gaping bag. Slowly I looked up and into her face. Although she was trying to maintain a neutral expression, I could sense she was worried about something, if her furtive looking over my shoulder was any indication. Maybe she thought I would attack her, you know, go crazy and try and make her hurt as much as I was hurting. But I don't do revenge. That isn't my style, even if I had the energy to slap her one. Truth of the matter was, however much I detested the nurse, it wasn't her fault that Maria was a lying, cheating bastard.

"Thank you." Those two words just popped from my mouth completely uncalled for. I don't know who was the most surprised—her or me. I wanted to gesture to my handbag, to make out that it was for helping me collect my things, but instead I said, "For telling me the truth."

Then I was gone, the sound of the door swinging behind me with a whoosh the only thing I heard.

All the way down to the car park I tried to stop the tears, tried to stop the breaking apart. All through the myriad of corridors, I tried to stop hearing Maria's voice, seeing her smile, seeing those blue eyes, so honest and open. Tried to shut my ears to the sound of her laugh, forget the feel of her lips against mine, the feel of her body against mine. All I can say is... I failed miserably.

Back in the car I let it out. Let out the beast that was climbing up my throat, the beast that was attempting to rip me apart in its urgency to take its place in the outside world...let out the grief that needed to be free.

Thirty minutes later I was home. Slipping the key into the lock gave me the first sense of peace I'd felt in hours, as I knew that when I got behind the door I could really let go of everything. And that everything was Dr Maria Moran.

It was half term the following week, and that is why we had planned on going away for a few days to the Lake District. But not now. Now I was going somewhere on my own, somewhere I could think, somewhere I knew no one could find me. Especially Maria. I didn't want to see her, or speak to her. If the nurse was right, she would try to explain her way out of it, reminding me again that she was the victim. As much as it went against everything I knew, I was feeling very much the victim this time around. How could someone who had told me how painful it was to be lied to, actually do the thing she professed to abhor? Was that some fucked up reasoning that I would never understand? More than likely. Was it a cover up? You know, like if I did find out what kind of woman she was, she could spout her story and make me feel sorry for her? Was there in fact a woman who had done that to her, and that, in turn, made her do this to other women? Serial killers say that, don't they? "She reminded me of my mother and that's why I killed her." I know she hadn't physically attempted to kill me, but the feelings I had inside definitely told me that Maria had maimed something deep within.

I know. You're thinking that I do victim well, too, although I have just said it goes against everything I usually believe in. But I do all the mental meanderings so fucking perfectly that sometimes I scare myself. I could go from having a coffee with someone to them strangling me with a pair of my own tights in the blink of an eye, or a flick from one neuron to another. The only way to know why Maria did what she did was to call her and find out, but, you see, I am too much of a chicken to do that. I could have sent her a text message along the lines of "Why did you fuck me about? TMBx" but even the thought of being a twat and doing that came to nothing. I couldn't find my phone for a start, though looking for the phone proves that I thought about sending a text.

So... The decision was that I was going to go away for a few days on my own, somewhere I could think, plan, and then come back and put my life into perspective. I loved Maria, but I could never be second, or even third choice for anyone. When I am with someone, I want it to be just the two of us, and accompanied by trust, truth, and respect. Not much to ask for.

A couple of phone calls to guest houses, a suitcase packed, and I was gone. Poof. Into my car and racing up the A47 and away from Norfolk. I didn't tell anyone where I was going, and with no phone, I couldn't be contacted either. This was "me" time. The time where I could get my head straight before I came back and faced the woman who I loved beyond reason, the very woman who had crushed any joy I could ever see in my future.

I ended up in the Peak District, Buxton, to be exact. I had to call back the places I had previously called about booking for the trip with Maria and tell them there had been a change of plan. I didn't do it to cover my tracks, as I doubted anyone gave a big enough shit about where I would be. It was more of a case of just driving and driving and driving until I felt the tiredness sweep over me and insist I stop.

So there I was: Derbyshire in all her glory. Such God-given beauty to soothe the eye and settle the soul surrounded me, but to tell you the truth, I don't think I looked at it. Everything was just a blur of green, and hills peppered with sheep. I couldn't even remember checking in; just remembered the feel of the bed underneath my body as I lay down. The feel of the coverlet over me was like a comfort blanket, acting as a shield against the world around me. I was crying, but I couldn't feel anything inside; I was numb. Thankfully.

Waking up hours later, I was surrounded by darkness and silhouettes of objects I didn't recognise. I momentarily felt confused; everything seemed strange and unfamiliar. As soon as I began to remember where I was, I also remembered why. And I began to cry again.

I was gone for three days. Three days, that's all. But they were the longest three days I think I have ever lived. Time always lasts longer when you are breaking apart, doesn't it?

So many times I lifted the phone to call Maria only to slam it back down again. By the third day I actually tapped in all the digits of her number before putting the phone back on its cradle, and that's when I knew it was time to face her.

After paying the bill, I stood outside the guest house and looked around me. It was the first time I had breathed fresh air in nearly seventy-two hours. My eyes were stinging both from the light and the hours of crying, and I knew I looked a mess; but I didn't care how I looked. If I had looked like a beauty queen it still wouldn't have changed the fact that Maria had lied to me. Five deep breaths, each one followed by a slow exhalation, and I was set to go. It was now or never...again. Only this time I hoped I could actually express what I meant to say.

Three and a half hours later I was pulling up outside my house. It still strikes me how a place you have lived for years can suddenly seem strange. My home had always been my place of refuge—my castle, so to speak—but looking at it now it appeared to be just bricks and mortar. Yes. I definitely think at that moment in my life, I was losing the plot.

As I opened the door, I felt something jam against the wood. A brown padded envelope was sticking part way under the edge. Bending down, I yanked it free and turned it over. On the front was my name, handwritten by a familiar hand, and the date. Friday's date. The date I had found out what had been going on. Initially I felt a surge of anger, as I honestly believed Maria had come around and wondered where her tart had gone to without telling her. I didn't straightaway rip open the packaging to see what web of lies she had concocted; I wanted to prepare myself first.

Passing the answering machine, I could see the light blinking rapidly like it was trying to get my attention in the way six-year-olds do when they want the teacher to notice them. I ignored it. It would either be Col, my parents, or Casanova herself. All of them could wait.

That seemed the best way to approach it, I thought—do things in my own time. I had waited all my life to meet someone like Maria and look where it had gotten me. Now I wouldn't be so rash as to let my heart go racing into things. First I would get myself ready for battle. Don't get me wrong, I wasn't going to go in there with guns blazing...firing off accusations left, right, and centre. That's not what I meant at all. What I wanted was for me to ask her what she had been planning to do, or hoping to achieve in this debacle that I had foolishly believed to be a relationship.

The next thing I did was to grab a coffee and slump down at the dining room table. Resting my elbows on the wood and nursing the mug in my hands, I couldn't help glancing over at the brown parcel sitting on the dresser. What was inside—a confession, an apology? I doubted it. It was more than likely a letter proclaiming how hurt she was that I had gone away and not told her where I was going. At least it could be another story she could peddle to her next victim.

Slam. Down went the mug, and I was out of the room and heading for a shower. Suddenly I felt dirty.

As the water pelted me, all I could think about were the things that had led me to this exact moment. How could Maria be a person who would do this to me? How? I wasn't that stupid, was I? And there was Trevor. Trevor didn't strike me as the kind of person who would cover for her, was he? The thought of going to her house on that very first day came back to me. The way she had dragged me out of the house when Trevor had shouted for her to stop should have been a warning. What had he said? Something about asking her to wait and then, "There's someone here you..." Someone here you know? Are shagging? Are screwing about? Has found out you are using her? I can't believe I never asked her, or him, or Colin, come to think about it. Had it been Colin who had been there? Maybe if I had insisted on meeting him, I wouldn't be in this mess now.

I could've spent ages going over every scenario, every single time something could've meant she had been using me, but what was the point? Enough of showering. I needed to ask her. Stepping out of the bathroom I decided it would be a case of dressing and leaving. I wasn't going to call her. This had to be done face to face.

As I was dressing, something caught my eye. Something sitting in the corner. Something trying to grab my attention from her place on the dresser. The crusty fur twinkled in the bedroom light, looking almost angelic. "You are an angel." That's what I had said to her just after I had fallen into the blueness of her eyes, just before I had flirted outrageously with her. Tears welled up again, and a lump the size of China formed in my throat. The next thing I knew, I was holding the rough coated teddy close to my face, the fur almost scratching my skin. Ugly Bear. The bear I had tried so hard to win, but failed miserably. I could still remember the way I had felt when Maria had presented to me the world's most ugly teddy bear and how

I had melted when she had said "I knew you wanted her, so I had a go." Were these the actions of a woman who was out to use me? "You were right, though. She was difficult to get." But not as difficult as Maria was, by the looks of things.

As I was putting Ubie back onto the dresser, another thought came to me. The way Maria had acted that day; the way she seemed to regress to being a seventeen-year-old on a first date. That wasn't the way someone who was cheating on her girlfriend would act, was it? And all this internal deliberation wasn't answering any of the questions I had. There was only one person who could do that.

After dressing, I raced down the stairs and into the dining room to pick up my car keys. I was going to confront her, ask her what the hell was going on. Find out once and for all if I could draw a line through these few months of my life and try to move on. Just as I was turning, I spotted the brown parcel. For a fleeting moment I was going to save it for later, but the nosy part of me wanted to know what was inside. At least I could prepare myself for whatever she was going to say.

I know what you're thinking. You're thinking I had already decided that Maria had been using me, and going to see her was a waste of time. But... Aw...maybe you're right. I had spent three days trying to come to terms with what had happened, and all based on the words of a typed letter and a conversation with a bitch. I know, there was the woman outside the hospital too—don't think I've forgotten that. How could I? That was the moment I had allowed it all to become real. However, the contents of the brown parcel put another spanner in the works.

The first thing I found inside the envelope was my mobile phone. The silver metal object slipped out, and for a split second I nearly let it fall on the floor. What was my phone doing inside an envelope from Maria? Why was it sitting on the palm of my hand when in truth it should have been lurking somewhere in my house? I hadn't seen it since Friday, and when I had realised I couldn't find it, I hadn't given two shits. It was only a piece of metal, after all. Clicking it on, I checked to see if I had any missed calls. Seconds later I was informed that I had missed twenty-seven calls, twenty-three of which were from Maria. Someone was panicking, and, more to the point, why would she call me if she knew I didn't have my mobile?

Looking inside the envelope, I found a letter. Slipping it out, I drew in a deep breath and prepared myself for what she was going to say.

Are you the kind of person that I am? Do you never say a wrong word to anyone (usually), but when you do, you know, have a go, you always find out that you are in the wrong? Like arguing in a shop about being overcharged and then realising you have read the sign wrong, or are mistaken about the oranges being minging. Or when you cut someone up who is coming out of the car park, and when they want to talk about it, nearly rip their head off? I couldn't blame PMS for everything, and this was another of those examples when agoraphobia could have been a blessing. It would have stopped me from marching over to the hospital and speaking to the nurse in the first place, for a start. But the thing I should work on, the thing that there are no pills for curing, was to not listen to an outsider until I have spoken to the person I need to speak to. I had allowed myself to be blinded by emotion instead of hearing Maria out; allowed myself to take the word of a woman who had made it clear she didn't like me, and didn't want me seeing Maria in the first place.

Are you thinking that I had already thought of this *before* reading what Maria had to say? If you are, then you have more faith in my good nature than I do. If you didn't, you seem to know me pretty well. It was in the letter. The letter written by Maria and hand delivered on Friday night. The letter that was inside the same envelope that contained my mobile, the same mobile that she found on the floor of the X-ray department when Maria was tidying up before coming to see me. Because she was always the last to leave, as we all know.

Funnily enough, when she had been tidying up, the nurse was just about to go herself. I didn't make this up; it was in the letter. And to save any more confusion, I think I should tell you what the letter said verbatim. It will save time in the long run.

So, here goes:

Gem

I don't know what's going on for sure, but I have a good idea. Tonight when I was finishing up, I found your phone on the floor of the X-ray room. At first I thought it was from my last patient, and only realised it was yours when I turned it on. I asked the nurse if you had been in, and she said no, but you had called. I didn't tell her I had found your phone, and by the way she was acting, I knew she was trying to cover something up. Can you please tell me if you called in and told

*her that you had to go away? She said you had been called
away for a private matter, and that you would contact me. She
knew that we were supposed to be going away this weekend, as
I had to change some appointments for next week. But I still
don't understand why your phone would be on the floor.*

*I don't know what has happened, and I hope I am not
speaking out of turn here, but I think we need to talk. There
are a few things I think I need to tell you—some things I should
have told you a long time ago.*

I did stop reading for a minute at this point—as one
does—and had a really good think about all the things she
should have possibly told me. One of which might have
been that she already had a girlfriend. I'm sorry, but I am
female. The next thing I thought about was that Maria
was in fact the last person to leave after all. Obviously my
brain had to pipe up with, "Who's the blonde?"

The nurse who usually works with me is not to be trusted.

Too right. She's a cow. But wasn't that something the
nurse warned me about—that Maria would try to explain
her way out of it?

*When I first came to work at the Norfolk and Norwich, I
thought she was a nice woman. She was the one who showed
me around. Not just the hospital, but the area too. It never
occurred to me that she might want something more than I was
willing to give.*

Want what? And who's the blonde?

When she asked if I wanted to grab a bite to eat with her, I never expected her to make a pass...

A pass! That fucking...

And when I told her I wasn't interested, I thought she was okay with it. Well, until I met you, that is. Then she seemed to change. It wasn't a case of what she said; it was more of how she said things. It is only now that I realise that I should never have listened to a word that came out of her mouth.

I was beginning to get the same feeling.

Why on earth I took her advice about not seeing you as much as I wanted to, I'll never know. She said you seemed the type of woman who needed space to breathe, and after the fiasco of you thinking I was stalking you (I guessed), I thought it would be for the best that I let you have your space. If I had followed my inclinations, I would have seen you every day—spoken to you every day. That's all I've ever wanted to do. Be with you, I mean. Part of me wonders if making you wait for us to fully express how we feel is a part of the problem. I can't tell you how many times I've wanted to move forward with that part of our relationship, and I was hoping we could've done so this weekend. I want to show you how much I want and need you. Whatever happened in the past, well, that's where I hope it can stay.

It was about now I realised I was crying. A splodge of wetness hit the paper and made the words "Be with you" blend, as if they too were trying to be together. A part of my brain was screaming out, "How could you ever have doubted her" whilst the other part was quietly insisting, "Who's the blonde?"

I don't know where you have gone, and I don't know what went on tonight; all I know is I love you. I think I've loved you from the very first minute I saw you dancing on the stage at The Castle. And I also know I should have told you this a long time ago, but like a fool, I thought I should wait. I also wanted to tell you when I was looking into your beautiful green eyes, green eyes that hover in front of me wherever I look. The same green eyes that haunt me, and I hope they will do so for the rest of my life.

She loves me? She loves me! She...loves...me. Me. The woman who ran a mile when doubt crept in...the same woman who is still asking, "Who is the blonde?"

Hopefully it is all a misunderstanding and you haven't been fed a pack of lies. I have to go out tonight as a colleague is leaving today. I won't be staying long—just long enough to toast her on her way.

Fuck. Again. And this time, a huge one. Was her work colleague blonde? And why was I still asking? Why would I doubt this woman who had told me she loved me? Was it because one person told me I shouldn't trust her, warned me that she would lie to me? The same woman who wanted Maria for herself? Did I have such low self-esteem that I believed no one would look twice my way, and if she did it was because she felt sorry for me? I had never thought that way before, so why now? Was it because I just didn't think someone as beautiful as Maria would like me as much as I liked her?

But she loves me. There it was in black and white, although beginning to smudge by this stage.

I will try to call you, both on your mobile and on your landline. As soon as you get back, can you let me know? Hopefully this is all a huge misunderstanding...

On my part, as it turned out.

...and the nurse was telling the truth when she said you had to go away. Whatever the reason you had for going, I understand. I just hope you are okay.

One more thing before I finish. I love you, Gem. I love you. Yours,
Maria xxx

I felt like a twat. I also felt like committing murder. I wanted to charge down to the hospital and throttle the life out of that lying, cheating bastard. And this time I didn't mean Maria; I meant the evil cow who thought it would be fun to fuck up people's lives because she didn't have one of her own.

Looking at my watch, I realised that it was too late to go careering down to snap the scrawny neck of the woman who had shot to the top of my most hated list, or, as the kids would say, "Bullet or Bolt" list. You can either shoot them, or fire a charge of electricity up their genitals. At this point I wanted to give her both. Obviously, the bolt first.

What was I doing? I was wasting time. AGAIN. Although I couldn't go and visit with Britain's Most Wanted, I could go and see Maria.

Grabbing my coat and bag, I raced to the door. As I got there, my mobile squawked. I was going to ignore it, but something told me to answer. Scrambling around in my pocket, I pulled out the singing object as my other hand reached for the door handle. As I pressed accept, I also opened the door.

Standing in front of me was Maria, *my* Maria, looking like her life had been sucked away. I'd never seen her eyes looking so dark, so lost. She was holding her hand up to the side of her head, and I did the only thing I could do.

"Hello," I said into the phone, but I meant it for her.

"Hello." Why did her voice seem to pour down my ear as well as hit me front on? "You're back then?"

"Yes." Still into the phone. I know; I'm an idiot.

"Are you going out? Is this a bad time?" Her lips were moving slightly ahead of her voice, and for a minute I thought I was dreaming it all. "What am I doing?" She lowered her hand, and I heard a distinct click in my head. "No point talking on the phone if we're standing in front of each other, is there?" Her question was followed by a nervous laugh.

Fuck. I'd been talking to her on the phone, as if you hadn't guessed.

"Did you want me to come back later?" There was something different about her, something that oozed what I can only describe as emptiness.

"No!" Too loud. "No." Better. "Please. Come in."

It seemed awkward, for some strange reason, like we didn't know how to act. All I had thought about since leaving the hotel that morning was seeing her, talking to her, asking her what was going on. I had even been in the process of going to speak to her. But now that we were standing face to face in my hallway, all I could feel was shame. Maria looked exactly how I had felt when I had received the letter on Friday—broken. And I knew I was the reason for it. I wanted to touch her arm, apologise, cry and beg forgiveness, but I didn't. I just stood there like a prick.

"I thought I would come and tell you it's okay."

What was?

"If you don't want to go away...or..." she swallowed, "...you've had second thoughts about us... I..." she swallowed again, "...I understand."

"Okay?" This was supposed to be a reiteration of what she had said, a kind of acknowledgement she had actually said what I thought she had said, but it didn't come out that way. It sounded like, "Okay—now get out."

And that's how she took it. Maria turned as if to leave, her shoulders sagging, her usual six feet of power seeming to shrink with every movement. It wasn't until she had opened the door that I realised what had happened.

"NO! WAIT!"

Maria stopped in her tracks, but didn't turn to face me.

"I love you."

She still didn't turn, but I saw her shoulders shrug up and down as if she was limbering up for a race.

L. T. SMITH

Grabbing her arm, I spun her round. Her face was scrunched tight and tears were flowing freely. The usually beautiful red lips were tight and trying to contain the sobs I knew wanted to break out and splatter. I could feel my own tears welling and seeping out of the corners of my eyes as I lifted my shaking hands to her face. Cupping her cheeks, I pulled her towards me, the wetness making it difficult to hold on to her as the sobs broke free. "I love you, Maria. I love you so much."

Then I kissed her. Not a passionate engagement, just an affirmation of all I was feeling for her, a punctuation mark for the words I had spoken. Soft, warm, wet lips cushioned my own, and I knew from that very moment that this woman was the woman I had always believed she was. This was the woman who I had willingly given my heart to...the woman I had decided to disbelieve at the drop of a hat.

Pulling away, I looked into her blue eyes, which were just beginning to bud open. The moisture in them made them twinkle even more than usual, and once again I was lost. So I did the only thing I could think of; I kissed her again. This time her mouth opened slightly, and I grabbed my chance. Tentatively, I slipped the tip of my tongue along her lips and luxuriated in the way they felt. They began to quiver, but not in the way that I wanted them to. Once again I pulled back and looked into her face. What I saw made an ache race up from my stomach, rattle my heart, and then stick in my throat.

She was crying. Big fat tears were galloping down her face and I knew it was my fault. Although it scared me shitless to say something, I knew I had to.

"What is it?" As if I didn't know already. "Come. Let's sit down."

Maria tried to answer, but the words clambering out of her mouth were not making any sense. Taking her hand, I led her into the front room and eased her onto the sofa.

Sitting down next to her, I wrapped my arm around her shoulders and pulled her to me. Her head resting on my chest, she really let go. Without thinking, I began to stroke her hair, the silken locks tumbling over my fingers with abandon. Part of me wanted to cry right along with her, but I knew that at that moment I had to show some semblance of strength. Shushing sounds seeped from my mouth, accompanied by tender words of comfort.

It must have been getting on for ten minutes that she cried. Nearly ten minutes of me wanting to apologise over and over again. And nearly ten minutes of waiting to explain why she would be better off without me in her life. I felt her begin to quiet down, as the sobs seemed to wane, and the shaking of her body slowed until finally it stopped. But still I waited.

The room was so quiet, the clock on the mantelpiece was almost deafening, and I could barely hear the sound of our breathing. But I could feel it. Feel the rising of her body against mine; feel us breathing in the same air in perfect rhythm. Feel the heat coming from her and melting into me.

"I'm sorry." Her voice sounded muffled as her face was still buried in the cloth of my top. And why was she apologising? I should be the one who should have been grovelling at her feet by now. "I usually don't cry like this."

I placed my hand underneath her chin and gently eased her face up to meet mine. Wetness was smeared all over and her nose had the delectable redness that accompanies wanton crying. When she sniffed, she reminded me of a child and I wish I could say that all I felt was motherly instincts. But being her mother was the last thing that I wanted to be. Her equal? Yes. Her lover? Definitely. Her all? Hopefully.

This was one of those moments when you say the most clichéd phrase in the world, and hope above hope that the person hearing it won't dismiss it as the oldest cliché in the book. "It wasn't you, it was me."

See? Older than old, but so true. It had been me, and my inability to recognise that this woman was in fact all she was cracked up to be. Maria was still looking up at me with the most engaging eyes I believe I have ever seen. "I... need...erm..." to get a grip and tell her what had happened. But how does a person explain that they didn't trust the one person they should trust the most, and would go on the word of someone else because they believed that's what they deserved?

Maria sat up and smoothed down the front of her shirt before leaning back a little. She was waiting for me to continue, but not in the "explain yourself" position that I think I would have used. It was a more "I'm listening."

"I received a letter on Friday." How lame is that? Many people received letters on Friday. It could have been from my bank manager for all she knew. Although if it was, I would probably have been laughing. "From a friend." Another waste of air. Many people received letters from friends on Friday...although email is more the hip thing to do now, or text messaging. And yes, just like I'm keeping you waiting, I was keeping Maria waiting. Maybe I was trying to word it right, or maybe I'm a dumb shit who couldn't string a sentence together with twelve foot of boat rope and Sellotape.

I walked over to where my bag was setting on the dresser. Rummaging inside, I pulled out the once white piece of paper, unscrunched it, and passed it over for her to read. Maybe she could get a glimmer of an explanation from that, as my conversational techniques definitely needed work.

Maria's forehead creased as her eyes read the words, *"Maria Moran has a girlfriend, and that girlfriend isn't you."* I knew she had read them, as her eyes flicked over the page, then back over the page, and then once again to make sure she wasn't imagining it. Then those eyes looked sharply up at me, before reading the line again. Her lips were moving, but nothing seemed to come out. Well, until...

"Why didn't you ask me?"

It seemed so easy when it came from her lips, but it wasn't easy, not by a long shot. I had wanted to ask her, still did, but wanting to ask a simple question and having it come out completely differently from how you envisioned it are two different things.

"Who's the blonde?" Why did I have to say it like that? It was okay when it was whirring around inside my fucked up brain, but those words hitting air and exposing themselves, and me, as stupid, was a different kettle of fish. Why couldn't I explain that I had tried to come and speak to her as soon as it happened, that I had seen her outside hugging and laughing with a mystery woman, then

I had gone inside to ask her again, but ended up believing the words of a vindictive bitch? Sometimes there is a miscommunication between the heart, the brain, and the voice box, and this was one of those times. My heart wanted me to take this woman in my arms and tell her again how much I loved her. My brain was screaming "Don't say it! Don't you fucking dare ask about the blonde!" The voice box won. Unfortunately.

"Blonde?" Her voice showed disbelief, the same kind of disbelief I found myself experiencing as soon as my heart and my brain realised what had happened. "What blonde?" Amazing to think that one moment I had been regretting my question, whilst the next I was pulling myself away from her and beginning to stand. "Friday. I saw you hugging a blonde." Maria still looked confused, and if I had mistaken the look on her face, the shaking of her head nailed home the fact she didn't know what I was talking about. "Outside the hospital. The woman you were clinging to, laughing with. I saw you." The last three words seemed to spew out of my mouth, and were followed by a definite feeling of growing anger. Did she think I was stupid? Blind? Gullible? Had I been too rash in disbelieving the nurse? Had Maria played the victim well?

"A blonde woman?" Was she doing this repetition to piss me off, or to give herself time to think up an excuse? "Friday?"

"Yes. Friday. Blonde. Outside the hospital."

"Just me and a woman, you say? Hugging?"

I think she was stalling, although I was still getting pissed off.

"Alone?" She was lifting her top lip now, and for a moment I thought she was snarling at me, but she wasn't; it was the expression of a thinker. "I was outside about six*ish* ... but I wasn't alone."

Damned right you weren't—you were all over another woman like a dose of the crabs.

"I was with Lisa and David..."

For once, or should I say for once *lately*, I stopped to allow my brain to actually tell my voice box to think about what it was going to say next. My brain was playing with two words. Lisa, being one, and David, being the other. Then through the process of elimination it concentrated on just one of those words. David. *Da...vid.*

"Da...vid?" There you go. Brain had worked in conjunction with my voice box and allowed the focused word to splatter forth. Then it seemed to gain momentum. "David and Lisa?"

"Lisa's blonde." Maria was leaning back now and watching my movements. "And if my memory serves me right, she was the only woman I hugged on Friday."

Fuck.

"It was her last day in the lab and I was saying a quick farewell."

Have you ever been in the situation where someone is explaining something to you and you know they are only doing it for your benefit? The pitch of their voice is enough to warn you that this wasn't a good thing. This aforementioned pitch indicated they were totally fucked off with you, maybe even classifying you as scum in the process. Well, that is the exact timbre she used as she continued to explain that Lisa was moving away and therefore was jacking in her job at the hospital. Maria had decided to say a private farewell at the hospital, as she knew that at the evening party, she wouldn't be able to speak to her friend properly.

What do you do when this kind of situation arises? Do you apologise? Cry? Laugh? Or do you allow the feeling of blowing everything you ever wanted to wash over you? Maria was beginning to stand now, and I had to do something. The only problem was, I was finding it difficult to think of something to say that could justify what I had done. The reality was—I had accused her of shagging about, that much was obvious. Once again I had allowed my insecurities to hamper what I wanted with Maria. The weirdest part of everything was I had never in my life acted this way before. I wasn't a jealous person by nature, and had always believed everything my previous girlfriends had told me. So what was the difference here? It couldn't be that I was jealous because I was in love with her, because that was the last thing that love meant. Being in love was the ability to trust without question, not be destructive and find reasons to doubt the person we profess to love above anything else.

"What are you implying, Gem?" She was in front of me now, her stature erect and intimidating, blue eyes that had seemed so soft and vulnerable a short while ago were now like chips of ice. "Don't you trust me?" She waved the letter in front of my face. "You believed *this* pile of crap?"

That was the problem, you see? It wasn't as if I believed it now, but I had done. And if this was the way I reacted when I couldn't find my arse with both hands, how on earth would I react when in the future we did encounter

something that would need me to be there for her and I
did the same thing? I felt a fool...bigger than a fool, in fact.
I had allowed this to come to this stage, first by believing
the letter, and then by even contemplating anything the
nurse had to say. Images of the nurse shot into my mind,
and I remembered the way she had nervously looked at the
door when she had been helping me collect the contents
of my bag. She wasn't being helpful; she had wanted me
out of there before Maria returned from saying farewell to
her work colleague. Pity I didn't think of that at the time.
Now everything seemed so obvious, so fucking plain as day
it scared me how easily I could be put off track and believe
the inner workings of someone who wanted what I had.
The nurse. But I couldn't blame her, as there was only one
person who was in the wrong on this occasion. Me. Once
again it was a case of me saying something when I was in
the wrong. I had fucked up, but this time I lost more than
my money for the minging oranges; I had definitely read
the signs incorrectly on this occasion. It was too late for
apologies, but I uttered one anyway. The "I'm so sorry"
seemed derisory, as it should have done. No matter how
many times I apologised, it would never change the fact
that I had allowed jealousy and insecurity to rule both my
heart and my head.

"Sorry?" After the word left her mouth, Maria snorted.
"*Sorry?*" again.

I know. Inadequate. So I repeated it, and then added
something else. "I'm so sorry...but I...we can't see each
other anymore."

Those words were so difficult to say. Each one seemed
to carve a niche in my throat as they passed on their way

to the opening of my mouth. As they arrived at her ears, each one of those words seemed to have the same effect on Maria, and I believe if I could have looked closely, I would've seen the gash marks on her cheeks. However, all I could see was disbelief accompanied by a flush of red. Maybe that was the evidence of the slap of my words.

"So, you think I am cheating, do you?" Her voice was low, and slightly shaky. "You believe the words of a person you don't even know and would give us up for *this*?"

A sob broke free, and she opened her mouth as if to say something else, but all I could hear were gulping sounds. Maria's face crumpled and another sob escaped. Lifting up the letter, she waved it in front of my face before gripping it between both of her hands. The tearing sound was deafening, and the paper appeared to flutter through the air. Tears were pricking my eyes, and I was swallowing repeatedly in order to control the tumultuous emotions racing through me.

"No. I don't believe the letter." *Now, that is.* But I didn't add that. I reached forward to grab her hand, but she pulled it away as if my touch burned her. Turning her back to me, I could see the control she had tried to muster was fading, as I could see her shoulders shaking. Her hands were against her face, and I knew she was trying to hide her suffering from the person who didn't deserve to see her in a moment of weakness. I tried to place my hand on her back but she shrugged it away, and I didn't blame her. I wouldn't want someone giving me comfort after they were the ones who had broken me apart in the first place.

From the safety behind her hands, her voice came out muffled. "So, that's it then?"

I couldn't answer. I didn't want this to be it, but what else could I do? I wasn't good enough for her. I knew she deserved someone who would never doubt what a wonderful woman she was.

"Goodbye, Gem." And she was off, snatching her bag from the floor as she went.

I hadn't explained to her why I thought it would be best if we stopped seeing each other; a little voice was trying to tell me that it would be better to let her think that I was just breaking up for no apparent reason. But that's not the done thing, is it? To allow someone to believe something because it's easier than telling them the truth? I had turned into Doctor Jennifer Fielding; I had hurt her to save my own skin.

She was halfway down my hallway by the time I realised I had to stop her. I honestly don't know where the burst of energy came from. Even though I don't exactly remember thinking I should leap over the sofa, that's exactly what I did. In retrospect, it would have been better if I had thought it through, because the next thing I remember was coming to with concerned blue eyes looking down at me. Maria's voice seemed to seep into my head, and she was asking me what day of the week it was. Fuck that.

"Don't leave me." I actually saw a reaction in her eyes, and if she hadn't been trying to check my pupils with her trusty torch, I would have been definite when I say I saw a glimmer of hope there.

"How many fingers am I holding up?"

"Please. Don't leave." I sat up abruptly, and in the process I felt the whirr of my brain smacking itself back into place. Looking around me, I was surprised to find I was still in my living room. The leap I had tried to perform had landed me about half a foot away from the back of the sofa.

"Be careful, Gem. You went down like a sack of spuds."

I turned to look at her and a slight smile flashed across her mouth. Was it because I had received my just desserts?

"You didn't have to go to this length to get me to stop. A simple 'wait a minute' would've done."

I tried to get up, but she pushed me back down again.

"Not quite yet. You took a bit of a fall, and I want to make sure you're okay before I let you do anything."

I started to speak, but she shushed me. "Just let me look you over before you say anything, okay?"

I nodded, and the movement made me groan.

"See?"

Maria continued to look into my eyes, and all the time I was staring right at her, I had the distinct impression I could see right through her. Inside her. And what I saw made my heart ache and melt at the same time. I loved her so much. So much. And I had allowed everything to get to this stage because I didn't trust her, didn't trust this burgeoning emotion inside me.

Like a good patient, I answered all of her questions, and as the time passed, her professionalism seemed to slip further and further away. Her hands were checking my legs to see if there were any injuries, but all I could feel were sparks of want racing through them.

"Does that hurt?"

Far from it. I shook my head.

"Can you feel this?" Her fingers were slipping over the tender skin of my thighs, and I nodded again, my eyes fluttering for a moment.

"How about this?"

Those delectable digits were on my neck now, and I allowed the sensation to envelop me. Click. My eyes closed and allowed me to envision those fingers there for a different reason than a medical examination.

"And this?"

Lips met lips, and I was absorbed by her. Completely absorbed. The kiss began to develop and I knew for a fact there was nothing at all wrong with any part of my body. I felt myself leaning back and taking her with me, the kiss becoming ardent and uncontrolled. Her hands were on my face now, and mine were gripping her waist, pulling her closer to me. Then her hands slipped down my throat and along my collarbone, experienced fingers tracing over goose pimpling flesh. Soft lips kissed my neck, and her breath was sending shivers along my body, making me tremble with need.

"We...need to...stop." Her words braced themselves on my skin and tingled and danced over and inside every nerve.

If we needed to stop, then why was she still kissing me? I knew we needed to stop; we needed to talk. Well, before we allowed things to get out of hand, I needed to explain what I had done. Maria had the right to know what she was getting herself into, for a start. And I was just about to pull away when I felt her hands playing with the hem of my top, felt her fingers delve underneath the material and make contact with my ready stomach, and felt the agony of lust race and dive into every crevice of my willing body. Reality was deserting me; confession was making an exit; and I was allowing them to do so. I felt powerless to do anything else.

"We...need to stop."

Her breath was now on my stomach, as her mouth replaced her hands and was making its way to my breasts. Anticipation was eating me alive, and I was hoping it was doing the same to her.

Still, I did the decent thing. I spluttered the words I didn't want to splutter. "I need to explain."

But she either didn't hear me or chose to ignore it. The kisses were becoming more forceful, but forceful in a good way; the kind of forceful that allows the mouth to lift my bra and push the material away. My nipples were standing to attention as the cool breath of her mouth slipped effortlessly over them, making them strain upward. Gently, those lips closed around the bud of my left breast, and I felt myself arch up and try to force the whole thing inside her mouth. However, she pulled herself away, leaving a flick of her tongue in farewell. Then on to my right breast, and if I thought the sensations were heavenly before, now I thought I was floating. This time she added a little more pressure, and alternated her tonguing with a slow, sensual sucking. Her hand came up and cupped my other breast, and I felt the air flee my lungs.

Looking down, I saw her face wracked with desire, those blue eyes looking back up into my own, eyelashes fluttering slowly with each suck, each push of her hand. God, but I wanted to take her, flip her over and ravish her there and then. In all the time we had been seeing each other, we had never reached this stage yet. The reason being was I didn't want to frighten her away, didn't want her to think I was just after sex. This was so much more than sex, so much more than anything I had ever experienced before in my life. When she shifted her weight, I felt her hip move into position between my legs. It hit the part of me that was so fucking wet I believed she would feel it through her jeans. Our bodies were moving in rhythm now, and I wanted to strip out of all my clothes so I could feel the silkiness of her next to me. But what I did still surprises me to this day.

I sat up, pushing her up with me in the process and nearly knocking her flying. "I need to explain." *But why now? Couldn't it wait?*

Maria was on her haunches and looking at me as if she wanted to ask the same questions.

That's when I knew I had done the right thing. "I need to tell you what happened and why I did what I did."

How noble. Although my southern region disagreed wholeheartedly; it was screaming out that I should keep my big mouth shut and continue what we had been doing. Maria had said twice that we needed to stop, so I assumed it was because of the same reason I had: guilt. My guilt, to be exact.

"We should stop, yes," I said. See.

"You've had an injury and we shouldn't...erm...do..." she waved her hand over our bodies, "in case you have a concussion."

Stuff the concussion, if I had one that is.

"Because I would hate to take advantage of the situation."

"Did my eyes look normal when you examined me?"

Maria nodded.

"Well, I haven't got a concussion then." And why was I trying to talk her out of stopping when it had been me and my conscience that had stopped us in the first place? A prime example of being a woman, I suppose.

"That's not why I stopped us...erm...this." I waved my hand over our bodies as she had. Why couldn't either of us say what we had been doing? Had we actually regressed to being teenagers? "I think we should talk about what happened before we...you know." Yes. I had become one of my tutor group, and it wouldn't have surprised me if I had asked "How do lesbians have sex?" in the very next breath.

Maria leaned forward, her breath hitting my face. "If you don't mind, I think that talking can wait." She brushed her lips over mine. "I have waited for you for so long, I don't want words, or concussion, to stop us from showing each other how much we care...how much I love you."

What would you do? Honestly? What would you do in this situation? I know you probably won't ever get into the same kind of situation as I was in at that moment, not the "wanting to show someone how much you feel" type, more like the "you're cheating, or are you? We should finish this, wham bang, extreme contact with floor and heading for concussion" situation. Would you stick to your guns and demand that this was the time that things should be spoken about, brought out into the open and dissected? Or even the "we should wait because I might be injured" scenario?

Well, let's just say—you're not me, and I'm not you, and I bet you are thankful for small mercies. I went for the only scenario I could, the one that was the right one for me, for her, for us. "Let's go upstairs."

Neither of us said another word as I led her out of the living room, down the hallway, and up the stairs to my bedroom. Her hand was gripping mine, and I couldn't help but look back at her as she followed me like a lamb. Inside I was shaking. Every organ was trembling in anticipation, and the blood was racing around like a mad cat. If I didn't calm things down, I would probably keel over by the time I reached the top step.

At the door of my room Maria stopped me, her hand pulling me back. For a split second I thought she was going to change her mind, but it wasn't until I turned around and looked up into her face that I knew that wasn't the reason.

She leaned forward slowly and placed the gentlest kiss I have ever received onto my lips. Almost instantly I felt myself begin to calm. But it was when she cupped my face and said, "It's only me, Gem. Only us," that I knew for certain that this union was not just an act of lust...a spur of the moment thing...a continuation of what had gone on downstairs. This was it. IT. This was what I had been waiting for all my life. This was the answer to the lifelong question: "Why are we here?"

When she nodded, as if to say, "Are you ready?" I didn't use words to answer her. What was the point? As I've said before, words are mere air, and as they always say, "Actions speak louder." So, I kissed her, then grasped the handle to my bedroom door and led her inside.

The room was dull, but not dark. As we stood together in the centre of my room, all the thoughts and fears that should have been racing around my head at this stage were pushed to the back of my mind. It was only her and me, me and her, us. There was nothing and no one that could infiltrate this meeting of two souls.

Standing in front of her, I could see those gorgeous blue eyes twinkling as they grasped the last vestiges of light from outside. My heart was hammering inside my chest, and I thought that at any moment it would burst from within and splatter all over her. Lifting one hand I tentatively extended one finger and traced the line at the side of her mouth. Maria's eyes fluttered shut, and then opened again to exhibit a change of blueness. The twinkle I had witnessed previously seemed to ignite, and so I allowed that lone digit to trail across her lips. Once, twice, three times, until she captured it inside her mouth and began to suck gently. Each tug on my finger was echoed by a tug deep inside me. Deep and low. Maria grabbed my wrist and began to inch her tongue down until it reached the palm of my hand, where she began to kiss the sensitive skin. A gasp shot from my mouth, which only incensed her to continue kissing my hand, my arm, the nook of my elbow. Short breaths hit my skin and these heightened the sensation of being thoroughly loved by this woman.

When her mouth reached the place where my top prevented her from going any further, I felt her hand come around to the front, the tugging sensation alerting me that it wouldn't be long until my shirt was slipped from my body. And it wasn't. Cool air hit my back, and goose bumps scattered over me. Maria slipped her free hand around my waist and pulled me towards her. I didn't want this. I wanted to feel her skin against mine, not just the texture of the material separating us. Her shirt came off easily, and before I had the chance to consume her form with my eyes, I was against her, luxuriating in the feeling of skin on skin, lips on lips.

Our mouths each devoured the other, slowly and surely. Bodies moved against one another in steady rhythmic movements until I thought I would explode. Wrapping my arms around her, I traced my fingers along the fabric of her bra and easily popped the clasps, whilst at the same time I felt the clasps pop and free my own breasts. Once again we pulled against each other, but this time the feel of her breasts was enhanced by the hardness of her nipples. Kisses were fiercely tender, and the movements of our bodies sharpened the want I had for her.

I didn't realise I had moved us both closer to the bed; didn't realise I was lowering her onto the cool duvet; didn't realise I was straddling her body. Not for one moment did I break away from the delectable contact of her mouth, and it came as a surprise when I briefly opened my eyes and saw her looking up at me. Her hands were on my back and holding me to her, her palms cool against my burning skin. The kiss stopped, and I lifted my face away from hers so I could commit to memory the vision beneath me.

Sitting up, my legs were on either side of her, her hands slipping further down and resting on the waistband of my jeans. Black hair fanned itself over the cream coverlet, and even though the room was dimly lighted, she was still a sight to behold.

"You are beautiful." The words hit the air in a whisper, but it seemed as if I had shouted them from the depths of my heart. Each word, each syllable, had wrenched itself from somewhere I didn't know existed until that moment. Maria's face, once serious, broke into a smile, and then twitched back to consternation again.

"Do you really think so?"

How could this woman ever doubt how perfect she was? How wonderful and beautiful and charming and exquisite she was? How could she lie there like a Renaissance painting—her hair fanning out, her eyes absorbing, her form desirable—how could she lie there and ask if I thought she was merely beautiful?

"No. I don't *think* you're beautiful," my hand slipped effortlessly along the crease in her abdomen before outlining the curves of her breasts, "I *know* you're beautiful."

Initially her face had clouded slightly, but the smile she gave me then was one of the ones I will remember for the rest of my life. And just as I was adding that image to my growing collection, Maria shot up and pulled me against her.

"And I *know* you are the most amazing woman I have ever met."

To be truthful, I was shocked when she said it. Me? Amazing? I was far from amazing. I was the one who had mistrusted her; believed someone else rather than believing in her. That wasn't amazing, was it? That was insecure, not amazing.

But I didn't get the opportunity to think of anything else, as she kissed me fully on the mouth, her hands slipping up my body, over my arms, and tangling in my hair. Nothing else mattered. Nothing. Everything could wait. It wasn't because I was ignoring what I had done; it was more a case of knowing that whatever happened after this, I would never again do what I had done, and I would spend the rest of my life, or for however long she wanted me, showing her how much I trusted her.

Pop. The top button of my jeans was freed from its slit, and I felt the zipper glide down. There was no way she would be able to slip them off me sitting in this posi—

Slam. Over I went, and Maria was on top of me, pulling my jeans and underwear away in one fluid swoop. For a moment I was shocked, but it didn't take me long to recover.

Slam. Over she went, and I performed exactly the same operation on her, making her giggle in the process. And there we were. Naked. Her underneath me and taking my breath away, again. The smile she had given when I had slapped her onto her back was still there, but frozen momentarily...until it slipped down her face and an expression of what I can only describe as hunger took its place. Maybe it was mirroring my own.

I lowered myself and placed my tongue on the smoothness of her stomach, drawing it slowly along her skin until it was sitting underneath the curve of her left breast. Then, even more slowly, I moved it around the curve and delighted in the shape of it. My abdomen was touching bare flesh, and I could feel the coolness of the air hit the wetness raging between my legs. Would she be as wet as I was?

There was only one way to find out.

Swirling my tongue around her breast, I moved my mouth to the crease where her neck met her collarbone. Lips pursed, I placed a kiss on the bone before opening my mouth and sucking it gently. As I was doing this, I rested my body against hers, the silkiness of her skin slipping effortlessly against my own. One hand reached up and pushed its way into her hair, whilst the other one made its way down to see if Maria wanted this as much as I did.

Stroking her hip, I slipped my hand around and caressed the curve of her ass. The languid movement made her gasp and jerk herself forward. So I did it again, but this time I made sure I was pressed as tightly against her as I could possibly be. Another gasp, or was it a groan? The next time I did it I went a little further, further along the cheek of her buttock and partly between her legs. Another groaning gasp. The feelings welling up inside me were beginning to think for themselves; all sense of control was being forgotten. I didn't want to be in control; I didn't want to rationalise or plan what we were going to do; I wanted to love her. I wanted to feel her. Taste her. Become one with her.

Again my hand moved across and down, and this time I could feel something else—something wet, something warm. Something I had craved for so long. And this something was there for me, because of me. Part of me wanted to slip those fortunate fingers inside my mouth, but I didn't. The other part of me wanted to take my mouth to this wetness, taste her essence straight from the source.

When I leaned away from her, Maria tried to move with me, tried to push herself into the bed and onto those fingers which were patiently waiting for admittance. But I slipped them away.

Blue eyes budded open and her mouth was parted. "Please, Gem. *Please*."

I wanted to do as she wished, but I also wanted to take her fully, and not just tantalise her opening with the tip of my finger.

"It's okay, love." I didn't have to say anymore; my downward movement alerted her to my intentions.

I was between her legs. Between her legs...between those beautiful, powerful, long legs, and lowering my head. My hands stroked her thighs, knees, shins, and back up to her thighs again, and by the time they had reached the topmost point, my face was against the soft downy hair of her sanctuary. I inhaled her deeply before slowly exhaling a soft breath onto her core. I felt her tremble against me, but I didn't want to rush this. I wanted her to know for sure it was me loving her. Cupping my hands underneath her thighs, I lifted her legs and pushed them further apart.

And there it was. Glistening. Perfect. Waiting.

I could feel myself begin to salivate with the expectation of the taste of her. Another deep breath, another slow exhalation, and I allowed myself to watch the dark hairs move in the rhythm of my breathing before opening my mouth and kissing her nub. I kissed her deliberately. Unhurried, I slipped my tongue past my lips and indulged in the most divine taste I have ever had. Sweet, yet slightly musky, and owning the sleekest texture I have known.

"God!"

Her one word alerted me that I was doing the right thing.

"Please! God!"

Two words that signified that I needed to do it again. So I did. Again. And again. And again. And each time she rasped out she wanted more, and who was I to deny her? Her hips were moving against my face and the wetness was smearing itself all over me, the juice from my mouth and her core mixing and blending and sending the both of us crazy with want. I needed more, she needed more, we needed more in order to tip over into the light that I knew was waiting in her thrusting body and my throbbing soul.

Moving my hand from her thigh, I once again slipped it between her legs. I held a digit at her entrance, softly swirling it in lazy circles as I lapped and sucked, sucked and lapped.

"Gem! Please! Gem!"

But, as I said before, I wasn't going to tease her opening with the tip of my finger.

I slowly pushed my finger inside her, just one digit, and it glided inside like a key into a lock. Opening my mouth, I captured her trembling bud inside before pulling the finger out and slipping it back in. A half cry escaped her mouth, and I pulled out from her again. A suck, accompanied by another push, followed by another suck and a flick of my tongue. The taste pouring from her was getting sweeter, yet it maintained the taste of her, and this excited me more, if that were possible. I tried not to go faster. I wanted this to last. I wanted to feel the build-up to her cumming as my mouth and hand worked in unison. But I couldn't. My hips were pushing onto the bed, and the ache between my legs was agony.

Another finger slipped into position and joined the first, and I heard her sigh with pleasure. I pushed inside her, moving my lips around her nub whilst allowing my teeth to graze the tender flesh in sporadic nips. God. This woman. This wonderful and beautiful woman. I could feel the smoothness of her walls, the juices easing my entrance, slaking my thirst for her.

Faster. Faster and deeper. Deeper and faster. Her thighs were gripping the side of my head, and her body was rising and falling frantically. Curving my arm around her leg, I pulled her closer to me, making breathing difficult. But that didn't matter. Breathing could wait. All I wanted was to feel...taste...hear her release. Sweat was coating our bodies, and this enabled me to glide easily, my shoulders banging the backs of her legs, each thrust pushing my face and hand harder into her.

I tasted the change first. Tasted the sweetness become muskier, become thicker in texture, become slick. Then she went rigid, briefly, and lifted herself from the bed, taking me with her. Finally came the sound, the sound of her cumming, the sound of her cry, the sound of her calling my name over and over again. I held my position, my mouth possessing her clit and my fingers buried deep inside her; and I waited.

Again. She pushed herself onto me again...and again... and again...riding out her orgasm on my face, my mouth, and my fingers. I wanted to see her, wanted to watch her face as she was calling my name, as she was cumming and cumming and cumming. Lifting my face, I was mesmerised by the sight before me.

Maria was now flat on her back, except for her head, which was raised from the bed. She had lifted her face up to look down her body and straight at me. Her eyes were hooded and fixed straight into mine. My fingers were still buried inside her, and I couldn't help pushing once more.

Throwing her head back, she released another gasp into the air, giving me the momentum to continue taking her. This time was different from before; this time I wanted to fuck her...force my fingers inside her and fuck her. And this time watch her face as I did so.

Each time I entered her, I could hear the moisture pulsate. Gripping her hip, I pushed and held her in place as I took her, but that didn't stop her from trying to lift herself up and against me. I wanted to lie against her, feel her body against mine, but if I gave in to that desire, I wouldn't see her face as she tipped over...couldn't watch her mouth as she said my name.

In...deep...out...and back inside again. Over and over again, I plunged into her, until I watched her mouth change shape. Those lips that had surrounded her open and gasping mouth seemed to twist—hold—and relax before one word slipped effortlessly from them.

"Gem."

And as that sole word hit the air, she opened her eyes and captured me once again before throwing her head back and giving in, allowing her second cumming.

I couldn't resist her, couldn't resist leaning down and luxuriating in the silkiness of her sweat covered body, which was still writhing with pleasure. As my lips met hers, I felt the words come out her mouth as well as heard them. "I love you, Gem." Her hands slipped up my back and pulled me closer. It seemed as if we clicked together, and all I wanted to do was to melt through the layers of our skin and live contentedly inside her.

The kiss was long and full, wet and satisfying, and I believe I could have kissed her forever. Well, until her hand moved down towards my butt. Sparks of desire raced through me, or I should say continued to race through me but more intense than I believed possible. Yes. That was more like it.

I felt myself beginning to lift, but it wasn't of my doing. Maria was raising herself up from the bed, and I was moving with her. I could feel the room tilting as I was turned over and onto my back. The process was so smooth, it came as a surprise when I realised she was now lying above me. One thigh was between my legs, parting them more fully. Instantly I felt the slickness of my need for her coat her skin and enable me to glide effortlessly up and down. Sensations rippled throughout me, starting at my toes and ending up leaving my mouth in a gasp, only to be sucked back inside and back to my toes again to repeat the process.

If I could put into words the way Maria made me feel, I would be a millionaire. Or should that be—if sensations were pound coins, I would be a millionaire? Either way, I felt rich. Rich because I knew this woman was everything my life wanted and needed. Rich because I knew that for once in my life, I had this woman loving me. Rich because I felt the same way back—I was loving her.

Her other leg was between mine now, and pushing them further apart to make room for her delectable body. Unlike me, Maria covered my frame with hers instead of waiting. It seemed as if I had a blanket covering me, a comforting one, a sensual one, the kind of blanket I hope everyone has the chance to have once in their life. Her lips were on my ear now. Little nibbles...licks...kisses...the breath coming out of her mouth in soft brushes. And each time I felt her mouth...her breath...her tongue, the desire in me pulsated and pushed my hips up to meet her body. I could feel the smile that broke out on her face before she did it all again.

I wanted to beg her, plead with her to take me, to make the contact of her against me more constant, but I didn't. Part of me was loving the wait. Maria inched down slightly, and I felt the tautness of her abdomen against the bundle of nerve endings that were screaming her name. Then she pushed against me. Then again. And again. And whatever I had said before about waiting for her to take me seemed to fizzle and fade. I needed her inside me, needed something more, needed something concrete and firm. Her fingers. That's what I needed. Those wonderful, capable fingers inside me, outside me...rubbing, collecting, nurturing, and holding.

But the sensation of her stomach...the pushing and pushing...the claiming and controlling...the feel of the rest of her body taking me, too...the strength of her muscles gathering to please and satisfy this hunger building within me, were enough for me to deliberate whether her fingers were needed at all.

Until I felt them. Felt them slipping past her stomach, slipping past the army of hairs guarding the place I longed for her to be, slipping down and separating the folds that held the wanting of my core and making me hold my breath in anticipation of what was to follow.

Tingles raced along my spine and evaporated along my skin, leaving bumps in their wake. She was at my opening, her hips moving slightly, her fingers in position and teasing. Then I said it. Said the word I didn't think I would say. "Please."

Thankfully, Maria understood. And the reason I say thankfully is because I couldn't think of any other words to say. My brain was refusing to conjure anything else; all it wanted me to do was feel.

Maria pushed her hand forward, two fingers entering me and inducing me to crave more of her. Two fingers burrowed deeply and stopped, permitting me to acclimatise to the ecstasy of having her there. Two glorious fingers that were now making their way back outside, only to plunge inside me once again. And again. And...again. Every time her fingers pulled out, I pushed my body towards her to try and renew the contact.

All the times I had made love in my life were nothing compared to this. This was the kind of sensation that you only read about in books or magazines, or what they imply when you watch films. I had never thought it was real... that these sensations actually existed. But they did, and they were all-consuming. The rhythm of our two bodies was completely synchronised; Maria pushed into me as I pushed into her. Her body was over mine, still between my legs, still making my heart pound against my ribcage in a bid to climb into her. I was gripping her hips...gripping and pulling her into me, and the sweat from her body coated my hands. Kisses upon kisses, kisses on throats, kisses on collarbones, kisses on shoulders; all accompanying the delectable thrusting of our bodies and her fingers.

The more I pushed, the more she took. The more she took, the more imminent my release. I could feel the tentacles of it gripping my insides and spreading outwards like a spillage. There was no way I could contain this; no way I wanted to control this fever of expectation raging triumphantly through every pore, every nerve.

It began as an exquisite ache then spread through me in thick, jolting lines. The cry I had been saving at the back of my throat began to clamour for release, but it held itself fast as it waited for the charge to expel it from within. And it did. I couldn't control the actions of my hips—or the rest of my body, for that matter—and I began to squirm and urge her fingers inside me as deeply as they could go. Maria pushed her body against mine, holding me in place. Her fingers began to stroke the inside of my walls, eliciting more sparks of pleasure that raced and tumbled and unfolded.

Heartbeats—two of them which blended blindly into one—were deafening. If I were going to die, now would be the perfect time. Blood chased itself around my ears, trying in vain to drown out the boom, boom, booming sound of the overexcited heart. My mouth was dry, and I licked my lips in order to speak, but no words would come. Maria began to blow cool air across my chest in an attempt to calm me, but it only made me want her again.

Lifting her head, she looked into my eyes. Such purity and love shone in her eyes that part of me wanted to cry whilst the other part was singing. It was as if a wand had been waved over us, as I felt all the urges to ravish her again leave me and a sprinkle of utter contentment take their place.

I couldn't help it, I swear. It was just too perfect to do anything but the next thing I did, the next thing we both did. We slept. Completely entwined in arms, legs, and hearts, we slept. And I think...no... I *know*...the sleep I had in the arms of my Maria was the best night's sleep I have ever had. A fitting end to a perfect evening, although I would never have thought it was possible three hours earlier.

And that reminded me. I still had to explain to her what had happened. All I had to do was to understand myself, and then it would be smooth sailing. Wouldn't it?

Chapter 10

MORNING CAME AROUND, AND I don't think I had moved at all throughout the night. Sunlight was pouring through the window, as I hadn't bothered to close the curtains the evening before. I had had other, more pressing things happening. Initially I felt a little confused, as my left eye was being blinded by brightness, whilst my right one was finding it difficult to open. It seemed as if something was pressing itself firmly against it and was refusing to budge. There was only one thing I could do; I could do the budging.

Leaning back, I also realised something else, but unlike the previous sensation, this one was more embarrassing. It must have happened in the night, whilst I was sleeping snugly against Maria. Although my eye had felt as if it was stuck to her body, or shoulder, as it turned out, it wasn't. But that didn't change the fact that my lips were jammed against her skin in a dried up, spitty mess. Trust me to fucking drool all over the woman, as if I didn't do enough drooling over her when we were both awake, figuratively, of course. If I could just unstick my mouth from against her without waking her up, then maybe I—

"Good morning, sleepyhead."

Shit.

"It's about time you stopped snoring and dribbling on me."

Her voice held humour, and if I wasn't so mortified with what I had done, I would have laughed. I snored? Me? As if giving her a spit wash wasn't embarrassing enough, I snored, too?

Wait a minute. Did it matter? Okay...it's not the best way to wake up in the morning, having someone's face glued to your arm, but it wasn't the end of the world. As for the snoring, I put it down to over exhaustion. Her fault. Simple. These thoughts enabled me to allow a lazy grin to emerge on my face and then a delightful yawn took control of my body, making me stretch and shudder.

"Good morning, you. Sleep well?"

She didn't answer me straightaway; she just leaned over to plant a soft, full kiss onto my mouth. Crap. Did I have morning breath?

"Perfectly."

Her face was so close to mine, I had to push back a little to get her eyes in focus.

"So, my snoring didn't keep you awake, then?" Why did I ask that? Why couldn't I stretch out like a sex kitten and make her mouth water? I think I am a romance retard.

"Not much. But it's cute." She swiped her finger over the tip of my nose and grinned at me.

I felt like a kid, but not in an "I'm being molested by a paedophile" kind of way, but more of the "I feel all cheeky and shy" way. I don't think it would have surprised either of us if I had started chewing my knuckle and swaying from side to side whilst squawking "On the good ship Lollipop." Talk about going off the point!

Okay. Let's get our bearings once again. There we were—the morning after. Both of us lying in my bed, naked. Me being a dipshit with, more than likely, a case of morning breath; her being gorgeous and making me feel too bloody special for words. The sun was coming up and the clock was struggling to point the big hand at six and the little hand at eight. And that only meant one thing.

"Shit! Get up! Get up!" And no. I hadn't added another bodily excretion to the mix. It was eight-thirty and Maria had to be at work.

Maria darted backwards and fell off the side of the bed, her legs sticking up comically.

"Come on... Get up!" Why didn't I laugh at her scrambling to her feet? The covers being pulled and thrown around? The way she kept on saying, "What's the matter?" in a panting, high pitched voice? "Work! You have to get to work!" I was off the bed and running for her clothes, frantically throwing them in her direction. She stood there, the clothes hitting her body and dropping onto the floor. Why wasn't she catching them?

"But it's Tuesday."

I know. A work day.

She was still standing there in all her glory, wearing only a smile. "Gem, I'm off."

Off where? To work? Had she finally gotten the message? By now I was at her feet, collecting her clothes and pushing them into her hands, and thankfully this time she held on to them. Well, for a minute at least, then she dropped them onto the floor again.

Grabbing my hands, she pulled me to her, making sure I couldn't gather her clothes again. "I'm on holiday, remember? We were supposed to be going away."

Sometimes I surprise myself at my ability to be a thick shit. Since Friday, all I had thought about was her and that we were supposed to be going away. And here I was acting a twat.

"Or..." I felt her grip loosen on my hands, "don't you fancy that now?"

Looking up into her face, I was surprised by the seriousness I found there. Her eyes were moving from side to side, as if they were trying to penetrate deep within me and exact an answer.

"I...I..." *am an idiot.* "I...you...well..." Case closed. There was no more wondering—I was certifiably the most stupid person in the world, if I could judge correctly given the circumstances of realising I was Britain's Thickest. I saw her lips move as if she was going to utter that she understood, and I went for a third go. "Of course I do!" Although, in retrospect, it was said rather loudly, I think she got the message. "Of course I want to go away with you. Stay here with you. Do anything with you." And for me, that was pretty close to romantic. The words seemed to fly straight from the pages of a Mills and Boon novel and, judging by the look on her face, I think I did good. Big pat on the back for me.

"That's okay then." Inclining her head, she pressed her forehead against mine. "Because I would love to just *be* with you."

Then a kiss. A soft kiss. An owning kiss. A kiss that said good morning, and welcome to the future. A kiss that was gradually leading into something a little more intense than an affirmation of a trip. It was the kind of kiss that welcomed the latter part, the part where we had both admitted this was something a hell of a lot more than a casual relationship. Then the kiss went on to become a stroking and touching and caressing combination. The kind of combination that precedes the ultimate connection, the kind of connection that leads to us both lying down on the bed and continuing this wonderful union of two people who had found a reason to get up, and then get back into bed in the morning.

Maria was flat on her back and I was spreading myself over her, our bodies remembering the joy of the previous night and craving it again. I could feel the want I had for her collect and spill from every part of me, and I wished above all wishes, that this hunger I had would seep into the very depths of her. My hands were on her breasts, and they felt as if that was where they belonged. The curve of them fit perfectly within the palms of my hands, and I could feel her nipples bud and grow just for me. I began to involuntarily move my hips against her, and even though the contact between us was limited, it felt as if she coated me.

But, you see, there is a mechanism within us all that tells us when we should, or shouldn't, do something. Mine was a voice this time...an annoying voice that was telling me that I should stop what I wanted to happen and tell her the stuff I had tried to push below the surface for a little while longer. I tried to ignore it. Tried to pretend it was the radio spewing out the usual morning shite, but to no avail. However, I did pick my time to come clean, and that time was exactly the time I was kissing her stomach, kissing that gorgeous bunch of abs that were flexing underneath my mouth.

"Maria?" I didn't say her name very loudly, lest she hear me and want to listen to what I had to say. It was a case of pretending to comply with the inner workings of a woman's mind. Unfortunately, a woman's mind, or conscience, cannot be waylaid or put off. I should have known this, being a woman myself.

Tearing my lips from her skin, I repeated her name. Then again. And again, until she realised I had stopped kissing her and blinked open her eyes.

"What's wrong, honey?"

And then I took my crown, my Idiot of the Year crown. Instead of saying I wanted to talk about the events of the previous days, I said something only a nugget would say at a time like that. "Need a drink. You thirsty?"

Baby need drinkie…baby need to go potty? Well, that's what it seemed like at the time. It seemed as if I had regressed into some childlike role, and if I hadn't been straddling a naked woman, and been naked myself, I would still claim to have had a flash of the ankle biters' syndrome.

Maria couldn't even answer. She was probably thinking of how she could sneak out without me seeing her. All she did was nod once before I scuttled off and out of the door.

When I reached the kitchen, I allowed myself to breathe again. There was no reason why I couldn't just go back up and begin the conversation, except that I wasn't too sure where to begin. Should I start with the letter, or start with why I was so insecure all of a sudden? Decisions, decisions…

After pulling the orange juice container from the fridge and filling two glasses, I stood in front of the counter and tried to structure how I would admit to her that I hadn't trusted her. It wasn't until I heard my name being called that I noticed the postman standing at the window. The look on his face showed surprise...no, shock, or was it mortification? I still remember thinking, "What's the fuck wrong with him?" before I realised I was standing in my kitchen completely stark bollock naked. I did the only thing a woman in my position could do at the moment. I quickly lifted the drinks and held them in front of my boobs. Then I thought about my lady garden, and that's when it went even more tits up than it had already. The glass decided it didn't want to piss about being a decoy, and realised it would be more fun to slip from my hand. My thigh thought this was the time it should try to lift itself up and try to bounce the aforementioned beverage into the air...and by the looks of orange juice all over me, my floor, and the kitchen surfaces, it would never play for England. Or perhaps, with their performance lately...

"Sorry, luv." Yeah...the postman sounded sorry, too. Must have been the laughter he was bellowing out as he buggered off that indicated his sorrow.

In fact, it was a good job he did leave at that point, because at that point, I decided that I would make a run for it, grabbing the tea towel off the side in order to cover my arse. I had failed to consider the floor. That's not quite right. I did consider the floor, but not in the orange sodden state it was now in. Therefore, it was a matter of seconds before I found myself tumbling through the air, the contents of the other glass flying upwards and straight back over me as I skidded across the tile on my bare backside.

I didn't have time to get up before I heard the sound of Maria running down my hallway, shouting was I okay. If sitting there on my kitchen floor, orange juice pulp dangling from my hair, after exposing myself to the royal mail, was okay, then I was perfect. When she appeared around the corner, I knew she would laugh, but what I didn't know was for how bloody long. It must have been five minutes before she took a breath and stopped pointing and guffawing, bending over to suck in air before starting all over again. Where was the helping hand? Where was the cloak thrown over the puddle (although it was juice, it still carried the same expectations with it)? Where was the "Are you okay?" I could have broken my neck, even though at this moment in time I wanted to break hers instead.

"You...you...you... Don't tell me. Let me guess. You fell over, right?"

No wonder she was in a high paying job.

"How did that happen?"

By magic. With the blessing of a fairy. By telekinesis. Lifting the tea towel, I wiped the sticky mess off my face before I could even consider answering her question. "I slipped."

Jesus. And I teach kids! Were our brain cells dying? Is that what happens after glorious lovemaking? "The postman was at the window and he saw me in the buff." Admitting that hurt both my throat and my pride. As if it wasn't bad enough that I looked like Tango man, I had to admit that someone working on Her Majesty's Service had clocked an eyeful before witnessing me perform a rumba with two tumblers. I did expect to hear more laughter, but to my surprise it was silent. Too silent.

Hesitant, I lifted my head to look up to her face. It seemed as if the journey upwards took forever. Even though I was already aware that she was tall, from my seated position, she seemed huge. When I eventually reached her eyes, there was no mocking gleam there. All I could see was sympathy. Did I want pity? If I did play the pity card, would I lose the last vestiges of my self-respect? And did I really think I had any self-respect left?

Her hand came out and hovered in front of my eyes, and I knew she wanted to help me onto my feet. But when I took the proffered hand, I didn't pull myself up straightaway. I couldn't. Not because I had caused myself an injury when I had gone arse over tit; that wasn't it at all. It was more of the case of being mesmerised that stopped me from jumping up and straightening my birthday suit. Or was it awe that paralysed me for a moment? Whatever it was, it gave me the time to totally soak up this gentle, beautiful woman who was standing over me, my hand claimed by her hand, one eyebrow raised in question. But the answer I gave her wasn't about standing up; it was an explanation of what had happened on Friday. Well, kind of.

"I'm sorry, Maria." She just stood there holding my hand and waiting. "For believing the letter and not trusting who you are."

A darkness flashed over her face before it returned to normal.

Tightening my grip, I pulled her towards me, until she was half bending, half crouching. "I just...well, I..." What to say? I was weak; end of story. "I know it's no excuse, but I felt as if you weren't as into me as I am into you." Jesus. Could I cock things up any more? With my track record, yes. "When I received the letter it felt as if I had been punched, and I can only put my resulting thoughts and actions down to temporary insanity." Why wasn't she saying anything? And why was she sitting down next to me on the cold tile floor? More importantly, why was she turning away from me and staring at the wall? I wanted to grab her face and make her look at me, but then the cowardly part of me reminded me that maybe her not seeing the person I really am was a good thing. Therefore I contented myself with the fact that she hadn't yet pulled away her hand.

"I need to explain...put things into perspective." And I stopped. I had to say it right for a change. "From the beginning, you swept me off my feet."

Maria turned towards me slightly, and I saw a small smile on her face.

"Even from the very first time I met you in the X-ray department, I felt you were special. And that was before even seeing your face."

She turned to face me fully now, a look of confusion taking hold.

"I mean...when you put your hand on my back, I felt... felt...safe, almost as if I had known your touch all my life."

At that point, Maria lifted my hand and placed it on the side of her face. A sad smile flitted across my lips and then disappeared before I continued.

"All I wanted to do was to get to know you better... think of any excuse to stay with you a little while longer.

But I couldn't even do that right. And when you thought I was going to faint, I seized my opportunity." I know it wasn't really as blasé as that, but that was near enough what had happened. "Then getting to know you a little bit over a coffee didn't seem enough, but I didn't know how to make our time together last."

"I gave you my number, and told you to call me." Her voice sounded distant, but not harsh. "Which you did, yet you didn't. I asked Liz."

Who the fuck's Liz? "The nurse? Liz." *Ah... Liz the demon lez...that Liz.* I wanted to ask if Liz was an abbreviation of lizard, but I was too busy trying to stop the hairs on the back of my neck from rising in anger. At whom, I was not too sure.

"But I didn't believe her."

Was she saying I was a twat because I *did*?

"But then again—I know what she's like. And what she was after."

The hairs on my neck were becoming confused. Was she siding with me or against me? Did she understand what had happened or not? Come to think of it, I hadn't really told her anything yet.

Instead of saying anything else at that point, I pulled her face to me, holding it close so we could look into each other's eyes. What I saw in those pools of blue gave me the courage to make the next move. I kissed her softly on the mouth, and the best thing was, she kissed me right back, just as softly. Only two small kisses, but they were perfect.

"Can we move? My backside is getting cold." Maria rubbed the cheeks of her rump to add to the effect, and I couldn't help but laugh, even though my face was beginning to stiffen because of the orange juice. I wanted to tell her more, but I knew us sitting on my kitchen floor, naked, was not the best way to have a heart-to-heart.

"Of course. Let's...erm... Could I just grab a quick shower? Then we can talk properly, okay?" And no. I wasn't playing for time. I genuinely was beginning to harden, although the hot water would probably also help to unstick my brain cells.

"Sure. I'll grab one right after, if that's okay?"

Why were we being so civilised? Was it because we were acting like adults? Before I could formulate any additional questions in my already question soaked brain, I found myself standing up and in her arms. The feel of her body next to mine was more than warming. I hadn't realised how cold it was sitting on the floor until I no longer was. "Go on then. Go grab your shower. I'll put the coffee on."

The next thing I knew I was closing the bathroom door, readying myself for cleanliness. And let me tell you one thing: orange juice is a bitch to get out of your hair.

Thirty minutes later we were both showered and sitting on the edge of my bed, sipping coffee. I had given Maria a T-shirt to slip into after she had dried herself off. I waited until I had half-drunk my coffee before continuing the saga of miscommunication and farce that accounted for the last few days. Plunking the cup down on the side table, I turned to face her.

"Okay. Where were we?" I didn't even wait for her to answer before I continued. "We have been seeing each other for three months, and I still wasn't sure where I stood

with you. It seemed as if you were blowing hot and cold."
Fuck. Talk about surprising myself. I hadn't mentioned the
"hot and cold" thing since the night after our first date.
And that might be where my problem laid—me not asking
the right questions of the right people.

Maria's face showed surprise, and I saw her mouth
open and close like a fish's, but nothing came out.

"I understood about what happened to you in
Cambridge, and I didn't want to rush you into anything
you would regret." I bet part of her was regretting ever
speaking to me at all by this point. "But what I didn't
understand was why you didn't want to see me as much as
I wanted to see you." There. It was out. Those little demon
words that had been gestating in my chest and waiting for
the opportunity to hit air so they could dance and prance
about in their mockingly stupid way were out. And all I
wanted to do was swallow them back inside. After I saw
her face, that is.

Blue eyes flashed and I saw those precious plump lips
tighten into a thin line before she squeezed out, "I thought
that was what you wanted. You didn't seem happy when
you thought I was stalking you."

It was my turn to open and close my mouth like that
poor little fish, but she didn't give me the opportunity to
deliver a response.

"I know. As I said in the letter—I guessed." But then
her mouth seemed to loosen a little…soften a little. "And
as I also said in the letter, I wanted to see you every day.
That's all I've ever wanted."

"Same here."

"I should have never listened to Liz."

"Same here."

"I should have trusted my gut instinct and believed in what we had."

"Same here."

It went quiet for a moment and then, mercifully, she said softly, "If I said I wanted to wipe the slate clean and start afresh, would you say 'same here' again?"

I leaned forward until my mouth was close to hers and allowed the words to drizzle out. "Only if you say 'same here' when I say I want to kiss you right now."

"Do I really want to kiss myself?"

My laugh burst out as I realised what she meant. Instead of talking, I did the next best thing. I grabbed that woman of mine and kissed her deeply. All the insecurities I had been feeling seemed to melt into nothing at the sensation of her mouth on mine. Nothing mattered except her and me, me and her. No one would ever come between us again; no one would have the opportunity to affect us, make us doubt what we had, because what we had was too special for that.

Feeling my T-shirt beginning to rise up my body, I lifted my arms to help it on its way. Next, I decided to remove the material trapping Maria's beautiful body, so I could trap it with my skin. I wanted to show her, again, how much she meant to me...how much "us" meant to me.

I gently eased her onto the softness of the duvet before sitting back and taking in the vision before me. Her hair had fanned out on just one side, making her seem as if she were posing. Red lips were wet, parted, and waiting for my mouth to cover hers. Arms were stretched above her head, making her breasts lift and her stomach taut. My mouth began to water at the thought of trailing my tongue along the line I could see etched down the centre of her body, a body that appeared as if it was made from marble. But unlike marble, this body wasn't cold to the touch, wasn't lifeless and hard. It was warm, pliable, delectable, and mine. Why was I spending time looking at her instead of touching? Because I could, that's why.

But, I'm the kind of person that doesn't live by the saying, "You look with your eyes, not your hands." I think to fully "see" what we have in front of us, we need to use more than just one of our senses. Touch, for example. And smell, for another. Taste is always a good way of deciding what we like and don't like. And last, but certainly not least, hearing. And do you know what the best bit is? The best bit is having all of your senses stimulated at the same time. It's not easy to do. You really have to concentrate, or, in fact, not concentrate at all. Anything in between gets lost in the attempt. I went for the not concentrating at all, mainly because the only thing I could focus on was being with her. That seemed like more than enough.

I cautiously stretched out one hand, and then one brave finger. This valiant finger chose its own path more than I did. It started its journey at her kneecap and trickled its way up her thigh. As it did so, all the senses I mentioned previously began to ramp up. Let's see if I can align them up in sensory order. Silk. Wonderment. Gasping. But that's only three. My poor finger; that lone digit that couldn't do everything on its own and was wasting two of the senses, and, in reality, an outsider would say it could only touch her. But personification is a marvellous thing when it wants to be. It can even give a lone finger the ability to see and hear. Alas, it would be taking the illusion too far to expect it to absorb her smell, to delight in the taste of her. So, another part of my body joined that plucky little finger, going to the spot it appeared to be pointing out. And this lieutenant had the ability to enjoy the musky aroma of her, gulping it down in deep panting breaths. I nearly had all five, but even though I could taste her by inhaling, it wasn't enough. I needed to taste her fully before I could safely say I had completely immersed myself in this divine woman.

There was only one way I could do this. Only one way to assimilate a full picture, a full understanding. And for that I needed to use my mouth, my lips, my tongue. Amazing to think that by using that wet, firm muscle I could achieve all the five senses at the same time. Silk. Wonderment. Gasping. Musky. Sweetness. But were they enough? No. However many reactions I had experiencing this woman, they could never be enough. If I spent the rest of my life loving her as I was doing now, it still wouldn't come close to being enough.

Maria's fingers were tangling in my hair—another feeling, another sensation for the growing list. My stomach was jerking and quivering. Again—another sensation. My mouth was moving against her core—sucking, kissing, tasting, and drinking the essence that poured like honeyed water from the very centre of her. Was I satisfied? No. I wanted more. I needed to give her more, take more from her. My hands were on her thighs, parting them, kneading the twitching flesh, but I wanted more; I wanted it all. I wanted to take and take and take until I lost my sanity in the knowledge that this woman had taken me too, taken me just by being her.

More sucking, more kissing, more pushing my mouth, my lips, my tongue onto her, into her. My heart was pounding in my chest and my breathing was erratic, but I didn't care. I knew at that precise moment that being there with her, taking her with this unworthy mouth, I had found my reason for being alive. Maria's thighs were pressing against my head and her hips were rising and falling with the rhythm of my mouth. My fingers were digging into her thighs, even the heroic one who had started the journey of sensation, but now had been joined by nine other soldiers, two palms, and want filling and spilling from every pore of me.

Maria's groans were coming thick and fast, changing pitch with every lick and suck. She was pushing into me with irregular thrusts and I knew it would be a matter of moments before I would taste the taste I needed to complete the wonderment of loving her. My ears were keen towards every noise, waiting for the ultimate note to alert me her cumming was near.

And then it was. It started as a silence. A stillness. An empty, vacant muteness which culminated dramatically in a low growl. Hoisting her hips towards me, I tilted her further before plunging my tongue inside her. The growl she had emitted transformed into a roar. So I plunged again, and again, and again, until her pelvis was twisting and squirming onto my soaked face. I don't know where I got the strength to hold her in place but it came from somewhere, and as I felt her movements slowing, felt the madness leave her, I released her from my grip. My mouth was kissing her gently now, and her hips were moving in lazy circles. Although her breaths were still coming in gasps, I knew she would be safe as I still held her. Moving up her body, I kissed her skin tenderly, reverently.

Then there they were. Those eyes telling me all I needed to know...opening up that inner sanctum reserved for our hopes and dreams for life...opening up so I could see deep within the soul I was beginning to believe I knew better than my own. Tears were glistening in her eyes, and for a split second I felt concern wash through me. But then she spoke.

"I'm so happy." Her words were followed by a sob, and then the repetition, "I'm so happy."

And so was I.

The rest of the day was spent in the glorious act of loving. That's all I can say really about the act part, being glorious, I mean. It is though, isn't it? "Glorious?" Or do I need to use a more defining word? "Magnificent" doesn't do it justice, not by a long shot. As for "splendid"...too British and usually preceded by "Would you like to come to my tea party?" "Glorious" has a ring of the celestial, doesn't it? I should get out a thesaurus and frantically search for a synonym for "glorious", but I think that's beating the experience to death. And "celebrated" doesn't quite cut the mustard.

I know. You want to know the nitty gritty, and are probably complaining that I have waffled for England, Ireland, Scotland, and Wales about everything else, but when it comes to describing what we did, how we did it, who enjoyed what, and not forgetting the where and when. All you need to know really was why.

And the reason why? Because that's what people do when they are in love. They show, and then show again how much in love they are. It's not a "proving" of love, it's more of a celebration of what we had found. Maybe the "celebrated" synonym isn't as farfetched as I first believed.

Anyway. As I was saying...writing...whatever...we spent the day together, doing what people do when they celebrate. See? That doesn't work, now does it? Imagine doing that when your footie team wins, or if you've passed an exam? It's different, isn't it? Okay. I will stop procrastinating and dissecting words and their meanings as found in the Oxford English Dictionary. I will tell you what happened. Maybe it's time for another "nutshell moment".

The day was magical. Perfectly magical. Even when nature said, "Hold up, sunshine. You need to eat, maybe take a toilet break. What about brushing your teeth?" we did so quickly and without fuss. It was gone midnight before exhaustion took hold and demanded we sleep. But, that didn't stop the kisses and caresses we found ourselves sharing in the middle of the night.

Morning arrived in her bright and breezy way, and we realised we still hadn't spoken about going anywhere for a break. Well, *I* realised it, actually, all on my own. It was now Wednesday and the week was quickly slipping away from under us. Then I remembered something else. And that something could definitely put a spoke in the works.

"I thought you only booked a few days off from work." Maybe I should have woken her up before asking her the question, and then maybe I wouldn't have had to repeat it three times. And even by the third attempt, I still got a grunt. "Work. Few days?"

The fourth time hit the mark. Amazing, really.

"Work!"

Why was she shouting?

"Work!"

And repeating.

"Shit!"

And swearing, whilst jumping out of bed and running around the room without doing much else.

"Shit!"

I know...you've said that.

"Shit! Work!"

Did this mean she was late for work?

"I'm going to be late for work."

I was lying back on the bed by this stage, watching her begin to gather her clothes whilst trying to dress herself.

"I really need a shower..."

"Maria."

"I must smell like sex."

You smell divine.

"I can't go into work smelling of sex."

Well, shower then. Obvious, really.

"But I have to go in and tell them I need some time off...and get through some appointments I have booked in." She stopped, sniffed under her armpits, and then realised I was watching her. Did I have to spell it out?

"Grab a shower." On one hand she seemed relieved I hadn't mentioned her inhaling her pits, whilst on the other, her face indicated she didn't have the luxury of having a shower. "It's only a quarter past six."

It was amazing to watch her expression at that precise moment. It's like when you wake up in the middle of the night all sleepy and see you still have a few hours before you need to get up. Yes. That kind of face. Her mouth moved around the words "a quarter past six" and then she deliberated over them briefly before she allowed the smile to crack across her mouth. The next move she had up her sleeve was to leap from standing and onto the bed, making me bounce on the mattress. Ardent lips met mine and I had to nearly push her off me before spluttering, "I thought you wanted a shower."

Maria lifted her face away from mine, and I watched with rapt fascination how her eyebrow disappeared behind her fringe. She didn't have to ask me; her expression said it all.

"Okay then."

The second eyebrow went to be with the first.

"I'll help you save water."

The grin spread before she kissed me quickly then promptly darted off the bed and held out her hand.

"Someone wakes up bossy, don't they?"

Her hand waved in front of me, before becoming stationary once again.

"Okay, Miss 'Get Your Arse Out of Bed' Moran. I'm coming."

As my hand slipped into hers, she responded, "It's *Doctor* 'Get Your Arse Out of Bed' Moran, thank you."

Then by some kind of magic, I was standing on my two feet. Or maybe it was just because she was so bloody strong.

An hour and a half later, Maria was showered, fed, and on her way to get into a clean set of clothes, and I was standing with my back to the front door with the biggest, most stupid grin on my face. Who would have thought my life would have turned around like this in such a short space of time? It was only five days ago that I thought everything was a big pile of donkey doo doo—shit, for the less cultured of us...me included. And look at us now. Was it only Monday night since everything had decided to go in my favour after all? Two itty bitty days ago?

What still amazes me is the way everything we should have been discussing had all fizzled into nothing once we became one. There were still many things we hadn't discussed, so many things we needed to examine in this relationship, but all of them seemed irrelevant. I agree that talking about things has its benefits, especially when it is one of those discussions that are called a heart-to-heart, but, to be honest, I'm not a heart-to-heart kind of girl. Confrontation is my nemesis. I would usually do anything rather than sit someone down and say, "We need to talk." As for opening up and spilling all, it is like nails down a blackboard. Even writing about it makes all the hairs at the back of my neck stand up and scream, "STOP!" But I knew it had to be done. Unfortunately.

Maria called a couple of hours later to tell me she had gotten the rest of the week off, and it was my job to find a place for us to go for a few days. Right at the end of the conversation, the tone of her voice changed slightly. Part of me was expecting it but I was still surprised when she actually said, "I've spoken to Liz." Then there was a slight pause. "She won't be sticking her nose in our business from now on."

I wanted to ask her what she had said, how the nurse had responded, if Maria had smacked her one—preferably in her big fat lying face. But I didn't. I should have, but I didn't.

Then she was gone again, with the promise she would be at mine at seven-thirty. That gave me nine hours to get cracking and find somewhere I could sweep her off her feet. Corny, I know, but I wanted the time away to be a chance for us to connect even more deeply than we had already; a chance for us to talk, to reflect, to move onwards and upwards and to better things. A sigh slipped from my mouth, but it wasn't a sad one. Far from it. It was a contented one. For once in my life I realised there were better things to come, even better than what I had already experienced with Maria. What a wonderful thought, a wonderful feeling, a wonderful everything. I had more to come. More of life with her. Now wasn't that something to sigh over?

It didn't take long to sort out a place to go, and although it wasn't out of Norfolk, it was still "away". I arranged a cottage at Sea Palling until Sunday, not the most romantic of places, but at least we could be away from the bustle of everyday life for a little while.

By ten past eight that evening we were unloading my car outside the small detached cottage near the dunes of Sea Palling. Maria loved the idea of not travelling too far from Norwich, and no one can say just over eighteen miles is too far, can they? The cottage was gorgeous. Small but compact, I think an estate agent would say. There was only one bedroom, situated in what used to be the attic space. Beams lined the ceilings, rugs spilled over the floor, a fireplace waited with logs piled, ready to be lit. I had gathered groceries earlier in the day, so we didn't need to go out once we had arrived, but who could resist a walk on the beach? Neither of us, that's for sure.

The daylight was almost gone as we stepped onto the cool sand. Stars were beginning to appear in the darkening sky, and a fresh breeze whipped across us making us both pull our jackets closer before we linked arms and began to walk in silence. There seemed to be no reason to speak; everything was perfect. Even though I was shorter than Maria, I matched each step she took, my feet sinking into the crystallised grains. And with each footstep, I knew I had to suck down my aversion to confrontation and tell her how I felt. It was time to break the silence, as there was, in fact, a reason to speak after all. I know. It's a woman thing.

"Can we sit down for a while?" Why did my voice sound nervous? Was it because it was showing how the rest of me was feeling? I was uneasy, and for the life of me I didn't know why. Or did I? Oh for fuck's sake! Maria just nodded and led me over to a half submerged rock near the sand dune. I think she knew it was coming even before I said anything. It must have been because I was beginning to shake like a shitting dog.

"I'm not always like that you know."

Maria looked at me, her eyes boring straight into mine.

"Jealous, I mean." A sigh escaped my mouth. "I can honestly say it was a new experience for me. One I don't want to repeat." But it wasn't jealousy that had made me react the way I did. At no time had I felt jealousy, had I? Yes, and it was quite a forceful emotion. Grabbing her hand, I swallowed and started again. "Well, not jealous...more like insecure. I...I...didn't know how you felt about us, you know...erm...if you...erm..." This wasn't turning out how I thought it should, you know, finding words to convey how stupid I'd been. Maria didn't help me out; she just gripped my fingers tighter. "I believed the wrong person... I didn't have faith enough to believe what we had was real..." Shit. This was going pear shaped. "What I mean is..." What did I mean? "I felt insecure." You've said that. "And I didn't know..." Please don't repeat that bit too, "...how you felt..." here it comes, "about us."

"Why not? Couldn't you tell by the way I looked at you...the way we kissed...the way my face would light up every time I saw you?" Maria wasn't being aggressive or challenging; she was stating the obvious. That is, it would have been obvious to anyone who wasn't an idiot like I was. "Gem? Do we have to go through all of this again? I thought we agreed to wipe the slate clean and start fresh."

I wanted to tell her how I felt when I saw her outside the hospital with the blonde, but what was the point? I knew it had been nothing, although I hadn't known it at the time, true. But now, now I think the picture was beginning to come into focus. At last.

Turning to face her fully, I lifted up her hand and kissed her knuckles before continuing. "One last thing and then I promise to shut up."

Her eyebrow raised and a slight grin skittered over her face.

"About this, I mean. I'll shut up about this."

A small chuckle came out of her mouth, enough to tell me she believed me but thousands wouldn't.

Sucking in a breath, I knew I had to make this part count...this part matter. "I trust you. I respect you. I love you." And then I fell silent, but I think Maria was expecting more, so like an idiot, I continued. "I will never jump to conclusions again. And I will never go on what other people tell me. I'll ask you instead."

What she said next made my ears prick up and nudged my brain into some sort of action.

"Going with our gut instincts is not a bad thing, Gem."

Huh?

"And listening to the advice of others can also have its benefits."

Was she deliberately shooting herself in the foot?

"Gut instincts are the things about us that keep us safe, protected, and in one piece. Without them, we are mincemeat."

Was it time for me to start panicking?

"But, and this is a BIG but, we have to recognise when it is time to fight and when it is time to flee."

This was going over my head a little. Were we talking about the same thing?

"You ran, Gem. You took the word of someone else and you ran. You didn't fight for us."

Fuck. Now I got it. Unfortunately.

"It goes with the taking advice bit. Sometimes it's beneficial, whilst other times—"

"The person isn't giving you advice at all."

"Exactly."

At this point I wanted to cry. It was true. I ran. I knew I made an attempt to sort it out, but it must have been half-hearted. I believed what I thought I was seeing, listened to what I thought was being said, and above all, ignored the real gut instinct I had raging inside me...and that was the love I felt for this woman, and the love I knew deep down she had for me.

"All I ask for in the future is that you come to me... you ask me. I will always tell you the truth." Her hand left mine and slipped around my shoulders to bring me closer to her. A soft kiss landed on my mouth. "But, to save you the trouble..." another kiss, "I'll tell you now..." and another. "You're all I'll ever want and need."

The next kiss she gave me started as another soft one, but I wanted more. Pulling her to me, I increased the pressure of our lips and almost devoured her before breaking it off suddenly.

"I promise. But, and this is a BIG but, too, I will never doubt you again." I expected her to laugh, to say something, to kiss me with happiness, but she didn't. For a fleeting moment I saw a darkness flash over her face before a small smile took its place.

Then she turned away from me and stared at the black looking sea bashing against the shore, watched as the fight between earth and water carried on its never ending dance. She must have stared at it for less than a minute, but it seemed as if it was a lifetime before she turned to face me again.

"Come on, you. Time to get back." Before I had chance to answer, she was on her feet, her hand lowered for me to take. "It's rather nippy out here now."

Slipping my hand in hers, she pulled me to my feet as if I was made of air. Not talking, we made our way back to the cottage. As you may guess, the thoughts rushing around in my head were a blur. Why would she react this way to me telling her that I would never doubt her again? Was she hiding something? And how long had it been from the moment I said I would never doubt her again, to me doing just that?

By the time we reached the cottage, droplets of rain were beginning to strike. Spitting drops, drops that were the size of pinheads, drops that were collecting together in groups of four or five to make big plodding drops. Needless to say, it was time to run, but we weren't fast enough to miss the downpour, and by the time I had fumbled with the key in the lock, we were both soaked to the skin and laughing. I do think the English have a way of coping with rain. Maybe it's because we are so used to the changing weather, we don't take it to heart when we suddenly get pissed wet through. At least it lightened the mood.

Inside, coats, boots, and jeans off, and there we stood in the hallway—socks, a T-shirt, and a smile were the only things we were wearing, all the rest sat in a heap at our feet. Water was dripping off my hair and trickling down my face, and the childish part of me wanted to shake my head like a dog. So I did, causing Maria to yelp as she staggered back.

"What's the matter, wuss? Scared of getting a little wetter?" God, I am so cocky sometimes, usually when I haven't got a cat in hell's chance of winning. But when I saw the change on her face, the laughter transform to a challenge, I realised that I wanted to run.

"Wetter? Me? Scared?" Maria's voice was low.

No, actually, *me*...scared...but in one of those giddy "Oh chase me" ways that make a person scream like a girl and run whilst waving arms madly. I snorted, as I couldn't speak. My chest was filling up with excitement. Could have been the rain...or the glint in her eye...or the fact she was walking in my direction, her lip curled back into a mock sneer. "I'll show you wetter..."

With that, I was off. The scream was tearing out of my mouth, and my socked feet slapping and skidding on the tiled floor. Maria was right behind me, and I darted around furniture to avoid capture. Trust me to pick the smallest cottage on the Norfolk coastline for a mini-break. However, I did surprise myself with how spry I seemed. I avoided capture all around the front room, the dining room, even the kitchen. I thought the stairs were going to be my undoing but I managed them fine, even though I could feel her right behind me on every one. That made it worse, as I thought she was going to grab my arse as I was pelting up the wooden steps two at a time. Not that I don't like her grabbing my arse, it's not that at all. It's the thought that she was behind me. Crap. I don't know how to explain it better than that.

Anyway...there we were at the top of the stairs. I avoided the bathroom because there was no way anyone could swing a cat round in there, never mind avoid certain capture. The only option left was the bedroom: the bedroom with it gorgeous sloped ceiling of a renovated attic; the bedroom where my reign as supreme runner came to an end. And no. I didn't knock myself out by smacking my head against the oak beams, although that bit surprised even me. If anyone was going to crack her nut on wood, it would usually be me. Nevertheless, there I stood on one side of the bed whilst she stood on the other. Our breathing was rapid and uneven, and it seemed as if we had run a mini marathon instead of around a two up, three down cottage. I needed to get fitter, that's for sure, as my usual fitness regime would not cut the mustard in future. Pushing pens, jumping to conclusions, and running around in circles were not the way to outrun this woman, who must have had the longest legs I had ever seen.

That was my undoing. If I hadn't been distracted by the length of her legs, naked legs, I might add, I wouldn't have found myself in a tight spot. There she stood in front of me, her hair wild, but not as wild as the look in her eyes. I felt like a cornered animal, just about to be eaten alive by the hunter. And it felt exciting…exhilarating… wonderfully dangerous. The room was full of the sound of our breathing, and I tried to see if I could get past her and back out of the door. Every time I moved, she darted into position, blocking my exit. It was on the third attempt that it struck me: why the fuck was I trying to escape?

With that thought in my head, I did what I believe was the only thing I could do. I threw in the towel by throwing myself onto the bed, my legs and arms all over the place… socked feet sticking up into the air. "I give up! You win!"

How old was I? Twelve? I didn't get the chance to think of anything else, because Maria made sure all I thought about was her. Wetness dripped onto my legs, and as I looked up, I could see her leaning over, her dark hair dangling over me. The look in her eyes was still the same, but also had a little sparkle of conquest. I liked that. I liked that a lot. Especially the part of me that is just below my stomach but above my knees; the bit that was becoming exactly what she promised I would be. Wetter.

She lived up to her promise.

The evening went by with us becoming closer, becoming one, over and over again. Morning came around but we stayed put, not getting up until gone lunchtime. This was the life. This was what every day should be like. I was so happy being with her, so contented, so...so...*whole*, that I didn't give another thought to her reaction to me saying I would never doubt her in the future. Why should I? I was trying to give up that part of my personality, you know, the one that questioned everything she said or did. Funny thing was, that wasn't part of my personality until I had received the letter from the Lesbian Shit Stirrer, who by now I definitely knew, through sheer gut instinct alone, was the nurse.

But, me being me, nothing else was said, and the remainder of our stay at the cottage was spent in delirious ignorance of what was going to follow.

Sunday afternoon saw Maria leaving me at my front door, as she and I both had to sort out things for work the next day. It hurt to say goodbye to her; I really wanted to make her stay with me for a little while longer.

As her car pulled away and turned the corner at the bottom of my street, I sighed and stepped back inside my house. It wasn't until I shut the door and leaned dreamily on it that I realised I hadn't planned any lessons for the following week.

Crap. And double crap. When would I ever learn?

Chapter 11

ORK WAS, AS USUAL, UNFORGIVING. Work didn't care that I'd gone through a drama, followed by a few glorious days away with the woman I loved. Work just sat there demanding to know why I was disorganised and vacant. In fact I think I was mirroring the students I teach, as they too came back disorganised and vacant. I hoped it wasn't for the same reasons I had.

The thing is, when you are working with kids you learn a thing or two as you go along. It's not a case of going to university for four years and coming away knowing everything, not by a long shot. Every day that I teach, I learn something new—something amazing, something fascinating, something that fortifies my armaments. And sometimes there are incidents that remind me of times past, or occasions that make certain things click into place.

Monday was one of those days for the latter: the "click click—oh shit" day, as it will become known.

I bet you are wondering what clicked into place. Many things, actually, but it's just the one I want to tell you about. It was something trivial that provided the spark that started it all. Something so tiny and insignificant, I would usually have dismissed it without much thought. Let me tell you what happened, and then I'll explain why it was so noteworthy.

It all started with a lying, spiteful pupil. You know the kind: brutish, thuggish, smarmy, racist, bullying, sly. Yes, I know that a few of the adjectives I have listed mean pretty much the same thing, but if you had ever met this boy, you would know why I would want to say some of them more than once. This boy was bad news. But the most worrying thing was that as much as I tried, and others tried, to pin anything on him, he always came out the victim. On the surface it seemed as if butter wouldn't melt in his mouth, but as soon as he knew that your back was turned...bam, blade in right up to the hilt...figuratively speaking of course. All the other teachers had his card marked, as did most of the pupils, apart from his little gang of sycophants (who were mainly his friends so that they wouldn't become his next victims). The only ones that still believed every word that came from those lying lips were his parents. And that was bad enough, considering they were just as bad as he was when it came to lying and bullying. When he was caught doing anything he shouldn't, the parents would step up and blame the teachers, the school, the other kids, everything except the fact their son was indeed a twat of the highest order.

I bet you are wondering how this all fits in, aren't you? Let's set the scene.

It was just after break on Monday, and I had been on playground duty. Not much of interest there, you may say. And you'd be right. It was boring, until a girl from my tutor group came and told me this not so nice individual (shall we call him Twat Boy to safeguard the identity of the little scumbag?) had made her feel uncomfortable in French. He had not spoken bad words to her in French, I mean their encounter occurred in the French classroom. Okay, that's cleared up. I had a free period next so I asked the girl to stay behind to dish the dirt on Twat Boy. What had happened was that as soon as the teacher had left the room to get another textbook, TB had called the teacher a bitch, quite loudly, by all accounts. He wanted to impress his friends at the expense of his teacher, believing that the teacher in question would never find out. But, ah... there's the rub. Nothing stays a secret when you have thirty teenagers and twenty-nine hate the remaining one. More to the point, where there's teens, there are no secrets, whether they like you or not.

The girl who came to get the load off her chest was a decent girl...a nice, quiet girl. It did not surprise me that she had become offended at such a display. What could I do? I was merely her tutor, someone who would do anything in her power to help out if the girl was upset. But I had already gone head to head with TB's parents, and they had threatened to have my guts for garters if I ever attacked their precious boy again. Unfortunately, for them I mean, I didn't give a flying fuck what they threatened to do. I had been waiting for this opportunity for a long while.

After sending the offended student on her way, I went to see the French teacher and told her what had happened. Next, we sent out a bulletin requiring all the students from that French class to return at lunchtime, without exception. Then I went to see all the other tutors of that Year group and told them to meet us in the French room...and also invited the Head of Year and the Head of Pastoral. I wanted as many witnesses as I could possibly get, and everyone was fed up with TB getting away with doing whatever the fuck he wanted.

Lunchtime came and the class filed back in, one by one. A tutor stood in each corner of the room; the Head of Year was on one side, and the Head of Pastoral on the other. I should have gotten the press in too, but time had not been on my side. And of course I'm joking. Even having the BBC as an impartial witness wouldn't have helped convince his parents of any wrongdoing on their son's part. I knew that. At the time, I didn't know that his own family members would be the ones who would carry the day. They didn't have a clue either.

So, where was I? Oh yeah. On the brink of solving a big problem; on the brink of exposing someone for what and who they were. How was I to know it would come back and bite me on the ass?

"I imagine you're wondering why you have all been asked back this lunchtime." The French teacher was cool and in control. She informed them of events that had occurred during Period Two, how it had come to her attention that someone had shouted out something in class that was not acceptable.

The students all looked at one another before glaring at TB, who sat staring cockily at the teacher.

"Okay. Our purpose for this assembly is to find out who heard anything they thought should not be tolerated."

I could feel the atmosphere in the room change from puzzlement to fear.

"Don't worry. It is going to be a secret response." The students were directed to place their heads on the table and not look up. Next, they were told to put their hands up if they had heard someone say something about the teacher that was negative. Amazingly enough, twenty-four hands went into the air. TB had five friends in that class... five of the six students in the school that would never do or say anything against him. The sixth cohort was him, of course. Just as the teacher was going to tell them it was over and done with, one of TB's mates, Tom Edwards, lifted his head and glanced quickly around the room. Shit. He would tell TB who had snitched, and there would be hell to pay. TB would get to them before we had a chance to.

"Right. Thank you. You may all raise your heads."

They all did, looking around them as they did so.

"Could all the people on the back row leave? Thank you for your time." This included Twat and his cronies, leaving twenty-two other students in the room.

I wanted to tell Edwards that he should stay, but then he would hear the rest of the conversation, so I did the only thing I could think of. "Mr Roberts, could you please escort these students to my room and make sure none of them speaks to each other or anyone else?" That was another mistake, as Mr Roberts couldn't organise a piss up in a brewery and wouldn't win an argument with himself. It was "show over" really before it had even started.

After the door closed, the Head of Year stood at the front. "Can anyone in here tell me exactly what happened?"

Talk about the flood gates opening. Every child had a story to tell about TB, most of which were not even to do with the present incident. One lad shouted across the mass, "What's the point? He'll only get away with it again, or beat the shit out of any of us who grass him up."

True, but I wasn't going to admit that aloud.

It turned out that they had all heard TB call the French teacher a bitch, and that he had also called the music teacher one on the previous Friday before deleting one group's composition work from the computer.

We made a list of everything we could, and after the students had been dismissed, the teaching staff assembled in my room to interview the perpetrator. We told the rest of his cadre to go, and then left TB on his own for a minute to have a stew. It was too much, even for him, to have so many adults accusing him at the same time. Therefore, it was up to me and the Head of Pastoral to confront him, sending the rest of the staff away with his mates to the office. Divide and conquer, or so we thought.

And that's when it turned into "click click—oh shit" day. It wasn't the fact that TB tried his hardest to wheedle his way out of it, although it was apparent that his mate had told him that the rest of the class had voted they had heard of something, something he had shouted.

I bet you are thinking, "Jesus, she usually goes off the point, but for fuck's sake...this is the worst to date!" But as I said before, it has a point to make. Funnily enough, it wasn't TB that caused my epiphany; it was "Looking Boy", actually.

Twat Boy wasn't giving in. Everything we said, he denied. He even ended up shouting in the face of the Head

SEE RIGHT THROUGH ME

of Pastoral, spitting in anger, tears of fury racing down his cheeks as he swore on his mother's life that he would never call anyone a bitch. I would have pitied his mother, and her suddenly imminent demise, if I hadn't already met her. I just hoped they would bury her at sea, as the number of people dancing on her grave would cause a mini earthquake.

The Head of Pastoral was quite calm; it amazed me how he kept his hands off TB. Thankfully, he wasn't taking any shit, and the next thing we knew we were on our way to the office to call for TB's parents to take him home. Five days exclusion, to begin immediately. Bonus. I wanted to laugh at the way TB danced and swore and shouted all the way to the office, and I wanted to dance too, as the evidence was piling up against him.

When we arrived at the office, I leaned over and whispered, "Tell you what, Jim, I'll have a word with Edwards whilst you call the folks, okay?" I wanted to get him to tell me how he had given TB the heads up and then ask why he would do that. The only reason he would have thought TB needed to know what the other students had revealed was because Tom knew TB had done something he should be prepared to answer questions about. Obvious, really.

I asked Tom if he had tipped off TB; he denied it. I told him that no one would ever know he had told me. He kept quiet. But then it happened...the realization I have been leading up to. The thought that hit me with such force that it didn't just go click, it went bam. It wasn't what Tom said; it was the way he looked that struck me.

"There's something you're not telling me, Tom." I watched his mouth move as if to voice a denial, and he looked away, looked back at me, then looked away again. His hands fidgeted and tugged at the cuff of his school jumper. "No one here will judge you; just get it off your chest." I knew that's exactly the way he was feeling—that he wanted to get something off his chest, but he was too scared to talk.

What bothered me was that I had seen the exact same look not very long ago, not long ago at all. Actually, it was the night when Maria and I had been walking on the beach... Even before that, if I were to be honest. Every time she and I had discussed things that were a little near the mark, that very same look had appeared on Maria's face. From the first time she had opened up to me about Dr Jennifer Fielding, she had had that look, had the same fidgeting reaction, gave off the same signals that she wanted to tell me something, but just couldn't.

But why? And more importantly, *what* was she hiding? I didn't want to go down the same path I had before, making assumptions. Look where that had led me. I couldn't just blurt it out and say, "What are you hiding, Maria?", and I definitely couldn't send her a text message asking her either. If I went in with all guns blazing, she would think I was a psycho. Part of me was beginning to think I was, too. Why would the actions of a teenaged boy make me doubt the woman I loved? And not just once, either. This was getting ridiculous. Maria wasn't hiding anything; it was all a figment of my overactive imagination, the same imagination that seemed to spew up loads of crap at any given opportunity.

"Are you okay, Miss?" Edwards was leaning forward, concern evident. I knew this was not the time to start ruminating about my own insecurities. Now was the time to do my job.

"Yes, Tom, perfectly fine." Thankfully my voice sounded normal; although it did contain the element most teachers can generate...the one that denotes disappointment. "You can go, Tom. And thank you for your time."

Edwards shot out of his seat and made his way to the door, but just before it opened completely and freed him, he stopped. He turned, then closed the door and came back to where I was sitting.

"Miss?"

I looked up from the work I was pretending to mark and smiled at him. I don't know how I did it, but I did.

"Can I tell you something?"

I nodded. At that moment in time, I didn't trust my voice.

"You promise you won't laugh?" By the look on his face I could see he was embarrassed.

"No, Tom, I won't laugh. You can tell me anything; you know that."

Before he could speak, his mouth seemed to lose the ability to function properly. The muscles went lax and his bottom lip began to quiver.

"Hey...what's wrong, Tiger?"

Edwards turned away from me, as no lad wants to show weakness in front of his teacher. For a moment, my own concerns about Maria were pushed to the side. "Here." I held out a tissue. "Do you want to go and freshen up before we start again?"

He shook his head, accepted the proffered tissue and blew his nose violently.

It seemed like ages before he reacquired the ability to speak. When he did, it was worth the wait.

"I'm scared, Miss." This admission must have been worse than the crying. "Ellis bullies me...bullies all of us."

From the mouths of babes, eh? Gary Ellis was, of course, TB. Just remember that it wasn't me who broke confidentiality and spilled the beans about his identity, it was Edwards.

"He...he...I mean...I can't tell you anything; he will make sure I pay for it." He apparently didn't realise he was telling me everything I needed to know. "There's no point relying on the school to do anything about it. He always gets away with everything. We end up taking the rap for him."

Standing up, I walked past Edwards, grabbed a chair, and plunked it behind him. "Come. Sit down." I didn't need to ask again; the lad sat straightaway. "I promise you, Tom, I will see him held accountable. Bad people always get caught out in the long run. It's the way of the world. Liars, cheats, and all the other scumbags always get their comeuppance. May take a while, but it happens."

Tom started to ramble about how he couldn't tell me anything and why he refused to grass Ellis up. Everything he said was another shovel for the grave being dug for TB. Not saying anything for fear of reprisals; the thumps Ellis gave all the other lads, which were supposed to be fun, when in fact no one else was laughing; the name calling; the leaving people out; the taking of belongings... I could go on, but you get the picture.

"Listen, Tom, I want you to know that we can't do anything about Ellis if no one actually tells us what is going on." I ducked my head to try and catch his gaze. It seemed as if he had shut off; the tears were beginning to dry on his cheeks. "He counts on you lot to back him up... take the rap, as you call it. But think about it this way..." he looked at me, "if you said 'no more', if you put your foot down and refused to bail him out, he would lose his hold over you." I paused to see if he was absorbing what I was trying to tell him. "And if you did that, if you showed that courage that I know you have by the bundle, then your other mates will do it too."

The room was deathly quiet for a moment, and then Tom spoke quietly. "I suppose you're right, Miss." There was a quaver in his voice. "Can I...can I think about it?"

"Of course, Tom." He stood as if to leave, but he waited for my permission. "And yes...you can go. But one more thing." Just about to escape out the door, Tom turned back to me. "I just want to say how very proud I am of you. You have shown courage today, and I hope you remember that." A nod and he was gone.

After the door closed behind him, I thought through everything he had said. The things people do to make themselves feel better, eh? Ellis must be one extremely unhappy lad to inflict all the things he did on his so-called friends. At least if Tom did stick to his admissions, Ellis would be out of school for good and then maybe he could get the counselling he needed.

I know, I know. You are wondering why I went into so much detail with this event, but it is what people call a "Bread and Butter" section. Although it is not interesting, funny, or insightful, it does help fill in the gaps. And it had certainly given me food for thought. Did Maria feel the same way as Tom? Did she want to get something off her chest? And if it was a "yes", then what was it? I knew she had been used and abused by her mentor, but that wasn't her fault. The woman was a pig—not only bedding Maria, but bragging about it too.

Something was playing along the fringes of my memory. Every time I thought of Maria telling me about what had happened in Cambridge, there was a niggling something that was just out of my reach. Resting my head in my hands, I thought harder. And harder still. But the only thing that came to mind was the inkling of a headache. If I just left the elusive memory alone, put my mind to something else, it would come to me.

Standing up abruptly, the chair slammed against the wall. If I went over to the office and told Jim what Tom had told me, at least I could clear my head of all the wracking and thinking about Maria that was getting me nowhere fast.

Jim was standing in the lobby near Reception by the time I arrived. His face looked old and tired. As he opened his mouth to speak to me, a sigh escaped before he said, "Ellis's parents are on their way. They said they want your head on a platter. And mine, too. Not to mention the head of every tutor and the Head of Year."

I couldn't help but laugh. Who did they think they were? The Mafia?

"I know. They are living in cuckoo land, but it doesn't make it any easier, does it?"

Grabbing his arm, I led him to the side of the lobby, making sure no one could overhear us. "Maybe we have got the little turd this time."

I told him what Tom Edwards had said, and he seemed to brighten up. All we needed was one pupil to speak out, to step forward, and then our hands wouldn't be tied by stupid by-laws and administration. I hoped Tom Edwards was the man for the job.

Unfortunately, he wasn't. By the time we collected Tom, he had changed his story. We all knew that Ellis's thug buddies had gotten to him, but what could we do? Disappointment flooded through me, and I could see Jim was feeling it too. Just as Tom was leaving, we got the call to say Bully Beef's parents had arrived.

Joy.

I wish I meant that. The day was progressing from bad to worse, then from worse to "shoot me". Sitting in the office with two smug and despicable people, I could see where their son had acquired all his characteristics. Once again, everyone but Gary was blamed, and as I took abuse from his mother I thought of her son swearing on her life. Pity the forces from above didn't speed things along, and then I wouldn't have to listen as she called me unprofessional, a bully, a shit-stirrer, and all the other epithets she had at her command, undoubtedly from frequent use. One thing in particular made my ears go ping, my eyes pop, and a bead of sweat bead form over my top lip.

"Can't you understand, Ms Hughes, that my son would never hurt another person, by words or deed?"

No, I couldn't.

"It's the same wherever we go. Gary gets the blame for everything. Bully? More like *being* bullied, and mainly by people like you." She leaned forward in her chair so her face was right in front of mine. I could smell her breath as well as feel it on my face. "I can take all you have to give me, Ms Hughes, but it's not just me being hurt here."

Bingo. Without thinking about it, the crucial element was there... "not just me she hurt". Maria had said that when she had been telling me about Dr Death's bragging. Who else had she hurt? Was she married? Did her husband or wife find out? But if that was the case, would she have bragged about it? Probably. If she was insensitive enough to give Maria the "Wham, bam, thank you, ma'am" treatment, the woman was capable of anything.

"Not just me..."

I didn't realise I had spoken the words aloud until I felt Mrs Ellis scream into my face. "As I see it...it is just *you*! You are a *fucking* psycho!"

Jim was trying to calm her down but his words weren't having any effect.

"All we want is for you bunch of wankers to stop picking on our son. It's the same thing...every school... every playgroup. Even the fucking neighbours have it in for him."

If only the woman could have heard what she was saying, maybe she would have realised there was a pattern there.

"But it isn't just Ms Hughes. I have a list of—" Jim didn't get the chance to speak, as the father had decided to show his true colours. A fist came out of nowhere and Mr Ellis struck the Head of Pastoral in the face. I heard the crack, as his jaw went one way and the rest of his face another. This wasn't good. Not good at all. Especially when Mr Ellis turned to me next, the fury blazing in his eyes. I knew he was on the verge of hitting me, knew it as surely as I knew that water doesn't run uphill. I did the only thing I could do; I screamed as loudly as I could. Ellis halted in his tracks, fist suspended in mid-air as the door to the office burst open. Numerous faces were there in an instant, staff and pupils alike. Caught red handed, literally, as Jim's blood was smeared all over his knuckles.

Do you know what they told the police? Go on, guess. They said it was self-defence. Self-defence! By all accounts, I had antagonised Mrs Ellis to the point that she felt threatened. She even indicated I had started to become physical, and her husband had stepped in to save her. Save *her*! They were going to report it to the school's Board of Governors, and demand that I be sacked...and Jim, too.

Twat Boy went with his parents, but even he had the decency to look embarrassed. As soon as the police car left the school, kids were lining up to grass Gary up. It appeared that they now thought they had a chance to get rid of their tormentor once and for all.

All in all, it hadn't been a very good day. The afternoon crawled by, and classes were held in an eerie silence—no pupils deciding to chat, thereby delaying doing the work set. All that broke this silence was my voice giving instructions, and even then it was clipped and to the point. Too much was going on in my head, and these thoughts didn't dwell on the threats imposed by Mr and Mrs Ellis;

I was more concerned about what I would say to Dr Maria Moran when I saw her that evening.

I had to stop by the police station after school and give a statement. That wouldn't have been so bad, but I also had to sort out work for the next day. I was attending a seminar at the University of East Anglia, and therefore I had to leave lessons for some other poor bugger to teach. By the time I got home that evening, it was gone eight o'clock.

As I slipped my key into the lock, I felt drained and beat. All I wanted to do was shower and then curl up in bed and let the day end. But I knew I had to see Maria. How could I not? I had given her my promise that if I had any doubts, I would ask her and not let my imagination run wild again, and believe me, wild was an understatement.

I went to pick up the phone and saw the answering machine flashing. Maria had called to tell me she couldn't see me that evening. She had to finalise some papers that had been waiting for her return and she hadn't had time to do it during the day. Maybe it was a good thing she was busy; maybe I was on the verge of disbelieving her; maybe I was a twat. Who knows? Part of me wanted to call her and just hear her voice, whilst another part of me wanted to call her and size up the situation.

Before I knew it, I was tapping in the digits I knew so well and waiting whilst the bell on the other end informed the person there that someone wanted to speak with them.

Click. The phone answered, and I heard the voice I knew so well.

"Hey, Colin." Sometimes I'm not that big of a knob. I didn't call Maria. That would have been untrusting, wouldn't it? "Fancy coming over?" I was knackered from the events of the day, but I knew I wouldn't get any peace until I had spilled my guts to someone. And yes, I know I promised I wouldn't go blabbing my mouth off to any Tom, Dick, or Harry, but this wasn't like that. Col was my best friend, and that's what best friends are for, isn't it: to discuss their love lives, forgive broken noses, ignore it when he or she inadvertently kicks your future girlfriend in the head whilst swinging from the rafters? Colin owed me big time, and he was about to pay.

"What's up, Twinkle?"

"Does there have to be anything up for you to come and see your best mate?"

"On a school night...after you have spent the day wishing you had planned your lessons? Yes."

True.

"So, what's up? Anyone need beating up?"

As if. Col couldn't fight his way out of a paper bag, not even if he was holding a pair of scissors in each hand.

He went quiet for a few seconds, a feat in itself for him, then he said, "I'll be right over."

Before I had the chance to say anything else, he hung up the phone and I was left listening to the disconnect tone supplied by BT. It would take Col about thirty minutes to get to my house, twenty if he thought there was a chance of gossip. Just enough time for me to grab the quickest shower in history.

It was just over twenty minutes later when I heard the doorbell sound. I was still towelling my hair as I answered the door.

Colin was standing there, his face flushed. "If I get mailed a speeding ticket, it's your fault." He stopped, rethought his greeting, and then planted a kiss on my cheek.

That's all it took for the waterworks to go into overdrive. "Hey, hey, hey... What's the matter, honey?" Colin wrapped his arms around me and pulled me to him.

That made matters worse; the sobs ripped out of me. I didn't want to be a drama queen but I couldn't help it. Truth is, I couldn't really tell you why I decided to let it all out, standing on the doorstep, in my bathrobe, hugging onto my best friend. And the other thing I couldn't tell you is why I was doing it. Was it because of the drama at school? More likely, it was because I was so scared of fucking everything up with my insecurities like I had nearly done the previous week.

It was both. Obviously.

I didn't even feel Colin move me from the door, was not consciously aware that he half walked, half carried me into the front room. All I seemed to take in was the softness of his voice, and the gentle way he held me. In his arms I felt safe. I knew he wouldn't judge me...knew that he would tell me the truth...knew that he would give me a slap if I needed, or deserved, it.

Colin held me as I cried, and kept holding me when the tears ran out. In all the time we sat on the sofa, he didn't say a word. For once he let me decide when I was going to share.

By the time that moment came, I had calmed down enough to say what I needed to say and wait for his response. The first thing I did was to tell him about the note...the *"from a friend"* one. It's all about structure, you see? Start at the beginning and all that. What I wanted to blurt out was "Is she cheating?" But I knew she wasn't... could feel it deep within. It would have been a case of words hitting air because they could, and not because they should.

"So...you think Maria is cheating, do you?"

"No." That stumped him. "We've talked about it. It was the nurse, I'm sure of it."

"Is this a case of 'The butler did it'?"

I glared at him and he mouthed an apology.

By the time I had finished telling him of how I had started out to confront Maria, but instead had a chat with the nurse, ran away to the Peak District, came back and had it out with Maria, Colin was looking more confused with every fact revealed. I knew he wanted to ask why I was still upset if it had all been cleared up.

"It was a kid at school." I knew as soon as the words came out that they didn't convey what I wanted them to. And by the look on Col's face, he was trying to contain the sarcastic comment that sprang to his mind. "Before you say it, he didn't take my dinner money, get me behind the bike sheds, copy my homework..."

When he laughed, I joined in. Good to know that the mood was lifting.

"Seriously. I was asking him some questions about an incident, and I could tell he was covering something up. And his actions reminded me of Maria." Col still looked confused, so I told him what I had thought and why I had thought it. "Then after Mrs Ellis called me an unprofessional shit-stirrer..."

"What!"

I shushed him, but I could tell he was seething. "She said something that reminded me of something Maria said to me once." Leaning over, I snatched a tissue from the box on the table and gave a huge blow, all the while feeling Col's eyes boring into me. He was dying to ask what it was, dying to hurry me up, but I took my time and blew my nose again. "She said, 'It's not just me being hurt here.'" Colin looked at me blankly, expecting me to continue, expecting me to explain what the fuck I was talking about. "I'm thirsty."

He didn't say a word, didn't huff and puff like I would've done. He just shot straight up, ran into the kitchen, slammed about a bit, and then came back to half fling the glass of juice into my hand. Then he nodded, as if to say, "Proceed."

After draining the glass, I placed it on the table and looked back at him. Would he think I was a weirdo? A psycho? A twatette? Would he consider making an excuse to leave on the grounds that I wasn't a full shilling, or that I was a sandwich short of a picnic?

As I was considering this, Col stretched out his hand and rested it on my wrist. That's when I knew for sure that he wouldn't think any of the things I had conjured up for myself. So, I told him. Told him how Maria had said the same thing after she had told me about Dr Jennifer Fielding, told him how she had acted the same way as

Edwards, and told him how I wanted to ask her why, but was afraid of the answer.

"You're a twat, Gem."

Huh? Where had all his sympathy gone?

"What on earth has possessed you?"

Wherever it had gone, I didn't think it would be coming back in a hurry.

"Maria loves you; you can see it all over her. The way she looks at you, the way she hangs on your every word. Why on earth would you think she is up to something, or hiding something from you? And even if she is keeping something from you, that doesn't mean she is doing anything bad." He grabbed my other wrist and made sure I was looking at him for the next bit. "Whatever has happened in the past should stay there. There's no point digging it up. What good would it do?"

That wasn't the answer I wanted to hear. I wanted him to side with me, like a proper best friend, and believe in all my conspiracy theories. Or did I? Was that the reason I had called him, so I could have a reason to confront Maria? Looking into his eyes, I knew the answer was definitely a "no". The reason I had called him was because, all said and done, he was my friend and I respected and trusted his judgment. Just like I should respect and trust Maria.

"You should ask her. If it's playing on your mind, ask her about it." Pulling me to him, he lowered my head onto his chest. "But don't make an issue out of it. Accept what she has to say and move on, okay?"

I nodded, my head tapping against his ribs.

"And what's all this about being a shit-stirring unprofessional?"

Looking up into his face, I saw the beginnings of a smile gathering at the corners of his mouth. I knew the conversation about Maria and my inability to show a spine was officially over, so I told him about the rest of my day.

And that was it, really. Col stayed for another hour before I told him I had to get to bed. He left, still spitting hatred about ungrateful obnoxious parents who couldn't recognise a good school when it came and bit them on the arse.

The next day was to be spent in a room full of English teachers arguing over punctuation, tests, and Shakespeare. At least I didn't have to plan any lessons; they were done. Thankfully. All I had to do was to get into bed and sleep. Sounds easy, doesn't it? Well, you'd be wrong. The night was not the best night's sleep I've ever had in my life, and, once again, I could blame someone else rather than myself. I just couldn't let it lie. All the worry about seeing Maria, asking her what she had meant when she had said, "it's not just me being hurt here."

The last thing I thought of before dropping off to sleep was that tomorrow I wouldn't be in work. Tomorrow I would be right next door to the Norfolk and Norwich University Hospital. And tomorrow, I would go to see Maria at work. There was no point in waiting until the evening to discuss it. I would take her to lunch, and over sandwiches, I would drop in the questions I needed to ask.

All I needed to do now was to think of those questions. I think trying to think of them was the reason I fell asleep at all. See? Too much thinking is not good for you. Makes you sleep and dream terrible dreams. I hoped that they wouldn't come true.

Chapter 12

TUESDAY MORNING WAS NOT A nice morning. She wasn't light or breezy or beautiful. Not that I would've noticed if she had been naked, as I was too busy shitting my pants to consider anything but talking to Maria.

I was up early, even though I didn't have to leave until later than usual. But how could I lie there in bed when I felt the weight of the world hanging over me? I was out of the door before my usual time, and sitting in the car park of the university an hour before check in.

The next thing I did was to start the car and make my way to the building next door. I wasn't being lazy; it would have taken me the best part of half an hour to walk to the place I wanted to go. Why I decided to sit there watching the front of the hospital building, I'll never know. But by the time I had to leave, Maria still had not arrived. It's amazing to think that in the beginning, I was the one who had thought she was a stalker. How the tables had turned. Now it was me doing the stalking: the one who had laughed about it; the one who had become freaked out and thought I would become a statistic on the evening news; the one who was nervously awaiting the arrival of the woman I professed to love. To say I was feeling like a prize one git would be an understatement. Knowing I had turned into the person I never thought I would ever become was not a very nice feeling. The next thing I knew, I was turning into the car park of the university again.

Weirdly enough I was late to my course. I must have sat in the car far longer than I realised, and that, believe it or not, made me feel worse. Needless to say, the rest of the morning went by without any help from me, and I couldn't tell you what they were discussing, even if you offered me money.

Twelve-thirty came around, and I was raring to leave. I hadn't brought anything for lunch like I had planned to do, and there was nowhere to grab something from, except Tesco's, and that was the ultimate romantic lunch, wasn't it? Therefore I turned up in G Ward empty-handed, my heart in my mouth and my stomach in my throat. If I was going to keel over, at least I was in the right place for it.

Walking through Reception, I heard the distinct nasal tones of the woman I had grown to despise. The nurse was trying to calm a woman who was robed in a hospital gown, telling her that she should have known that leaving her clothes unattended had not been the wisest of moves. It would have been funny if I hadn't felt the bile rise up my throat when I spotted the woman who made me want to choke the life out of her. How could I speak to her? How could I summon that part of me that should comply with the rules of the game and brave the conversation? It wasn't as if I had to be nice to her. All I had to do was to ask if Maria was in her room, and then leave. It wasn't as if she would tell me the truth. She would more than likely spin me another tale.

Stop. Not you, me. It was up to me whether I believed her or not, wasn't it? I didn't have to fall for her lies, her stories, her shit-stirring. I was a grown woman, who was in love with another grown woman...two grown women in a grown up relationship. One thing I knew for certain was that I loved Maria, and I also knew she loved me. I also knew that I trusted her. Yes. With all the whinging I have been doing, I forgot to tell you that. Now I had arrived at the ward, and was moments away from confronting Maria, I had realised it didn't matter what she had done in her past. It didn't matter that she had looked uncomfortable when we had discussed things. All that mattered was now. The here and now. And within this here and now, there was her and me.

Just as I was about to turn and leave, the nurse called me over. Part of me wanted to ignore her, but it was too late for that. Slowly, I turned back to face her, and with extreme effort, I dragged up a smile. The irate patient was nowhere to be seen. It was just the two of us.

"Good afternoon." I hesitated whilst I swallowed the vomit racing up my throat. "Is Dr Moran available?"

I watched as her eyes half closed as if she was assessing me. I knew that for the briefest of moments she had forgotten who I was, and I was hoping it would stay that way.

Then she snorted. "I thought you were out of the picture."

Here we go.

"Considering she's got another woman in her room..."

My fists were clenching into balls, pressing my nails into the palms of my hands until it hurt. But I didn't respond. "Don't you ever listen to advice? I did try to warn you away from her, on more than one occasion."

"I'm sorry to interrupt you, but I haven't got long. Is she in or not?" I was proud of myself at that moment; I felt in control...powerful, even. The nurse had tried to rattle my chain, but I stood my ground and gave her nothing in the way of reaction, unlike the last time we had seen each other. That being said, it didn't change the fact that I wanted to punch her squarely in her fat, lying face. I was controlled, but I wasn't infallible. "Shall I just pop down there?" I began to back away, but the next thing she said surprised me, or, more to the point, unnerved me.

"Sure. But don't say I didn't warn you." She continued filling out forms, almost giving the impression I wasn't there.

I didn't get it. Why would she back down so easily? Why hadn't she pressed home the point of Maria being unobtainable? Why had she spelled out that there was in fact someone in there? If it was a patient, when I burst in, Maria would go crackers and throw me out. Or was it... Aw for fuck's sake! There was nothing going on! The nurse was trying to freak me out, reverse psychology and all that bollocks. She wanted me to doubt what I was going to do, wanted me to leave and worry about who the woman was in the room with Maria, or go in and disturb her when she was working. And there was no way I was going to stand there and second guess everything she said, or everything she implied. I had to understand that no matter how hard I tried to decipher what the nurse was trying to achieve,

I would always fail miserably. All I knew was that she wanted what I had.

Now that was a cheerful thought, cheerful enough to enable me to thank her for her time and begin to walk down the corridor to Maria.

I knew the troll was watching me, and I really wanted to turn around and give her a little wave, but that would have been rubbing it in, wouldn't it? Of course it would. So, of course, I did it. How could I resist? I am a woman, after all. I don't think she was a happy bunny, and I'm definite that if she hadn't been in her place of work, she would have given me the two-fingered salute.

Just as I reached the door, stretched my hand out to grab the handle, someone spoke behind me. "I wouldn't disturb her, if I were you."

That fucking nurse was back, and this time my control had buggered off. "Will...you...*leave*...me the fuck alone!"

She started to grab my arm, but I pulled it away. "And don't you dare try and touch me, you fucking knob rash." Knob rash? "Can't you get it into your thick head—I don't care what you say about Maria...don't care if you want me to believe she's in there fucking the brains out of someone else."

She was beginning to back away. I don't think she had expected me to fire up quite as much as I had.

Neither had I, come to think of it. Instead of letting her scuttle off to her coven, I followed her, my voice becoming louder and louder. "Just because Maria wouldn't touch you with a ten foot pole soaked with a bottle of disinfectant, don't try and stir things up." All the time I was walking towards her, I was jabbing my finger closer and closer to her chest. I didn't want to touch her; I wasn't wearing rubber gloves. "You need to get a life...your *own* life instead of someone else's."

That did it. I actually saw the spark of hatred ignite into something that could easily become physical. That's all I needed. Me scrapping with her in the corridor of the X-ray department.

"You think you're so fucking clever, don't you? Eh? Coming in here thinking you know more than I do." She was no longer backing away, she was coming towards me.

Shit.

"All I've tried to do was warn you about her, but oh no...you know better." A snort came out, making her face twist. "We *all* know what she's like." When she said *"she"*, her hand jabbed in the direction of the closed door. "Why do you think she left Cambridge and came here?" Another snort. "I suppose she told you about Dr Fielding, didn't she?"

How did she know about that?

"As I said...I know a lot about your *precious* Maria."

I was against the wall now. Where had my spine and gumption gone?

"Did she tell you how she slept with Fielding whilst she was seeing someone else? Did she tell you how that poor woman was devastated? No? I'm surprised, considering you think you know it all."

As she spat out the last words, she lifted her hand, and I knew she was going to hit me. Should I hit her first? Surprise her? Surprise myself? I'm not one for violence at any time, but I knew if I did hit her, it wouldn't just be the one time. That's the bit that scared me the most. Instead of clouting her, I blocked her hand...and blocked the second strike, as well. After her two attempts to knock my lights out, we found ourselves at a stalemate. I was holding her wrists, and she was struggling to free herself. The next thing we did was pause, stare at each other, and conjure up evil warrior faces before struggling like crazy.

I didn't care if people saw us; didn't care that I was in the middle of the hospital scrapping like a teenaged girl. What I did care about was letting go of her hands, because by letting go of her hands, I would be allowing things to escalate.

"Listen, bitch, even if Maria had slept with Fielding whilst seeing someone else, it has nothing to do with you." I was still gripping her wrists, but this time it was because I knew if I let go, I would wipe that stupid smile off her face.

"But..." she leaned into me, "it has everything to do with you." Then she laughed. "And that woman...the one she used...is the one who is with Maria in her room. Call it 'for old times' sake'".

That did it. I threw her backwards into the opposite wall, and just as I grabbed hold of her top and began to shake her, I heard a voice behind me telling me not to do it. Fuck that. She had pushed me too far. This time I was going to make sure she got the message.

"Stop shit-stirring! Maria is not shagging someone else behind my back...and she has never cheated on anyone else! Got it?" Slam, again. The nurse bounced off the wall, but I held her fast. "And don't you ever say it again...or send me another note telling me she has someone else... and never, and I mean never...say you are my friend."

Although she looked scared shitless at that moment, she still looked surprised. Her mouth moved around the word "friend".

"I know it was you. Don't try and deny it."

"It was me."

Why hadn't her lips moved again? How could I be hearing this confession when her lips weren't moving, when there wasn't any sound coming out?

"It was me."

Why did it sound as if it was coming from behind me?

I slowly turned my head to see a woman standing there. *What the fuck?*

"I sent you the note. Maybe if you'll let me explain..."

But who was she? Where had she come from? Looking past her I saw the door to Maria's room was now open, although there was no sign of Maria.

Still grasping the nurse, I asked, "Who are you?"

"I'm Kate. Maria's ex."

I felt all the strength leave my body; my legs felt as if they were made of jelly and my hands didn't have the ability to keep on gripping the nurse's blouse. I suppose you could say that was my main mistake.

The pain hit me before the blackness. I couldn't say for sure, but I could make a good guess. Because I was distracted, the nurse had taken her opportunity and thumped me in the back of the head. I still remember the sight of the floor coming up to meet me, but the darkness took hold of me before I could feel the contact with the tile floor. I could hear voices, but they seemed far away. But when I felt a gentle touch on my face, I allowed the blackness to completely take over.

I bet you are thinking that I am prone to passing out, aren't you? If you think about it, I'm not. The first time, I tripped; the second, I was knocked out. For argument's sake, we could agree that both incidents were my fault. One, I shouldn't have jumped over the sofa; two, I should never have turned my back on the nurse. And yes, now I will continue.

When I came to, I wasn't lying on the floor in a pool of my own blood being jeered at by the nurse and the ex. I found myself inside the X-ray room, lying on the bed, with very anxious blue eyes looking down at me. All that I had been through to end up at that point should have made me want to shoot up and give Maria a piece of my mind, but I didn't want to. In fact, I felt safe now that she was there. At least I would begin to get some answers, and not just from her.

I wet my lips and attempted to speak, but the words stuck in the dryness of my mouth. I wanted to know how long I had been out.

"You were out for only a few minutes, love." Her voice was like silk. "And yes...I will tell you everything when you feel better. Kate is just getting you some water."

Kate. The ex, Kate. And on that thought, she reappeared from the back room carrying a glass. She held it out and I took it in my shaking hands. It felt as if all my nerve endings were on red alert and as I sipped, I looked about me. The nurse was standing in the corner, glowering in my direction.

For a while no one spoke, and I felt it was up to me to inform everyone that I was feeling better and wanted to talk about what had happened. Obviously, the first person I directed any comment to was Maria. "Why didn't you tell me about Kate and Cambridge?"

Maria sighed the sigh of the defeated, but before she could answer, Kate spoke. "Can I just explain something first?" She aimed the question at Maria, before looking at me and nodding. "I sent you the note."

Maria lowered her head and stared at the green paper sheet covering the bed.

"I wanted someone else to hurt as much as I hurt at the time...the time when...when...I found out about Fielding."

Maria turned away, and I knew she was hiding her embarrassment.

"It's not all cut and dried, though. Maria didn't cheat on me. Well, she did, but she didn't. And I'm not making any sense."

At this point, the nurse tried to speak, but both Maria and I glared at her. Kate continued. And we listened and listened and listened. When Maria and Jennifer Fielding had the one-night stand, Maria and Kate had split up nearly a week before. The reason for the split? Maria had explained that it wasn't working between them, that she needed space, needed room to breathe. So when the gossipmongers spread it about that Maria had slept with her mentor days after saying she wanted to be on her own for a while, well, hurt is an understatement of how Kate felt.

"But why send me that note?" It seemed a reasonable question.

"Because when I found out she was seeing someone else, I wanted her to remember what she had done to me. I didn't care if it meant you two broke up. You meant nothing to me—I didn't know you—it didn't affect anyone but me and Maria."

And me. Don't forget me.

"I wanted her to hurt. Childish, I know. But I felt stupid more than anything else. Everyone knew before I did."

It *was* childish, and wouldn't be out of place in my tutor group. It was exactly what a group of teens would do—"I hurt, so shall you" philosophy.

"But I don't understand. How did you know who I was and where to send the note?" As soon as the words came out, I followed the gazes of Maria and Kate, and those gazes landed on the woman standing in the corner. "But how? You didn't know her, either."

Kate began to explain how she had called the hospital a few times to try and speak to Maria, but the nurse would never put her through. *No change there, then.* She thought that if she made conversation with her, befriended her, even flirted a little, then maybe she would get to speak to the person she wanted to speak to—the good doctor herself. "And when Liz told me that Maria was dating again, I wanted to warn you. And remind her of how she had hurt me; maybe let her see what it felt like."

I turned towards where the nurse had been standing, but she had inched further away along the wall, her expression closed.

"The next thing I knew, Liz was giving me your address. She got it from your records. Told me I would be doing you both a favour, too, since doctors shouldn't be having relationships with patients."

True. But I wasn't a patient when we had started. And where did the nurse get off giving out my personal information? Once again I turned to where the she had been standing, but this time all I saw was an empty wall. I scanned the rest of the room, but she was nowhere in sight.

"I'll have her cards for that." It was the first time Maria had spoken since Kate had started, and it seemed weird to have her in the same room and talking about her if she wasn't there. "And you should press charges." She stretched out her hand as if to stroke my face, but changed her mind, and I watched as it fluttered down to rest on the edge of the bed.

Leaning forward, I grabbed her fingers in mine and squeezed her hand. Whatever had happened in the past between these two was where it should stay. In the past. Why would I allow something, or someone else, to jeopardise what we had? That would make me a fool, wouldn't it?

Kate coughed, and I think it was one of those clearing of throats that are used to alert other people they are still there. For a moment I stopped staring at Maria's hand in my own and looked in the direction of the woman who was waiting for me to listen.

"That's why I'm here today, although Liz didn't know that. She thinks I'm here to stir things up a bit. I wanted to apologise, tell Maria what I had done." She nodded at Maria as if asking for confirmation. "But I had only told her part of it when we heard the shouting outside. Both of us came out to see what was going on."

The next bit goes without me telling you anything else. I remembered hearing Kate having a go at the nurse. When she got there, I was doing my impression of a starfish. Maria had been the one who knelt next to me, the one who stroked my forehead, the one who, with Kate's help, had gently moved me into the X-ray room.

"I know it's not anywhere near enough, but I'm sorry for everything I've done." Kate picked up her bag from the side of the table and moved toward the door. "If you need a witness..."

"Thanks. That would be helpful," Maria said. "I'll call hospital security now. Can't have Liz thinking she's gotten away with it." Maria went to make the call in the office at the back of the room, leaving me alone with her ex.

What could I do? What should I say? On the grounds that she was hurting, this woman had tried to break Maria and me apart, for the hell of it. I wanted to have a go...tell her she should have thought through her actions before she decided to play about with people's lives, but when I turned to face her, it was evident that I didn't need to. Kate was feeling bad enough without me adding to it.

"She's a good woman, Gemma."

I know she is.

"And she thinks the world of you."

How could I have a go now?

"When...when we were...erm...an item, it wasn't right between us from the start. But we tend to ignore such things don't we?"

I didn't, although that was my problem. I dissected things, blew things out of proportion, allowed my overactive imagination to take control and fuck up my brain, and anything else that got in its path.

"We only went out together for a couple of months."

Was this an awkward moment? How many of us have chats with our partner's ex girlfriends? Please, God, don't let her start telling me about when they had sex.

"When Maria ended it, I already knew it was coming. But, as I said, we try to ignore things."

Yes...you've already said that. And now let's have some uncomfortable silence.

"Dr Fielding is not a nice person."

Tell me about it. More silence, followed by a wish that Maria would come back.

"They're on their way," Maria's voice came from behind me.

Wish granted.

"They'll want to ask you some questions, although I know Liz has left the building. Security saw her driving out of the car park like the hounds of hell were after her."

Maria and Kate were still talking with security, but I had to finish my day at the UEA. When I was leaving, Maria pulled me to one side and asked if it was okay if she came around to see me after work. "I need to tell you my side of the story...need to make sure you know I'm not the kind of person who—"

I placed my hand over her mouth. "Listen to me. I trust you. Let's leave it at that, shall we?" And I did trust her. No one and nothing could change my mind about that. I knew from the very pit of my stomach that this woman was the one I had been waiting for my whole life. I knew she wasn't the kind to screw about; knew that whatever happened in the future, I would be there at her side. I also knew she would be at mine. I think that was enough knowledge for anyone, don't you?

It was just turning seven o'clock when my doorbell chimed. I knew it was her even before I answered. I could feel her, feel her presence, her life, her energy. Feel the love seeping through the door. After all that had happened, I should have felt nervous about seeing her, but I didn't. I just wanted to pull her into my arms, inhale her scent, kiss her, and never let her go.

"Hey, you."

Either she said it or I did. Who cared? I certainly didn't. She was here, and that was all that mattered. Amazing to think that she looked even more beautiful than I remembered, and it had only been the matter of hours since I had left her at the hospital.

Holding my hand out towards her, I gasped at the connection as her fingers slipped into mine. Sparks of energy fizzed up my arm and dispersed throughout the rest of my body, and the door was still closing as I pulled her into me.

Perfect—the fit, the smell, the sensation of having her with me. My arms wrapped around her, and hers embraced me. Pulling closer, it seemed as if I couldn't get enough, couldn't be as close as I needed to be. Words were unnecessary, definitely redundant.

We stood there for God knows how long, as time seemed to fade away. What was the point of counting minutes and seconds when every one of them was perfectly spent? I had everything I needed in my arms. Maria was not just what I needed; she was also all I would ever want.

A soft breath hit my neck and the hairs on my body stood to attention. Then a sigh spluttered onto my skin. "We need to talk, Gem."

I didn't want to talk. I wanted to stay like this, stay in the protection of this all-consuming embrace. If we talked about what had happened, would this perfection change? Would it end with her telling me that she couldn't deal with someone who was so insecure? This time it was my sigh that released itself, just as I withdrew myself from her arms.

Turning slightly, I was stopped by her hand on my arm. Looking up and into her eyes, I didn't see an expression of disdain or accusation. All I saw was what I believed I was mirroring: love. Simple. Love in all its glorious wonder.

Then she kissed me. Full, hungry, and deliriously decadent. Arms circled and held, and I melted again.

After we eventually pulled ourselves away from one another, we moved to the front room, slipping beside each other on the sofa. Laying my head on her chest, I waited for her to begin. And waited. Then waited some more. Eventually I realised it was up to me to start, up to me to make some sense out of my actions before expecting her to share her side of the story.

"I'm sorry, Maria." What a fantastic start! I should quit teaching and become an Ambassador for the World.

"No. Don't be sorry, Gem." Craning my neck, I looked up at her. "And don't ask me to forgive you."

Why? Was I too far gone for forgiveness?

"I should have been straight with you, should have told you everything from the start then you wouldn't have felt like you couldn't trust me."

No. That wasn't right. We don't need to know the ins and outs of a person's life to know whether or not we should trust them. Whatever has happened in the past should be just that, in the past. Trust is earned, isn't it? Respect, too? "But—"

"No buts. We are here now, aren't we? Together? Happy?" She leaned down and brushed her lips across mine as confirmation. "Aren't we?"

"God, yes." Slipping my hand around her neck, I pulled her down to possess those delectable lips. Heat and moisture spread through me, from her to me, and then back to her again. A shift of bodies and she was lying flat, my smaller frame covering hers. I know I should have continued to talk, continued to explain what had happened and why I had acted like a dick, but I couldn't. All I could think of doing was showing her how much she meant to me, and hope beyond hope, that if I showed her well enough, she would know I wouldn't make the same mistake again.

Hands slipped inside clothes, fingers trailed along skin, committing to memory the texture and the heat. Mouths moved in synch and desire inched hungrily inside of me. Air hit my skin as my top was released, quickly followed by my jeans. Then her clothes disappeared as if they had evaporated into the molecules of the air around us.

She was underneath me, eyes sparkling like ice blue chips, her lips moist and waiting for me to claim them. So I did, our skin slipping effortlessly against each other sparking desire, need, longing to be fulfilled. Hips moved, the rhythm building, the sensation rippling like water washing over us. Harder, firmer, deeper, the kisses were becoming primitive, as were the gyrations of our bodies. I needed more of her, needed to take her, needed to claim her, possess her, love her, just like I needed the same from her.

Maria pushed me backwards, leaning over me. I knew what she wanted; I wanted it too. Mouths were still engaged in taking, as hands slipped between ready thighs, as fingers pushed between wetness and dragged along soft supple flesh. Groans slipped from one mouth to be swallowed by the other.

Circling. We were both circling, and coating our fingers with the essence of each other. Both teasing and taunting, both aching to be filled.

Two fingers. In. Two fingers plunging, taking, curling and dragging. Two fingers owning and possessing. But the ache continued. The agony of needing her deeper, needing to be fully inside her made each of us push against the other. And push. God. And push. We were so close to each other, so connected, that when I opened my eyes to look at her I felt love surge through me as I saw those blue orbs looking intently into mine.

Breaking the kiss, I whispered, "I love you."

Slowly and deliberately, Maria closed her eyes, a smile spreading over her mouth, her head nodding with the rhythm of our loving. Then they opened again to show the change from blue to almost violet, half hooded, pupils dilated, and deliciously addictive. "I love you so much, Gem. So much."

Fuck. Fuck. And fuck. This was it. This was what I had been searching for, yearning for. This woman. This Goddess loved me as much as I loved her and everything was perfect. Positively perfect.

Fingers still searched and excavated, still penetrated and plunged. But this loving was more than mere loving; it was an affirmation of everything that was to follow. Whatever happened after this we would always know that we were one, we were us, we were Gemma and Maria. And that's all that really mattered in this life after all.

When we came, we came together. When we cried out in synchronised gasps, they mingled in the small space that had appeared between us before becoming trapped within us again. Fingers gently slipped from inside, coated with our future. And as she fell forward and into my chest, I caught her and pulled her down to me, circling my arms around her and pulling her close and into the heat of our skin.

This is the place where I wanted to stay, wanted to live out the rest of my life. Being with Maria was the only thing I would ever want and nothing would ever happen in the future to shake my trust in her. I love her too much for that.

Amazing to think how time flies, isn't it? I mean, time has that slippery way of acting any way she goddamned pleases and we just take it on the chin or moan about it. But you see, I don't want to moan about the time I have spent with Maria. Far from it. In fact, I want to celebrate it... give it a slap on the back...an award...something to show it that it is very much appreciated. The time in question is all of the time Maria and I have shared since we first met.

Since the incident at the hospital, four months have passed. See how quickly that went? Nearly as quickly as I feel it has gone. When Maria came around to my house after work, we didn't chat about any of the shit that had happened. We found another way to move forward, although some people would prefer to discuss incidents to death instead of trying to show how they feel.

What is the point in dissecting stupidity? Life is definitely too short to worry about things that have gone by, too short to fill itself with anger, hatred, and regret. If you find the woman, or man, you want to spend the rest of your life with, then cherish that—don't dig and dig and dig until you find the smallest shred of evidence that something in the past has been hidden from you. It is who that person is now that matters. That is the person you are in love with. Trust her. Believe the woman when she tells you she loves you and wants to be with you and only you. I know it's hard, but what do your actions say if you don't? And can you really say you're in love if you totally disregard trust?

Even though time has skipped by, I think I need to clarify some stuff for you, otherwise you'll have my guts for garters and my intestines for a necklace.

Nursey...AKA   Shit-stirrer...AKA...Liz   the   Lez... AKA... I know—I'm getting on my own tits now. Let's start afresh. Nurse Liz was given her marching orders. Her pin was taken off her and she left the Norfolk and Norwich in disgrace. Last thing I heard, she was working in a care home in Dereham. I didn't press charges; I believe she got her just desserts. Part of me felt sad that she had spent so many years training to become a nurse, and then just threw it all away by giving out patient information. And for what? So she could gloat over the fact she had split apart a relationship she envied. Why would someone want to do that? To this day, I can't understand it. It's okay to fight for the one you love, but when she doesn't love you back—when she loves someone else—isn't that the time to let go and let her live her life? Treat that as a rhetorical question.

Maria and I are doing well. Very well. Exceedingly well, in fact. Since all the palaver at the beginning of our relationship, we have grown stronger, happier, more relaxed in the knowledge that we are one. So much so, that, as of tomorrow, we will be living under the same roof. You got it. Moving in together. Becoming the start of a two-person family. Well, when I say we're moving in together, what I mean is *I* am moving in with *her*. What about Trevor? I hear you cry. Trevor is fine. Trevor is now living with Colin—God help him. At least Col told him about pink not being his colour.

So, you have stayed with me until this point. I would say till the end, but it isn't yet. I still have to gob off about my philosophy on life, love, and the future. I can hear you again, but this time you're not concerned about my stargazing friend, are you? No. You're muttering, quite loudly actually, that you can do without the lecture, and could I please just finish so you can go and read something decent. Wait up. I won't be long. I promise (and no—I haven't got my fingers crossed behind my back).

Okay, here goes. Are you holding your breath? Well, don't. I would hate to think of you turning all blue and passing out, maybe cracking your head open on a sharp piece of furniture in the process. I know, I know…I'll shut up…erm…well, continue with my sermon from the mount of my armchair.

Firstly—life. The ultimate question: why are we here? And the answer isn't forty-two, I think. Even though that's what the computer came up with in *The Hitchhiker's Guide to the Galaxy*. The meaning of life is what we want it to be. Whether it is standing in the rain at train stations, marking down numbers in our train spotter's pads, or attempting to beat the baked bean eating record, it is whatever makes us happy. If being single is what floats your boat, then go float it. We are all different; we like different things, different kinds of people. We act in ways that are unique to us. All our idiosyncrasies are precious, and we should rejoice in that instead of envying what others have or hating them for it.

Secondly—love. The ultimate four letter word, but in a good way, I believe. Love is not static, not choosey, not a four letter word to mess with. Love is something we experience all the time, a word we seem to use so easily with no thought to what we are saying. "I love this song… I love Italian food… I love… I love… I love." But do we actually know what this word means? Are we in love with the song…the lasagne? Or do we use the word willy nilly to show we like something? When the real "love" shows her face, do we embrace it? Recognise it? Fear it? Check it over like a worn book, trying to find fault before deciding it's not the genre we like before putting it back on the shelf without realising we are actually the ones on that shelf? Love is not solid. You can't hold it in the palm of your hand and say, "Aw...look at it...it's so tiny." Love is abstract. You can't touch it, but it can touch you. You *can* feel it, and even though it's invisible, you can also see it, you can see it everywhere, if you have enough faith to look.

The thing about love is that although you know it's there, sometimes you disbelieve it is there for you. A classic case of low self-esteem, methinks. But here's the tip: if you allow yourself to love who you are, then maybe you would get a good idea of what love is about. Take the nurse, for instance. She thought she loved Maria, yes? But you have to love yourself in order to love another. Hers seems to have been a classic case of her not loving herself enough to recognise what love truly is. I am not innocent on this score either. You know why? Easy. I doubted Maria *and* believed she was hiding something. Was that a case of not thinking I was good enough to be loved by such an amazing woman? Or was it me being a knob, like usual? A bit of both, I think.

Finally, the future. Now with this I could rattle on for hours about what could happen, or what I want to happen. But in truth, I haven't a clue. One thing I do know is that I don't fear it. The future is what we make of it, as the old saying goes, and we get what we deserve, or believe we should. Maybe it is Karma, maybe it is just my philosophy, maybe the nurse will get her comeuppance one day, and Gary Ellis, even Dr Jennifer Fielding will shag one too many, or brag about copping off with the wrong person. Who knows? But we also must remember that what happens in our past is something we should learn from, not dwell on, and maybe the lesson learned will help us to avoid making the same mistakes again. Mainly, what we need to do with our futures, our lives, and loves, is to take that leap of faith and trust that everything turns out as it should. I think I did mine in stages, leaping the sofa before the faith, but eventually I ended up in the place where I wanted to be. At Maria's side.

I promise, this is the last thing I am going to say. Well, not that, this. I could go on all night, as if you hadn't noticed.

Sigh.

In one of my oft mentioned nutshells...

We all have the ability to see through someone...see *right* through them. But to see *into* them? Rarely. To allow someone else to see right through *us*...even rarer. But, you see, if we don't knock down those walls that we erect within us, how can we let others in? Just as importantly, how can we let ourselves out? We have to learn to trust, allow ourselves to ignore the demon voices within us that try to break us down with negativity and insecurity. We are worth more than the value we place on ourselves...a lot more. I know I didn't erect a wall when it came to my feelings for Maria, but it had the same impact. Love slammed against it and was reflected by doubt and lack of faith in ourselves and the one we want to give our heart to.

When we find that one, that special someone who makes us feel as if we can give our all to them, then we must give our all. It's the way of the world, and if we ignore it, the world will stop and we all fall off. Or so I've heard. Colin told me. And we all trust Col, don't we?

One more thing. I have my life, my love, and my future, and they all point to the same thing: Doctor Maria Moran. The woman, who from the very first time I saw her, saw right through me and made me the woman I am today.

And do you know what kind of woman I am today?

A happy one.

About L.T. Smith

L.T. is a late bloomer when it comes to writing and didn't begin until 2005 with her first novel *Hearts and Flowers Border* (first published in 2006).

She soon caught the bug and has written numerous tales, usually with a comical slant to reflect, as she calls it, "My warped view of the dramatic."

Although she loves to write, L.T. loves to read, too—being an English teacher seems to demand it. Most of her free time is spent with her furry little men—two fluffy balls of trouble who keep her active and her apologies flowing.

E-mail her at fingersmith@hotmail.co.uk
Facebook: https://www.facebook.com/LT-Smith

Other Books from Ylva Publishing

http://www.ylva-publishing.com

Hot Line

Alison Grey
ISBN: 978-3-95533-048-4 (print)
Length: 114 pages

Two women from different worlds.

Linda, a successful psychologist, uses her work to distance herself from her own loneliness.

Christina works for a sex hotline to make ends meet.

Their worlds collide when Linda calls Christina's sex line. Christina quickly realizes Linda is not her usual customer. Instead of wanting phone sex, Linda makes an unexpected proposition. Does Christina dare accept the offer that will change both their lives?

L.A. Metro
(2nd edition)

RJ Nolan
ISBN: 978-3-95533-041-5 (print)
Length: 349 pages

Dr. Kimberly Donovan's life is in shambles. After her medical ethics are questioned, first her family, then her closeted lover, the Chief of the ER, betray her. Determined to make a fresh start, she flees to California and L.A. Metropolitan Hospital.

Dr. Jess McKenna, L.A. Metro's Chief of the ER, gives new meaning to the phrase emotionally guarded, but she has her reasons.

When Kim and Jess meet, the attraction is immediate. Emotions Jess has tried to repress for years surface. But her interest in Kim also stirs dark memories. They settle for friendship, determined not to repeat past mistakes, but secretly they both wish things could be different.

Will the demons from Jess's past destroy their future before it can even get started? Or will L.A. Metro be a place to not only heal the sick, but to mend wounded hearts?

Something in the Wine

Jae
ISBN: 978-3-95533-005-7 (print)
Length: 393 pages

All her life, Annie Prideaux has suffered through her brother's constant practical jokes only he thinks are funny. But Jake's last joke is one too many, she decides when he sets her up on a blind date with his friend Drew Corbin—neglecting to tell his straight sister one tiny detail: her date is not a man, but a lesbian.

Annie and Drew decide it's time to turn the tables on Jake by pretending to fall in love with each other.

At first glance, they have nothing in common. Disillusioned with love, Annie focuses on books, her cat, and her work as an accountant while Drew, more confident and outgoing, owns a dog and spends most of her time working in her beloved vineyard.

Only their common goal to take revenge on Jake unites them. But what starts as a table-turning game soon turns Annie's and Drew's lives upside down as the lines between pretending and reality begin to blur.

Something in the Wine is a story about love, friendship, and coming to terms with what it means to be yourself.

Walking the Labyrinth

Lois Cloarec Hart
ISBN: 978-3-95533-052-1 (print)
Length: 267 pages

Is there life after loss? Lee Glenn, co-owner of a private security company, didn't think so. Crushed by grief after the death of her wife, she uncharacteristically retreats from life.

But love doesn't give up easily. After her friends and family stage a dramatic intervention, Lee rejoins the world of the living, resolved to regain some sense of normalcy but only half-believing that it's possible. Her old friend and business partner convinces her to take on what appears on the surface to be a minor personal protection detail.

The assignment takes her far from home, from the darkness of her loss to the dawning of a life reborn. Along the way, Lee encounters people unlike any she's ever met before: Wrong-Way Wally, a small-town oracle shunned by the locals for his off-putting speech and mannerisms; and Wally's best friend, Gaëlle, a woman who not only translates the oracle's uncanny predictions, but who also appears to have a deep personal connection to life beyond life. Lee is shocked to find herself fascinated by Gaëlle, despite dismissing the woman's exotic beliefs as "hooey."

But opening yourself to love also means opening yourself to the possibility of pain. Will Lee have the courage to follow that path, a path that once led to the greatest agony she'd ever experienced? Or will she run back to the cold comfort of a safer solitary life?

Coming from Ylva
Publishing in Winter
2013 and Spring 2014

http://www.ylva-publishing.com

Puppy Love

L.T. Smith

Ellie Anderson has given up on love. Her philosophy is "Why let someone in when all they do is leave?" So instead, she fills her life with work and dodges her sister's matchmaking.

Then she meets Charlie—a gorgeous, brown-eyed Border Terrier. Charlie is in need of love and a home, prompting Ellie to open the doors to feeling once again.

However, she isn't the only one who is falling for the pup's charms.

Emily Carson is her rival for Charlie's affection, thus starting what can only be classed as a working relationship.

By allowing herself to love Charlie, can Ellie open her heart to anyone else?

Broken Faith

(revised edition)

Lois Cloarec Hart

Emotional wounds aren't always apparent, and those that haunt Marika and Rhiannon are deep and lasting.

On the surface, Marika appears to be a wealthy, successful lawyer, while Rhiannon is a reclusive, maladjusted loner. But Marika, in her own way, is as damaged as the younger Rhiannon. When circumstances throw them together one summer, they begin to reach out, each finding unexpected strengths in the other.

However, even as inner demons are gradually vanquished and old hurts begin to heal, evil in human form reappears. The cruelly enigmatic Cass has used and controlled Marika in the past, and she aims to do so again.

Can Marika find it within herself to break free? Can she save her young friend from Cass' malevolent web? With the support of remarkable friends, the pair fights to break free—of their crippling pasts and the woman who will own them or kill them.

Crossing Bridges

Emma Weimann

As a Guardian, Tallulah has devoted her life to protecting her hometown, Edinburgh, and its inhabitants, both living and dead, against ill-natured and dangerous supernatural beings.

When Erin, a human tourist, visits Edinburgh, she makes Tallulah more nervous than the poltergeist on Greyfriars Kirkyard—and not only because Erin seems to be the sidekick of a dark witch who has her own agenda.

While Tallulah works to thwart the dark witch's sinister plan for Edinburgh, she can't help wondering about the mysterious Erin. Is she friend or foe?

Coming Home
(revised edition)

Lois Cloarec Hart

A triangle with a twist, Coming Home is the story of three good people caught up in an impossible situation.

Rob, a charismatic ex-fighter pilot severely disabled with MS, has been steadfastly cared for by his wife, Jan, for many years. Quite by accident one day, Terry, a young writer/postal carrier, enters their life and turns it upside down.

Injecting joy and turbulence into their quiet existence, Terry draws Rob and Jan into her lively circle of family and friends until the growing attachment between the two women begins to strain the bonds of love and loyalty, to Rob and each other.

Hearts and Flowers Border
(revised edition)

L.T. Smith

A visitor from her past jolts Laura Stewart into memories - some funny - some heart wrenching. But she needs to deal with all of them before she can open the door to allow her past to shape her future.

A story starting in the present day, narrated by a woman who needs to retell her past before she can move on with her future. There is no fantastic underlying plot, just a simple retelling of events leading to the present day. Most of us will recognise the uncertainty of youth and the first flush of love.

See Right Through Me
© by L.T. Smith

ISBN: 978-3-95533-068-2 (Print)

Also available as an e-book

Published by Ylva Publishing, legal entity of Ylva Verlag, e.Kfr.

Ylva Verlag, e.Kfr.
Owner: Astrid Ohletz
Am Kirschgarten 2
65830 Kriftel
Germany

http://www.ylva-publishing.com

First edition: November 2013

Credits:
Edited by Judy Underwood and Cheri Fuller
Cover Design by Amanda Chron